Balsam Sirens

Titles by Keith Weaver

An Uncompromising Place

The Recipe Cops

Balsam Sirens

Balsam Sirens

Keith Weaver

IGUANA

Publisher: Greg Ioannou
Editor: Mary Ann Blair
Front cover image: Courtesy of Unsplash
Front cover design: Daniella Postavsky

Library and Archives Canada Cataloguing in Publication
Weaver, Keith, 1947-, author
     Balsam sirens / Keith Weaver.

Issued in print and electronic formats.

Issued in print and electronic formats.
ISBN 978-1-77180-204-8 (softcover).--ISBN 978-1-77180-205-5 (EPUB).--
ISBN 978-1-77180-206-2 (Kindle)

I. Title.
PS8645.E2175B35 2017   C813'.6   C2016-908164-8
                                               C2016-908165-6

This is an original print edition of *Balsam Sirens.*

A Note on History

Readers might infer from *Balsam Sirens* that the author shares some of Mark Whelan's views on history.

They would be right.

The only non-fictional character in this book is George Laidlaw. George Edward Laidlaw, eldest son of entrepreneur and railway promoter George Edward, was a tireless student of local history.

Balsam Sirens **is** a work of fiction, but I want to acknowledge some liberties that I have taken in writing the book and to flag one very important piece of background.

The first gold rush in Canada occurred near Madoc in Ontario in the mid-1860s, but the date has been shifted slightly in the book.

Rory McCleod is entirely fictional and represents no real person.

The island in Balsam Lake that was once called Ghost Island is now Hogg Island, but Ghost Island sounds better.

In the nineteenth century, there was limited steamboat traffic on Balsam Lake. But the timing of this traffic has been shifted about 10-15 years earlier than was the actual case.

The steamboat *Coboconk* did exist; however, no steamboats named *Jackson*, *Daniella* and *Damsel May* ever sailed on Balsam Lake.

The establishment *Le Repos de Champlain*, placed in Rosedale, does not exist. Too bad.

The village of Largs (the one on Balsam Lake) also doesn't exist.

Finally, and in many ways most importantly, I have tried to express, through the thoughts and speech of Mark Whelan, statements I have come across on the present and past realities of First Nations peoples, the appalling history they have had to endure, and the need not only for this situation, but also the First Nations' central role in the reality we call Canada to be recognized and acknowledged, and for reconciliation and justice to be sought. Having said that, the character John Longfeather / John Woodhouse is fictional.

Dedicated to the Memory of Geoff Ogram

Colleague, Kindred Spirit, Friend

One

It promised to be a warm late spring day, the sky bright and sunny, and a light breeze flirting with still virginal leaves.

Ideal for a trip to the morgue.

Mark Whelan, Private Investigator. That's me. And I was here, at the Toronto morgue, at the request of one of my clients who wanted moral support in the task of identifying his brother.

"Bankers' hours, eh, Whelan?" The speaker was Detective Sergeant Bent Cromarty. I had interacted with Cromarty a few times. Decent sort. Hard to read. Apparently impossible to get to know. But I would choose Cromarty to work with over many other detectives. His one hot button – well, warm button – brought out a prickly reaction to anyone who didn't respect his turf.

Cromarty wasn't the hard-boiled, chain-smoking, larger-than-life bad-cop stereotype, someone headed for an early seat on the emphysema express. He was lean, had close-cropped auburn hair, and wore suits that looked a bit severe, but that were an attractively snug fit to his athletic form. There were always, it seemed, a few remarks stored behind his deadpan expression, ready for delivery. But he was fully rooted in the police system and did not release projectiles, verbal or otherwise, that could bounce off his superiors and result in self-inflicted wounds.

I let Cromarty's dig pass without any response or acknowledgement. Other thoughts were occupying me just then, and there was the problem of time. Waiting seemed to be one of my most frequent occupations – in this case, waiting for my client to turn up. The combination of the prospect of unstructured time lying before me and of stooging around next to Cromarty caused my mind to make its escape and dodge down a frequent byway into one of the many quirky mental spaces that are a necessary part of my life. My own collection of quirks, contradictions, and puzzles populated that space. The puzzles, human nature puzzles, intrigued me most. One such unexplained puzzle was the large percentage of parents who made it to peaceful old age. I had ruminated for years on the apparent low rate of parricide. There seemed to be all kinds of reasons that would nudge people toward that particular crime.

Cromarty was walking about aimlessly. I pulled out my cellphone and made as though I was checking appointments. What I really wanted was to avoid any attempt by Cromarty to drag me into some meandering discussion that would help him fill *his* time. Hiding behind my phone, I resumed my own mental wandering.

Where was I? Oh, yes. Parricide.

High on the list of these plausible reasons for parricide were the many serious rub points between the generations, and one of the most prominent of these rub points was names. Not for the first time, I wondered what gave rise to the mental fog that engulfed parents as they sat down to name their children. The names that some parents chose! Many of the given names were fine on their own, but a name always has two or more elements. Given names chosen, apparently, in blissful isolation, can team up with surnames to produce aberrations that range from oddly peculiar to unbelievably ghastly. The possibilities were legion. Instances of infelicitous alliteration, asinine assonance, and podunk handles adapted from commercials and sitcoms. There were far too many instances of ill-matched monosyllables that jostle together in hard brutal clunks. One cringed at assaults by meanderings of vocalic jumbles, too rich in vowels and requiring more than one breath to utter. Bentley Cromarty was a good example, his given and family names together offering a hopscotch lilt, a tipsy linguistic ramble in some undocumented musical time signature, like the totterings of a horse that has just sampled the sour mash. And presumably, it explained Cromarty's preference for "Bent". But then "Bent" trailed a haze of its own problems…

I was always grateful for my own given names: Mark Alessandro. But that was just the luck of the draw, having been inspired by a rather unlikely mix of biblical and Botticellian enthusiasms. It could have been otherwise: Winston Whelan, Galen Whelan, Dylan Whelan…

But this recurring fret over names was just a minor compulsion, chronic but easily resisted, nothing as imperious as the invitation presented by a chipped tooth to a tongue. In due course, my client would turn up, allowing me to terminate this diversion into a world of personal fantasy.

Cellphone fiddling and musings worked well as bulwarks against intrusions from Cromarty, and eventually, my client George arrived. George was a stressed-out fifty-something bundle of hesitations. I greeted him, offering a gentle smile and a reassuring hand on the shoulder, but this did little to counteract the hidden causes, or the psychological effects, that perhaps were reflected in his ruffled salt-and-pepper hair, his red eyes ringed in grey, and the unrelenting Pontius Pilate hand actions.

"Okay, George?" I asked gently.

George Barbour was one extreme of a classic office worker, someone appearing to have no past, no future, and no access to happiness. He returned a faint nod that was little more than an automatic response to my question.

"This won't take long, George. Then we can go somewhere and have a talk."

Nod.

A body lay before us, covered by a sheet. A mortuary staff member asked, by way of a gesture, if we were ready. I looked at George and raised an eyebrow. There was another nod, much more hesitant and anxious this time.

Identifying a dead loved one is a shock, but George's sudden vocalized intake of breath when the dead face was revealed was far more reaction than I had expected. Something prompted me to move closer to George, which I did just in time to grab him round the waist before his knees buckled.

"Is that your brother, Harold Barbour?" Cromarty asked. George stood immobile. I squeezed his arm gently, he nodded vigorously several times, croaked out a "yes", and looked around in near panic, as if seeking a corner to which he could run and hide. I led George away, and as soon as we were in a neutral corridor, I pulled out a hip flask, unscrewed the cap, and put it to George's lips. Not knowing what else to do, George took a sip, coughed delicately, and seemed to regain some colour and strength.

"Let's go and get a cup of coffee", I suggested, and led George away without waiting for a reply. We left the morgue and found a coffee shop a couple of blocks away. I sat George at a corner table and went off to order two cups of coffee, one having a good shot of espresso. Over the coffee, we talked for about fifteen minutes, while I got the whole discussion kick-started through snatches of narrative that had nothing to do with death, during which George graduated from nods, to reluctant "yes" and "no" responses, and eventually to short sentences. Our coffees finished, I announced with some gusto that I was hungry, even though it was by then still only late midmorning, and I invited George to come with me to a good breakfast place nearby. George nodded, rose, and followed passively.

Forty minutes later, we had both finished whopping plates of omelettes and pancakes. George looked much more human by now. As we left the restaurant, I scanned the street for a cab.

"I … Will there be some … paperwork?" George asked in trepidation.

"Yes, but I'll get it all ready so that all you need to do is sign. We can leave that for a few days. I'll call you, George."

A cab pulled up to the curb, we climbed in, and went to George's apartment building. On the way, I passed George my card, and fixing him in a direct gaze, said forcefully that he should call me if he had any questions, or even if he just wanted to talk.

George smiled faintly. "Yes", he said. "Thanks", he added, after a short delay.

"Off you go, George. You need some rest."

I had the cabbie wait until George reached the front door of his building. We waved to each other, then I told the cabbie the address of our condo – Andrea's and mine – in the old part of town. Back in our condo, I immediately changed into shorts and a T-shirt, went out onto the terrace, and flopped into a large cushioned reclining chair. I had some thinking to do.

George's case had come to me entirely by chance through one of my bush telegraph connections. I had just finished a tightly bunched group of commissions, was tired, and let it be known to a few of my fellow PIs that I was taking a week for myself. Just staying home, enjoying the weather, doing some reading…

Then came a call from a colleague, hinting at a favour and mentioning someone's name. There was something about the way my colleague described the case that grabbed my attention. I agreed to allow my name to be recommended, and a day later I had George as a client. I had contacted Cromarty and got the information that was available. I had then called George, we had a somewhat one-sided telephone discussion, and I assured him that I would take him on, even though I wasn't sure at all just what it was that he thought I could do for him.

The event before us was the death of the man George had just identified as his brother. The notes on the case called the event "a boating accident". There were a few lines of description but little else. However, that wasn't what caught my eye.

The accident had occurred in Balsam Lake, on the shore of which slumbered my home village, Largs, the place where I had spent my youth to the age of eighteen.

More significantly, from even the little information I had been passed by the police, I was all but convinced that the accident had been no accident. It seemed more probable that Harold Barbour had been murdered.

Two

We both sat there looking at her, feeling like two students being chided for not working hard enough, and waiting for her pronouncement.

"I really don't think you two have a problem", the marriage counsellor said, leaning back in her chair and setting down a pen that so far had been used just to carve half a page of doodles.

"Well, we're here, aren't we?" I replied, slightly annoyed.

"Yes, but by your own admission you don't fight over things. There's just this haze of mild disagreement. Surely you don't expect every situation to resolve instantly into crystal clarity. I think", she said, leaning forward over the desk in a pose that spoke of reaching a conclusion, "I think that you are allowing situations to define who you feel you should be rather than the other way round."

The two students looked on dumbly, as though the meeting had suddenly switched to ancient Greek.

We had been talking with the counsellor about all and sundry. It wasn't really any sort of crisis management. We weren't teetering on any brink. It was just that, without actually arguing or fighting, there seemed to be an uncomfortable number of things that Andrea and I didn't really either agree or disagree on.

Before the end of our first session with her, I had the frustrating sense that we were getting nowhere, and this wasn't helped by the relaxed and apparently unconcerned aura that surrounded our counsellor. Our session was now obviously wrapping up, and I'm sure that the summary statement she embarked upon now was meant to reassure us both, but it didn't do that for me.

"People tend to be followers", the counsellor began, "and some of the things that influence people most strongly are social mores. And, by the way, this has little to do with intelligence. Nobody is particularly good at analysing their own situations, so the information we as individuals work with tends not to be of the analytical sort. We usually get it elsewhere. People can form impressions independently, or impressions can be transmitted unconsciously to us, somehow, from others, through expressions, gestures, odd words, and phrases. And we have expectations. Some of these we formulate ourselves, but many of them we pick up, perceive, from what's around us. We're all social creatures, and all of us, but some much more than others, are sensitive to cues, hints, and non-verbal suggestions. Usually without realizing it, we detect social expectations, the collective expectations of others, and our responses, too often, are that those expectations have to be met as is, without questions being asked. And this is a dynamic that many people are never aware of."

A further short discussion led to the conclusion that Andrea and Mark should go away and think about things. Then we left.

The ride home was quiet.

We both knew, I'm sure, that we had things to work through. But first, we had to bring our situation into focus.

During that trip home, my mind raced through the events that had preceded my first contact with George. It wasn't that George was in any way a precipitating factor. He was just an arbitrary stake in the sand. Going to see a counsellor inevitably caused a lot of reflection. It was this reflection, welling up into consciousness, that made me shine a bright light inward on myself.

What that light revealed was that George was just one more of those odd random chunks of reality that continuously litter what I seem predisposed to consider my linear well-engineered path through life. But I knew that I was just fooling myself, or trying to. Sometimes, I would awaken at 3 am and be appalled, when I looked at it carefully, at what a crash site my working life was. My arrogant departure from the police force, where I did have a future, had led to my current existence, which was … what, exactly?

It had seemed straightforward back then, and my blithe confidence greased the quick decision to become a private investigator, my police background being ample preparation for such a role, or so I thought. Being honest with myself, or what passes for honesty amid 3 am desperation, my livelihood was indeed lucrative, but at the cost of sifting through the sordid detritus of other people's disintegrating lives. This had become background music, definitely atonal, to many of my days, when at least daylight, sunlight, managed to dissipate most of my metaphorical grey mental fog. During these periods, I was indeed able to focus on the day's work, and ignore the question in Peggy Lee's song line that challenged me regularly. "Focusing" and "doing the work" was rarely much of an effort owing to the fact that most of my cases fell into one of four or five standard formats: divorces, affairs, financial irregularities, dysfunctional families, and virulent personal situations, the development of which were almost always powered by suspicions, feelings of inadequacy, and smouldering hatreds. In any assignment, focusing on the patterns and avoiding being psychologically engulfed by the gruesome details was essential. Once I had found the standard pattern that matched the particular events before me, the past, present, and future of the case became as evident as an unfolding Harlequin romance. I could just concentrate on the pattern, work the problem.

So I was mystified to discover that, even though George's case had only begun, it was already throwing curves at me and refusing to fit into the simplest of my patterns. It was occupying my time excessively.

And *there* was the problem.

I had got myself stuck almost completely in the mechanics of my working life. And this wasn't good because there were other things that should have been taking up a good deal of my time. Those things all centred on Andrea and me.

That evening, Andrea and I had a long heart-to-heart. I could see the concern and anxiety I had been causing her, and that hurt. But then I guess that's the idea.

In the end, we decided that time away together would be the right course. And that's what led us to be on the point of spending two weeks in Largs. Beautiful Largs, my home village.

Perhaps as early preparation for those two weeks, we spent quite a few hours revisiting images from our six years of marriage. I recalled how surprised and delighted I had been that Andrea's mother had wanted a small and intimate wedding. Andrea smiled once more over the thought that she would be married to a landowner, a baron of sorts. Of course, that referred to my inheritance of properties in Largs, and while that didn't leave me struggling to keep up appearances while in genteel poverty, I was far from being an aristocrat afloat on cash and facing the perennial decision of which stately home to live in.

A long chunk of the past flickered through my mind. It was a pastiche of episodes drawn from early in our marriage. I had replayed several versions of this to myself.

"I still remember you telling me about Largs not long after we met", Andrea reminded me through a smile. *"Frankly, I didn't believe a word of it."*

"But then we went there. Just for a look", I said. *"I'll never forget the expression on your face. And I do remember rubbing it in."* I grinned smugly.

"And then", she continued, *"during our first holiday in London, you insisted on a side trip to Glasgow, but all we did there was pick up a rental car. Then we drove to Largs, the original Largs, just west of Glasgow. We walked through the town, a beautiful place, and you told me about William Thompson and his mansion, Netherhall, the grandest building in Largs, and when I asked about how old the place was you just*

said something about a mist-shrouded past and hairy, smelly Caledonians swinging nasty instruments at one another."

I had smiled at Andrea, remembering it all clearly.

"I was delighted at how strongly you responded to the cottages in Largs, I mean in Balsam Lake Largs", I said. "I remember you wanting to look inside every one of them."

"Yes, well, it was magical. It is magical."

"And then", I continued provocatively, "we spent a couple of weekends there. In sin. That loosened a few tongues."

"Oh, come on, Mark! You don't know that! You keep saying that just for effect!"

"Not at all! Largs is deep in Protestant country! Anyway, I walked you through the history of the place, as I know it."

And I did tell Andrea about Rory McCleod, who emigrated to Upper Canada in 1836 as a young Scot, and how he parlayed his skills as an instrument maker, apprentice engineer, and general organizer. He was soon the owner of a transport and trading company that had ships operating all along the north shore of Lake Ontario and links to the early rail network.

She had seemed fascinated that someone could accomplish all that he did, starting with the village itself. I recall during her first visit to Largs, walking through the village, looking at the big house and the cottages I owned, running a hand over the deeply weathered stone, sensing the solidity of the place.

"He was imaginative, and very much a driven man. But in those days, you just got off your duff and did things. There was little or nothing apart from nature and physics to stop you, and nobody would do it for you."

"But the stone for all these buildings!" she said, looking around. "There are tons of stone here!"

And I explained about the stone being quarried near Coboconk from a limestone cliff close to the eastern shore of the Gull River, then rafted downriver to the site McCleod had chosen for Largs. We went to visit the old quarry, now heavily overgrown and hard to find, but the amount of work that had been done was evident.

It was during one of those first weekends we spent at Largs that Andrea asked about my family. I related the story of my mother, old McCleod's great-granddaughter, her marriage to Howard Whelan, a union that held together just about long enough for me to come along, my mother's sad death by drowning in 1983 when I was just two, and how one of my mother's friends in Largs, Mrs. Hastings, successfully made a case to the courts to take me in and raise me.

"Was it an accident? I mean, your mother's death. Do you know?"

I shook my head.

"Don't know. Probably it was. But she might have been depressed … I just don't know."

"What? Suicide?"

"It's possible", I said.

Family histories can be interesting, but mine seemed to fascinate Andrea. I showed her the two large photo albums and the scant twenty-six-page written family history my mother had put together. This included the sad tale of my great-grandfather and grandfather, both of whom seemed to be lazy and dissolute. They would have been quite happy to allow Largs to degrade and decline, but my great-great-grandfather, old McCleod himself, had taken measures to safeguard what he had built up.

"You mean he knew that his son was no good?" Andrea asked.

"It certainly looks that way."

She looked through the albums, lost in thought, the way people do when faced by history just beyond the limit of living memory.

"Why did he choose this spot? I mean, why did he build Largs just here?"

"Good question. The only answer I can come up with is that he just fell in love with Balsam Lake and this spot. Can't think of any other reason why someone would pour as many resources as he did into a place that has no geographic or economic reason to be here."

"Who looked after the place after your mother died?" Andrea knew by then that I had no siblings.

"A trustee. A man named Gary Aldred. It was all laid out in my mother's will. She had been the sole surviving member of the McCleod line, so she bequeathed everything to me. There was a clause in her will saying that if she died before I reached the age of eighteen, the estate was to be managed by a trustee."

"A far-seeing woman."

"Yes", I agreed. "And I've regretted more than once never being able to get to know her. Almost everything I know about her has been through Mrs. Hastings."

We looked at the two extant pictures of my mother, neither of them particularly flattering.

Andrea asked me how McCleod had paid for all this, meaning Largs, and I told her about his very successful business.

"He was a wealthy man", I said. "He had more than enough money to fund all this. But he was also very practical, and he soon used Largs as a base for his steamboats on the lake."

"Steamboats?"

"Yes. He had all the metal parts fabricated in Toronto, had them shipped north, and his boats were assembled in Fenelon Falls. He used

those boats for freight and passenger traffic to all the villages he could reach and to supply lumber camps around the lakes."

It took very little time for Andrea to buy into Largs in a big way, and as our initial attraction to each other quickly deepened to love, she learned all the details of my boyhood and youth, what I regarded as my idyllic early life in Largs, and my attachment to Balsam Lake. Andrea was the first adult I had ever explained all this to, and hearing the words come from my own mouth left me feeling mildly embarrassed.

Andrea soon learned about the complex relationship I had with Balsam Lake, how I had learned to swim early, and soon was almost amphibian, and how the lake became my exploration zone, classroom, playground, companion, and friend. I knew the fish in it, and I knew its moods, from all the time I had spent on it in my canoe, day and night.

She often ribbed me about it, in a good-natured way. But after we had been married long enough for her to spend time at Largs, she too came to know the lake in the flush of mornings and in the languor of evenings. She could thrill at the roaring and booming of the ice in winter, and she was fascinated by thunderheads that built up out over the water on hot summer afternoons and by the electrical storms that followed.

Closing out that long reverie once more, I reflected on how Andrea had come to recognize what Balsam Lake means. It has always been an exotic place for me. It's large but shallow, so when strong squalls hit, it can be dangerous. Grand Island changes with the mood of the lake, now hard and stark in the clear bright air, now diaphanous and floating at an indeterminate distance. The lake is serene in the purple haze of evening, beguiling in the pink mist of morning, and masterful, untamed, when churned to vigorous life by the wind. It forms an echo chamber for the ineffable call of the loon. And the whole integrated and apparently timeless backdrop of water, trees, and islands reminds one that a tall, handsome race of people once lived here…

It was in Largs that I also learned about boating accidents, having seen a number of them up close over the years. That's how I knew there was something seriously wrong with calling Harold Barbour's fatal injuries "accidental".

Three

Cromarty heard me out, but he wasn't going to agree.

"Just like that? You say it wasn't an accident, based on your own experience, and you expect me to throw away what I've got and start over?"

"No", I said. "It's your case. I know that. You'll deal with it as you see fit. I'm just adding my own observations."

"Well, thanks, but I think I'll just record your views and move on."

"Suits me", I said, and got up to leave.

"What are you going to do now?" he asked, a hint of challenge in his voice.

"I'm going back to work. Unlike some people, I don't get paid unless I'm doing something." It was a pointless dig, but it made me feel better.

"What about the case?"

"What case?" I demanded, really letting my annoyance show. "Look, Bent. You can't have it both ways. You've said you want to run the case your way. Fine. Go ahead. But I'm not going to stand here flapping my lips and watching the clock go 'round. If you ask for my input, I expect you to take it seriously. You haven't, so we're done."

And I walked out, signalling that our non-meeting really had wrapped up.

Back at home, there was a rambling telephone message from George Barbour. I called him.

"George. Meet me in the Stonecutter's Arms in half an hour."

"Yes, well, but, okay. But I don't, you know…"

"You can drink ginger ale, George. Half an hour", and I hung up before he could field another whine.

I got there in fifteen minutes, figuring that being a pint ahead when he arrived was the best means of steadying myself against what was likely to be a frustrating hour and a half. Twenty minutes after I had sat down and was a third of the way through my second pint, George pushed his way past the door as though apologizing to it. He looked just about as much at home as a tadpole in the Kalahari.

An inner voice said suddenly, *Park it, Whelan. Don't be an asshole. He's your client.*

The voice was right. I stood, flashed a big smile, and waved him over. I was only about twenty feet from the door, but it took several minutes before he was settled at my table.

"What can I get you, George? Would a Sprite be okay?" He nodded, and rather than wait for either the server or a change of mind, I went over and placed the order.

Despite the fact that I knew small talk was a dead end for George, I threw in a few of those utterly meaningless but universally acknowledged dollops of conversational grease. George's standard reply to all of them was "Okay. I guess." But he seemed to be a little more chipper, the image from the morgue probably having faded slowly during the day.

George's Sprite was delivered, I raised my pint, and our glasses clinked solidly, my judgment being that a loudish clink was needed to ward off the horde of shades that seemed to be hovering about us.

"Tell me about your brother, George." I knew this was next to pointless, of course, but one needs to start somewhere, and I had to find out what George knew and get some background. George began speaking, but he wandered like a broken gyroscope. I intervened at one of those painful dead-air pauses that often seemed to characterize George's utterances.

"What was he doing on Balsam Lake?"

"I really … I can't … I really don't know. He…"

"When did he leave to go there?"

"He said he was going to take … I think … three weeks' holidays."

"When was that? Do you remember?"

In a sudden access of clarity, George said that it had been about ten days ago.

"So", I said, constructing a timeline in my head. "Today is June 9. The best guess is that the accident happened three days ago, on June 6. And we can suppose that Harold decided on his holiday about May 29 or 30. Does that sound about right to you, George?"

"I guess … yes … I suppose so…"

There was a long pause here.

"So … I suppose … that's it, I guess … or – "

"No, George", I said firmly. "That's *not* it. I want to know more. I need to look into this business more closely."

George fiddled with his napkin.

"But I, you know … I don't … I can't pay you much…"

"Don't worry about all that, George. We'll take it one step at a time. You won't get any financial surprises."

We sat there in companionable silence for a few minutes, then I began to chatter in a way that I hoped would fill some time, make George feel more comfortable, and perhaps – against all reasonable expectations – find some topic that would animate my client. He nodded from time to time to show he was listening, but he took advantage of my undemanding conversational stream and just sipped his Sprite. As he began to relax, I took some time to study him.

He was quite a nice-looking man, and he could have been moderately handsome if his swirl of internal uncertainty hadn't shown itself in his expression, his eye movements, and his hand fidgeting. His hair was mildly flecked in grey and clung naturally to his head in a way that hairdressers and barbers yearn to copy. His grey eyes would have been arresting if he could have stopped them flicking about. He had a strong jaw, masculine angular temples, good teeth, and lips of just the right fullness.

"Did the police tell you anything about the accident, George?"

"They … I don't … No, they didn't."

"Did you talk to Sergeant Cromarty?" Pause. "Tall man, auburn hair. Looks like an athlete", I added, when George's expression made it evident that he was having trouble placing Cromarty.

I got back a mumble.

"Did you speak to anyone from the police about it?"

Another, somewhat longer mumble.

So. Nobody had spoken to him about the accident itself. They probably had just asked questions about his brother's movements. It looked as though the case, such as it was, would turn into a waiting game. But it was clear to me what was likely to happen. They had a body. They had a number of facts. By now, they would have determined how Harold got there, found his car, and whether and where he had rented a place to stay. They had no leads. There were no witnesses. The case was dead. All they needed to do was wait a decent length of time, then declare it closed. Accident under unknown circumstances. Move on.

"Do you have any other brothers or sisters, George?"

The sudden change had caught him off balance. He blinked a couple of times and looked around, perhaps expecting the answer to be written somewhere on a wall.

"No … no, I … no, no brothers, no sisters."

"Parents both dead? Aunts? Uncles?"

No living relatives, apparently.

Pondering all this, I took a different tack.

"Harold lived here in Toronto, didn't he, George?"

"He … yes. Yes, he lived here."

To my question of where, I eventually got an address on Cosburn Avenue.

"What did he do, George? Where did he work?"

A long broken mumble, but there was something about a depot.

A bit more prodding fleshed this out to a UPS depot, where Harold assembled shipments of packages to be delivered by the couriers, and he had worked there for about five years. There were several other obvious questions, and there were things I would have to get George's help on checking out, but that was enough for one session. George was beginning to resemble someone just subjected to an eight-hour security vetting complete with polygraph and cavity search.

I nodded, took another swig of beer, and looked at George in what I hoped was a friendly way.

"There will be things to do, George. I'll help you, if you want. How be I make a list and then contact you tomorrow so we can go through it?"

George looked up and gave the first hint of what might have been a smile.

"Yes. Thanks ... I ... thanks..."

We finished our drinks, I paid, and we rose and made for the door. Outside, we both squinted in the bright sunshine. I pulled out my sunglasses, while George just shaded his eyes with one hand.

"I'll walk home with you, George. It's not far."

He nodded and made no objection, and as we began strolling along the street I had the feeling that I was gaining George's confidence.

Four

Andrea and I were lying together in bed, in contact from shoulder to ankle, just a single sheet over us to allow the heat from recent exertion to dissipate. There was a good feeling between us for other reasons as well. We had discussed, earlier that evening, the details of our upcoming two weeks in Largs, starting the day after tomorrow. I was looking forward to it, and my impression was that my interior-designer wife, despite being something of an overachiever at work, was looking forward to it as well. But before we went any further, I needed to navigate us into another area of discussion.

"There's a lot to be done there", I said, in reference to our properties at Largs, at the end of a long and pleasant silence, expecting to shunt the discussion adroitly from principles to practicalities.

Andrea's raised eyebrow was far more eloquent than any question.

"A lot of windows and window frames need replacing, there are electrical problems throughout some of the cottages, all the cottage roofs need to be checked, parts of floors in at least four of the cottages need replacing, and there are a hundred and one cosmetic improvements crying out to be done. Requests to use the church for weddings have doubled over the past three years, and parts of the inside are starting to look sad. Plus, the sprinkler systems in the church and administration building need upgrading or we're going to be hit by higher insurance premiums."

As I stumbled through this laundry list, Andrea fixed me in an expressionless gaze.

"We're not seeing a lot of net cash flow from Largs as it is", she said, by way of a caution. "If we're not careful, we'll be sliding into the red."

"True", I agreed, "but we'll be in the red anyway if we don't stay on top of things. And there's the potential to go solidly into the black if we tackle the problem systematically in a long-term plan."

Andrea stirred under the sheet, signalling her rising impatience at not seeing clearly what point I was making.

"And who's going to do all this work?" she asked neutrally.

Here it was. Time to place my bet, put everything into the pot, up the ante.

"You are", I said, as calmly as possible.

She was up on one elbow in a flash.

Short digression here.

I'm probably a fairly normal, well-educated male. I like discussion. I respond to intelligent people. Informed individuals, both women and men, turn me on mentally. Because of my background, growing up in what I still consider a perfect idyllic environment, living in a village that was constructed having substance and durability in mind, and most of all having had my own private Beatrice to guide me (my Beatrice being Balsam Lake), I tend not to be attracted to, or impressed by, ephemera.

But...

Then there's that flighty part of masculinity. I have blind spots that shift unexpectedly and suddenly occlude whole areas of rational awareness. It was getting to know Andrea that made me conscious of my hormonal existence, and this upset my prior simplistic view of myself considerably. Realizing at last, in an honest, visceral way, that I am subject to random bursts of testosterone that can take me from lofty mountaintop contemplation to roiling in a fetid swamp, all in five seconds flat, was, well, revealing. Hearing the words "you can be difficult to get along with" took some time to square with myself.

As I regarded Andrea now, resting in challenge on one elbow, I could see all the things that were so attractive about this person who is my soul mate but definitely her own woman: the open expression that revealed a clear, compassionate mind, the inquiring, ever-curious air that had helped lead us sometimes into long, sharply focused but labyrinthine discussions, sometimes into short, sharp-edged debates, and often into paroxysms of laughter, the sandy hair, cut to a plain mid-length that framed her oval, light olive face, the almond-shaped grey-blue eyes that were portals into an active intelligence, the firm but relaxed mouth that was never far from breaking into a range of smiles, the…

But I was also keenly aware of all the aspects of her body: the bewitching sweep from shoulders to waist, the slender perfectly formed hips, the smallish breasts that were so inviting precisely because they were in such sweet proportion to the rest of the…

"Me?"

I couldn't read her expression, but I was pretty sure it wasn't anger. More surprise than anything, but beyond that her expression was opaque.

"Me? Did I just hear you right?"

"Yes. It's time I made my admission, Andrea. I'm good at conceptual stuff – planning, seeing what needs to be done and in what order. But I'm no good at all with my hands. Whenever I try to drive a nail, it bends over like someone about to be decapitated, and the board ends up being a case of terminal battery. On the other hand, you're a natural with your hands, and I know you like doing that kind of work."

"Where is all this coming from?" she asked, but from her expression I thought she had a good idea.

"This is my take on what the marriage counsellor said. She told us we had no real problems, but that we should, you know, think about some adjustments."

"Adjustments."

"Yeah. Both of us move to our strengths."

"Odd. I didn't hear her say that."

Ignoring that comment, I was about to plunge on, but she got there first.

"So, I'm going to be doing everything now, is that it?" Once again, more a question of curiosity, surprise, and confusion at not seeing something coming, but no real hint of rising anger.

We had now reached the second breakpoint, and it was time to play my ace. Not without danger, I thought, and offering a little prayer to St. William, patron saint of stone cottages, I let go my handholds on our better-than-average marriage and dropped into what could end up being relationship free fall.

"No. We just need to reorganize who does what. And it's me who needs to take on a lot of the domestic stuff, particularly meals and cooking." All I could do now was wait for the shotgun blast that would take my head off.

"So, you think I can't cook, is that it?" This surprisingly mild rejoinder bolstered my courage a little.

"No. You're a good cook, but so am I. And I love cooking. And I've had the feeling for some time that I'm not pulling my weight in this household."

She fell back onto the bed, folding her arms across her chest in an adult pout. We lay there, looking at the ceiling, my thoughts becoming darker, wondering whether I had miscued the whole thing, wondering if this entire initiative was going to crash and burn. I had worked out in my head what a reasonable readjustment would look like, and it seemed fine to me. So I thought. But, as I knew from experience, brilliant nighttime flashes of insight, when exposed to the cruel sunlight of midday, can turn out to be just watery redundancies or hazy mental confusions that don't even pass the laugh test. Maybe I had tried to go too far on my own in search of the ultimate marital mantra. Maybe we should both start from square one. Maybe I was just digging a misadventurous hole…

My jumble of looming cumulonimbus thoughts was interrupted as Andrea suddenly rolled over on top of me.

"So that's the way it is, is it?" she said in challenge. "You could have given me some warning. What do we do now?" The question was half complaint, half inquiry.

"You mean right now, or…"

A hand started doing things to me.

"What we do right now should be pretty obvious, even to someone as poor at taking hints as you. What about later on?"

"Later on. Well…"

The hand was seriously at work now, and it was becoming difficult to think straight.

"I phthink tongorrrow we ngake song lists ang theng go out ang guy song tools", my pronunciation being warped in that predictable way when one's lower lip is caught between a set of teeth.

"Tools?" she asked impishly.

"Tools."

"Big tools?"

It was about then that the primal night took over once more.

Five

When I awoke next morning, the sky was full of light, and the air resounded to those avian declarations generally referred to as "songs" but which are actually open challenges, naked threats, and war cries. Andrea usually worked for an hour or two at home before going to the office where she and her two partners run their business. But it was still only a little before six thirty, and she was sleeping soundly, so I climbed carefully out of bed, grabbed my watch from the night table, my shoes from the floor, and some clean clothes from my closet, and I headed off to the shower. Our condo is in one of the old warehouses in the east end of old town Toronto. It was rescued from oblivion and converted to residential use about five years ago and was ahead of the curve in refusing to label the units "lofts", despite the wonderful fourteen-foot ceilings. Andrea convinced the developer to let her do all the interior design for our unit, and she did such a fantastic job that even at the initial drawings and artist impression stage, the developer wanted to use our unit as the basis for their advertising and sales literature. We accepted, for a small fee, of course, and it was that fee that allowed us to install the pool at Largs.

I knew that by the time Andrea came down to our breakfast corner, I would need to have ready the details from last night on our proposed new division of labour, so over coffee and a freshly buttered kaiser roll, I set to work. By eight o'clock, I had a list of ten large tasks broken down into subtasks. I had made a list of the supplies and tools needed to finish those subtasks, highlighting the tools we didn't already have at Largs. It wasn't a huge list, although three of the items on it were bulky, and there were a few vanity items. I had printed off about fifteen pages from the Lee Valley Tools website, circled the items needed, and swallowed a bit at the $7000+ total. A first rough schedule for my ten tasks would stretch over more than two years, and the equipment needed could be purchased over that time. These calculations and small pile of figures would be enough to pinch off any snap accusations that I was shooting from the DIY hip.

I could hear Andrea surfacing, and before she began her descent to the breakfast area, I had tucked my little pile of notes and calculations into a drawer, was deep into the morning paper, a typical male who, in the grip of a late-night testosterone inflammation, had made sweeping promises and commitments, and then almost immediately forgotten about them.

"Ahh!" I said in greeting, folding closed the paper. "Coffee?"

"Yes, please", Andrea said, as she went to the fridge for a yogurt. Returning and sitting in front of the cup of coffee I had just set down at her place, she pulled the plastic lid off the small yogurt container, took a spoonful, and smiled across at me.

"Any further thoughts on what we discussed last night?"

"What?" I said, looking up and playing dumb.

"Tools."

"Oh! That!"

Without saying anything in reply, Andrea rose, found a small roll and some butter, and returned to the table. Looking down at the notes and calculations that had materialized beside her placemat, she frowned, then smiled slowly and looked up.

"So! You really are serious!"

"We can go through that list of tasks today, take a look at the buildings tomorrow when we're at Largs, and you can decide which one of them we should tackle first. Then I suggest we work out a detailed plan for that task, do a tabletop walkthrough to check that we haven't missed anything important, and then make a final list of all the tools and fittings we'll need right away. Before we head off to Lee Valley…"

"Hang on!" she said, holding up one hand. "This is all going a bit fast."

"Okay. We can slow it down."

"Not just that. I want to think about it."

"You can't think in a vacuum, Andrea. We need to pick something concrete, get our heads around it, try to see how we would do it, then we think about it. Really. We need to look at something specific at Largs."

"And if I decide it's not for me, not something I really want to do?"

"Then we find another way." We looked at each other for a few seconds. "We spent the time and effort sitting with that marriage counsellor", I began, breaking a lengthening silence. "She was very positive, and she did suggest a way forward. I'm all in favour of just trying something. If it doesn't work, or we don't like it, well, then we try something else."

The particular pattern of wrinkles on Andrea's brow was easy enough for me to read, although from experience I knew not to make it too obvious that I could tell what she was thinking.

"What?" I said.

"You know very well 'what'!"

"Okay. This is new for me too. I'm not entirely comfortable with it. I'm not certain that it will work. But I'm not prepared just to do nothing. Maybe what I've suggested isn't that good. Maybe there's a better way. If so, let's find it."

Her continued hesitation was a good sign, since she is strong-willed enough just to say "No dice" to something that she is sure isn't right or won't work.

"On the other hand", I chirped happily, after a silence had stretched out between us, "we could just default to what we do best and go back to bed".

The spoonful of yogurt splatted across my face, but Andrea's smirk robbed it of any offence.

"Sometimes I wonder why I put up with you."

"Ah! It's just the celestial music we make together."

Andrea's expression cleared, then she rose, got a piece of paper towel, and carefully cleaned the yogurt off my face. "Okay, hunk. Let's go."

"Back to bed?"

"No, you twit. We both need, or at least one of us needs, to go to work. But I know that I'll be thinking about Largs all day now."

I knew that my attention would be drawn likewise, but the small smile on Andrea's lips as she left the condo told me that feeling compelled to think about Largs would be no hardship.

In the background, George and his brother and the "case" surged once more, demanding my time and attention.

Six

There isn't any place I would call my office, except for our condo. That's where my filing system is, an important component to be sure, but for me to be able to work, the essentials are just a cellphone, a laptop, a notebook, a pen, and, some way down the list, a car. I had established an early rule that people connected to jobs I'm working on don't get invited to our condo. There is such a thing as mental contagion, and I don't want any of it in our home. It's not that I feel I'm susceptible to any particularly jaundiced view of the world, quite the contrary, but my work now, and previously in the police force, necessarily exposed me to the darker sides of our society. At the worst of times, almost all the people I come across seem to be from the "dark side", dark not only in the sense of being constitutionally ill-equipped misfits, luckless, or feckless, but also unsavoury, dangerous, even satanic. I don't work for the worst of these people, but they infect the lives of my clients, and the contagion can spread easily.

In the population at large, the fraction of people who are actively dark, the psychopaths, is small, just a few percent, and the majority of people seem able to field the right elements of temperament and motivation that allow them to find a path through life leading to some form of contentment. But everybody has a dark side, and under the right conditions that dark side can show its face. I guess my ongoing concern is that if I spend too much time exposed to those on, or tainted by, the dark side, and have no safe refuge from all that, such as our condo, the bright backlit face of the world that I'm always ready to perceive, the goodness, the wholesomeness, the real joy in life, could fade and die for me.

As I cleared up the breakfast things, I roamed vaguely through my own life path to date: studying science at university, deciding I'd had enough of that by the time I had achieved a first degree, spending an appalling and excruciatingly boring year being a desk jockey at a chemical company, having a sudden enthusiasm for police work, being a beat cop and finding that I enjoyed it most of the time, moving up through the ranks quickly, being turned off by the internal politics, spending a year at Largs to regroup and to work on my property inheritance, meeting Andrea one night at a lakeside restaurant, being married, and then hanging out my own private investigator's shingle. It all seemed a bit like a random walk when looked at from a distance, but as each change in direction occurred, that change seemed obvious, intelligent, and judicious. That was my sun-drenched happy-face self-image.

I had worried about Largs for more than two decades, and I had struggled for more than ten years to bring the properties I owned there to a higher level of maintenance, appeal, profitability, and long-term viability. We were getting there, but the threat of some horror surging out of the murk and tipping us over into serious debt was never far away. Just selling up and being free of it was always a possibility, but even the thought of doing that was like putting my own arm on the chopping block. The place had a much-too-powerful grip on me. It was my refuge, my paradise, my own little continuously reappearing Brigadoon. Largs had been one of the few bright linings in what I came later to understand had been my mother's otherwise generally unhappy life. So I had complex feelings for the place: visceral connection, responsibility, love. But, really, when I came right down to it, Largs reflected, and it has always felt right that it should reflect, my basic optimism, and Largs was always where I went to recharge that particular wellspring.

Having thus dithered and procrastinated, not being able just to sit down and enjoy a Wednesday off, I slid into what turned out to be a partial working day at low revs on the terrace. My first call was to George. The end result, the kernel of intelligence, garnered from four minutes of pauses, hesitations, and backtracking, was that no further information had come to him from the police. I told him I would keep in touch.

Bent Cromarty was less than ecstatic to receive my next call, but I did eventually manage to extract a promise from him that he would keep me up to date every two days or so, along with an acknowledgement that I was acting on behalf of George and that information on the case should be shared with me. Extracting blood from a stone fell well short as an accurate characterization of that discussion.

Apart from my work on George's case, my intention was to stick to my plan and take the week off. That message certainly hadn't reached my telephone, which seemed to ring every fifteen minutes. In the end, three people said they would call me back in a few weeks, and I committed myself to three more jobs, but none of them would start for two weeks.

I had two books on the go, but somehow reading didn't seem to be the cure for what ailed me, and I couldn't raise the interest to open either of them. Watering the plants on the terrace seemed like a good idea, and that took five minutes. Breezes lifted the leaves of the large trumpet plants that Andrea likes and brought the occasional scent from the herb garden to me. The watering finished, and being out on the terrace, it was natural just to collapse into a reclining chair. More breezes puffed into the terrace, and I slid down into the chair, put on my sunglasses, and enjoyed the morning. Lying there, behind my shades, was so reminiscent of the house at Largs, the trees that stand all around whispering *bons mots*, the lake resting happily in one of its surreal dreams, and the pool we had installed there. It's a small pool for relaxing only, not large enough to do any swimming. We have the lake for that. But the pool is special, not least because of the features Jimmy had added.

Jimmy is our handyman. He's been around for years, and I agreed to let him live in the cottage that had been my home in Largs in pre-Andrea days, while I was in university and still had the large house rented. He gets the place rent-free in exchange for being available as needed to do any odd jobs that crop up. He also does larger jobs, but I insist on paying him for them even though he feels all his needs are met if he can see a couple hundred dollars a week. These needs became even more modest once he had the rent-free cottage.

When I first floated the idea of a pool, Jimmy was mystified. He looked at me, he looked at the lake, then he looked at me again, clearly thinking I had gone barking mad. But when I showed him where I wanted the pool, that I wanted it heated, and that I wanted it to have access and sightlines only from the house, he became more interested. We dug out the space where the pool would be located, and then Jimmy put in the basic structure, the lining, and the large tiles surrounding the pool on three sides. Jimmy had had no idea what an "infinity" pool was, but when I described it, he shrugged, made a couple of vague hand gestures that said clearly enough "Okay, if that's what you want", and did the work. But it was his plan for heating that really surprised me.

The picture Jimmy drew for me was of a length of hose fastened in a back-and-forth switchback pattern to a lightweight steel frame. I made a few changes to it, and Jimmy took the whole thing from there. He bought four hundred feet of garden hose, put together the rectangular frame out of lengths of tubing, had a local welder fabricate a strong base and support, bought the small pump, connectors, electrical fittings, temperature measurement, and flow control gear, and assembled it all. When he had finished, we had a solar heating array aimed at a specifically chosen point in the sky and a system that drew two streams of water from the lake. One of these streams was heated and one wasn't, and when they were combined using flows determined by the temperature control scheme, the resulting warm water was fed into the pool. An equal flow of water slipped over the infinity edge as a film sliding down the angled exterior pool wall that faced the lake, passed through a small filtration and treatment device, and then was returned to the lake. Jimmy's solar heater was hidden from view behind an eight-foot hedge. Andrea had been skeptical of the whole venture, but became increasingly interested as it took shape, and ultimately became by far the most frequent user of the pool.

My thoughts by this time had shifted fully to Largs, and I spent half an hour pondering which of the ten projects I had outlined for Andrea we should start first. She would have her own ideas, but would expect me to offer my suggestions. Reflecting on all this, eyes closed, smiling stupidly at the sky, not bringing to bear any real mental discipline, meant that I was subject to some wandering. And even though I had said to myself that my earlier telephone calls would be the end of work for the day, that I would spend no more time thinking about work, my mental wandering soon led me back to George's brother's "accident".

The facts of the case were very skimpy indeed, and a single page, obtained from Cromarty, was more than adequate to contain them all. Harold Barbour's body had been found wedged among rocks in a small inlet on the east side of Indian Point. The body was clad in bathing trunks and one diving fin. Apart from the deep wounds across the back, evidently caused by a boat propeller, there were numerous marks elsewhere on the body, presumed by the police to have been the result of waves bringing it repeatedly into contact with rocks on the shore where it had been found. This presumption struck me as being too quick, too easy. No consideration appeared to have been given to the possibility that there could have been other much less innocent causes for more than one of those marks. Because of the body having been immersed in water, time of death had to be determined based on measures of decomposition, and from this it was estimated that the body had been in the water two to three days.

That was it. No physical evidence of anything. No witnesses. No suspect boats. No reports from anyone. *Time to become proactive*, I thought, as I pulled out my phone once more.

"Hi, Kate? Yes, it's me, Mark. Yes, fine, thanks. Both fine. We'll be at Balsam Lake tomorrow afternoon. Any chance of getting together? Yes, The Repose would be fine. We can be there by late afternoon, let's say about five thirty. Excellent! See you then."

We chatted a bit more.

"Yes, there is something else, Kate. Somewhere out on Balsam Lake, a canoe has gone missing. Could you keep a look out for it? No idea. No, I don't know what kind or what colour, but it might be somewhere along the shore of Indian Point. No. Not sure. What? Oh, yes, you can start looking whenever you like, the sooner the better actually. No. Sorry. I can't be any more specific than that."

Kate had a few more questions.

"I know, it does seem like a very odd request, but I'd rather fill you in when I see you at The Repose. Yes. Looking forward to it. And I know Andrea is as well."

Seven

The remainder of the day loped past. I dozed on my reclining chair, moving every half-hour or so either to be in or out of the direct sun. At two o'clock, I fished out the window-washing gear and cleaned the terrace windows. There was no real need, but it made me feel better. Andrea keeps a Mediterranean schedule, so she wouldn't be home before seven thirty or eight. Responding to a vague unease at just flopping all day, I strolled past my shelves of books, but decided that my energy levels had dropped too low to start into anything more demanding than *Dick and Jane*, the stress of relaxing being what it is. I watch very little television, and in any case the tube's normal mindless content would have plummeted even further to its midafternoon amoebic level.

It would still be a long way to dinner, but my new roles of provisioner, chef, and kitchen staff were more appealing than anything I had come up with so far today, and I pondered what to make us for dinner. It took barely twenty minutes for an enticing menu to assemble itself in my mind.

Something tasty but not too overwhelming.

(But even so, my client's problem kept raising its head in the background. Harold's death wasn't an accident, of that I was almost certain, and I was hoping that finding the canoe might clarify things one way or the other.)

Artichoke hearts in extra-virgin olive oil, a few crushed capers, a grind of pepper, and a decent sprinkling of coarsely grated Asiago promised to do yeoman service as an appetizer.

(If it wasn't an accident, then my best course would be to take whatever evidence I had to the police and let them deal with it, wash my hands of the matter.)

Then would follow smoked salmon and pasta in a white sauce made using mascarpone and a dash of vodka, completed by strips of red pepper, finely separately broccoli florets, and sugar snap peas, the vegetables all lightly steamed and mixed into the salmon and pasta just before serving.

(I would still need to help George come to terms with things, since that appeared to be the humane thing to do.)

And we would drift through dessert on a raft of my own *tarte au sucre*. There was the right amount of time available to do a good job on this, which meant going out and getting what I needed, allowing the appetizer components (except for the Asiago) to sit and infuse for a couple of hours, and making the *tarte* far enough in advance that it would be cooled by the time it was needed.

(But then there had been Cromarty's reaction – one-track, bull-headed, and evidently fixated on driving through what it seemed to me that his superiors had decided would be the fate of this case. Was I just going to give it my one best shot, then say to hell with it all if Cromarty remained intransigent? I was reminded again of an Andrea comment, raised more than once, that I pursued problems beyond all reasonable limits, then justified myself by saying that's what my clients expected.)

After getting the ingredients at the market, I put together the appetizer, prepared the *tarte*, and got the elements for the main course lined up. By then, it was time to check that the wine glasses still worked, and it seemed that a good rosé would match all the courses well.

I bounced back and forth in increasing frustration between cooking and client. At six thirty, I took the *tarte au sucre* out of the oven, smiled back at it, and went off to check my e-mail.

To my surprise, there was something from Bent Cromarty. The bare essence of his message, which took a fair bit of boiling down to reach, was that the police had exhausted all leads in the Harold Barbour case, the prospect of further advance was expected to be zero, and the case would be closed in the morning. He also noted in the message that he had sent me an e-mail attaching some notes on the Barbour case. That was the news I'd been waiting for. I called George, and he confirmed that Cromarty, or somebody, had contacted him. Keeping George on the telephone, I opened the attachment to Cromarty's e-mail and read it quickly.

They had found Harold's car near the shore of Balsam Lake, off a rarely used stretch of dirt track on the east side of Indian Point. There were some notes on the site investigation that had been carried out by the police. The police had also learned that he had been staying at a cheap, rundown, and dispiriting holiday cabin outside Fenelon Falls. The police had collected Harold's things from the cabin and towed his car to a garage in Coboconk. The car and suitcase were there waiting to be claimed. I related some of this to George, told him about Harold's car, and said that I would look after reclaiming it, but that George had to authorize me to do it. This appeared to pose for him a major conceptual hurdle. I was amazed when he told me that he had an e-mail account. I said I would send him the text of a message that he should then transmit to the police, to the garage, and to me, using e-mail addresses that I would also send him.

"You should do that today, George, and let me know if you have any problems. Okay?"

"Yes … okay. But, I … there's … something else has happened."

It took another five minutes to get out of George that he had received a letter from a lawyer saying that he, the lawyer, had Harold's will and that George should collect it.

"How did the lawyer find out this quickly that Harold had died?" I asked George. "Did you know that Harold had prepared a will? Do you know what it says?"

He didn't, on all counts.

To my alarm, what I heard next was a wrenching sob.

"Mr. Whelan, I'm not … I ca- … ca- … Harold was … my brother! I can't do this … Mr. Whelan!"

"I'm very sorry for what's happened, George, and I will help you. Where is this lawyer's office?"

George managed to give me the address.

"Okay, George, here's what we'll do. Tomorrow morning, I'll meet you at your place, and we'll go together to the lawyer's office and pick up Harold's will. Don't worry, George. I'll be with you all the way."

George sniffled a bit, said thanks six times, and I assured him we would work out a plan to look after everything. I got George to tell me that he was okay, and I told him he had to get himself something to eat.

"Order in a pizza, George, or some Chinese food. Things will work out. You'll see."

We talked a bit more about inconsequential stuff, and I said he could forget about the e-mails since he and I would make the arrangements needed when I saw him in the morning.

"You sure you're okay, George? Get yourself something to eat, and get a good night's rest."

He mumbled something and said thanks a few more times.

"See you tomorrow, George. Ten o'clock at your place."

At least the mumbling now sounded less agitated.

"Good night, George."

Seeing someone in that much distress always disturbs me. Especially when the someone doesn't know where or how even to begin in coming to terms with it. I keep a case notebook, and I opened it now and jotted a page and a half of items based on our conversation and what looked at the moment to be some of the implications of what I had heard. What had started off looking simple was quickly seeming much less so.

Acting on one of the notes I had made, I sent a quick text message to Kate, confirming our conversation earlier, and making my request more specific. At that point, I had to put the matter behind me. Andrea would be home soon, and there should be no gloomy moods or downcast expressions. A number of things were beginning, and in the expectation of bringing them to completion, I cued up the first movement of Beethoven's Fifth as a warning to the forces of darkness that I would persevere and victory would be mine. Or something like that. Seven minutes and four seconds later, through the intervention of von Karajan and the Berlin Philharmonic, my personal sky had cleared.

The rest of the evening flowed smoothly. Andrea arrived home at quarter to eight, I snatched her bulging briefcase from her, steadied her while she kicked off her shoes, and led her to a comfortable chair, in front of which just happened to be some appetizer and a glass of rosé. By this time, all hard edges in the room had been softened by Richard Stoltzman's liquid relaxation. The meal flowed without a hitch, although Andrea was oddly quiet, and I was pretty sure it had to do with more than just tiredness. A sense, perhaps, that the job of putting food in front of us, an activity she had regarded as essentially hers, had been usurped? But from the first bite of dessert it took less than half an hour for the *tarte au sucre* to begin tugging Andrea's eyelids down. She was beat. We climbed the stairs and crashed happily, just like two people ready to escape to the country for a couple of weeks.

Well, one of us crashed. I lay awake going through the catalogue of things I would be pursuing on George's behalf, but also totting up a list of events and situations, loosely interconnected, but all associated in some way with Harold Barbour.

Eight

Andrea loves her work, and she is tenacious, very committed, and single-minded in her approach to any job. Her work is brilliant, arresting, sublime, and various combinations of these and other things, as the case demands. She spends a lot of time querying, nudging, and offering suggestions to her clients. This is draining, and it often shows in Andrea's expression at the end of a day.

I awoke fully refreshed just before six o'clock, and I spent a minute or two looking at Andrea in the bed beside me, very deep in sleep, her face neutral, completely relaxed, and bearing no signs of tension, as her remarkable system recharged those reservoirs of energy and optimism that were among the first things attracting me to her. She would sleep for at least another hour, and during that time I would make some of the preparations in readiness for our trip to Largs later in the morning. It was a working day, Thursday, so there was no point in making an early start and having to fight the rush-hour traffic. We would aim to leave at eleven. That would put us in Largs at about one thirty. We would open the house, get settled for our two-week stay, and go out and buy locally the provisions we would need. I would check with Jimmy, see whether anything needed doing urgently, and he and I would go through the list of things he was working on in the long-term effort to raise gradually to a higher standard the properties Andrea and I owned at Largs. I knew that Andrea would take some work with her, because for her and her two partners the business never really slept, but one of the first things she would do at Largs would be to have a long soak in the pool and gaze out over moody Balsam Lake. I never objected to Andrea taking work to Largs, since I was often caught up by that need myself, and today, in particular, I had to be at George's place early in order to meet the lawyer at ten.

At eight o'clock, Andrea was up. I had already had a scratch breakfast, so we shared morning coffee at eight thirty and agreed on a schedule for our departure for Largs. Although it would take me less than twenty minutes to get to George's place, I set out at just before nine. Not having any idea what George was like in the morning, or how long it would take him to do anything, I erred on the safe side, since I wanted to be ready and waiting for the lawyer at ten, and back home by eleven. My precaution was justified.

When I arrived at George's place, he was partly ready, but adrift in a massive cloud of confusion, some of it probably natural and some of it no doubt due to present circumstances. Somehow we managed to be free of his place by nine thirty, and we were at the lawyer's office at quarter to ten.

The lawyer's name was Hawley, and his operation appeared to be a single-person affair, but judging from the neatness of his office, the amount of space given over to filing, and the fact that he had two assistants who clearly were busy, he had a thriving and efficient practice. He rose to greet us as we were shown into his office, and he said "Mr. Barbour?" as he looked from one to the other of us. I inclined my head toward George, who began stumbling and dithering right away.

"Mark Whelan", I said to Hawley, extending my hand and dropping my card on his desk. "I'm assisting George as he tries to come to terms with what's happened."

Hawley took my hand, but the puzzled look on his face told me right away that I had missed something.

"I'm not sure I understand", Hawley said, looking again from one to the other of us. "What *has* happened?"

"The recent death of George's brother, Harold. Isn't that what you wanted to see George about?"

Hawley looked bewildered, but recovered quickly.

"No. I wasn't aware that Harold had died. Please accept my condolences, Mr. Barbour."

"It's evident that we've misunderstood something, Mr. Hawley. Could you explain, from your point of view, what led to this meeting?"

"Yes. Certainly. Last week I was instructed by Harold Barbour to pass these two envelopes to his brother, George. He said specifically that there was no rush, and that sometime within the next ten business days would be fine." As he said this, Hawley indicated two sealed envelopes lying on his desk.

George was suddenly pale and withdrawn, probably fearing another experience like the one at the morgue, or even worse.

"So, you weren't aware that Harold had died?" I asked.

"No. Absolutely not."

Hawley hesitated here, and before he could carry on, I jumped in again.

"What is in the envelopes? Do you know?"

"One of them contains Harold's will. I don't know what the other one contains."

"Why would Harold want George to have a copy of his will while he was still alive?"

"I asked him that. He said that he had never spoken to George about his will or what it said, and he just wanted his brother to be aware. So now I'm passing these letters to you, Mr. Barbour", picking them up and reaching them toward George as he said this, "and I will ask you to sign, acknowledging receipt."

George recoiled as though he were being handed a poisonous snake.

I felt I had to jump in again. "Harold was found dead four days ago on the shore of Balsam Lake, a victim of what the police are calling a boating accident. It has come as an enormous shock to George, and he has asked me to act for him, help him get through this. Do you agree to me taking the letters?"

"As long as Mr. Barbour signs, I have no problem."

I took the form acknowledging receipt that Hawley was holding, looked it over quickly, placed it in front of George while handing him a pen, and asked him to sign. In deep water and unable to touch bottom, George hesitated and cast me the pleading look of an unhappy spaniel. I smiled at him encouragingly, and he took the pen and signed.

"I'm going to open these now on your behalf, George. Do you agree?" George nodded, wearing a let's-get-this-over-with expression.

I opened the will and read. It was simplicity itself. Harold left everything to George, and in an attachment there was a list of the major items: the contents of his rented apartment, his car, the money in his bank accounts, and the contents of his safety deposit box. The other letter contained a single folded sheet of paper. On the sheet were four pairs of numbers:

-0.0009	0.0199
-0.0212	0.0168
0.0113	0.0203
-0.0053	0.0392

Nothing else.

"I'm going to hang onto these for you, George", I said. Without waiting for a reply, I turned to Hawley. "Could you make a copy of each of these and keep them until I ask for them again?" Hawley nodded, and asked one of his assistants to make the copies.

For George's sake, we needed to wrap this up. I thanked Hawley. "If anything further comes up", I said as I rose, "could you contact me by phone or e-mail?" Hawley nodded, he shook hands with me and then with George, and I ushered George out of the office.

There were two things I wanted to do practically right away. One of them was to pay a flying visit to Harold's rented apartment. Harold's personal effects found in his car, including his wallet and keys, had been sent to Toronto with his body. We had collected them from Cromarty at the morgue, and they were now in the cloth bag I was carrying, since I had hoped to pass them over to George. Change of plan on that. The second thing was to talk to Andrea, and she wouldn't be thrilled at what I was going to suggest.

Outside Hawley's office, I flagged a cab, and we went to George's apartment, where I asked the cabbie to wait. What we had to do there took only five minutes, thanks to me bullying George and him being in shock. Back in the cab, we drove to Harold's apartment building. It took a few minutes to find the right keys on Harold's key chain, but we got into the building, then into Harold's apartment. I didn't expect Harold's flat to be neat and tidy, and it wasn't.

The place had been comprehensively ransacked.

Nine

"But you don't even know him!"

"That's true, Andrea, but he is my client, and he – "

"This was supposed to be time off for us!"

"And it will be. He won't be in our way. It's only to get him out of town, and because it's really not safe to leave him on his own."

There was a long eloquent silence.

"I'll look after him, Andrea. You won't need to speak to him or have anything to do with him. He won't be in our way. I promise."

My cellphone abruptly went dead.

George and I arrived at our condo building. I paid the taxi, took him in the elevator straight to the parking garage, walked with him to my parking space, and asked him to wait in the car. A normal person would have been surprised or offended, but George was meek as a lamb.

Upstairs in our condo, Andrea was tense and bristly, an earthquake just waiting for a trigger. She grabbed the bag she had packed, leaving mine to rest by the door in telling solitude, then we locked up in silence and walked toward the elevator. The air in the hallway chilled by a good fifteen degrees as we passed through it, and I expected hoar frost to form on the buttons in the elevator. As we approached our car in the parking garage, we could see George sitting in the back seat immobile as a crash test dummy. Andrea cast me a sideways glance that challenged my decision to leave him here, alone, in a soulless parking garage, but I picked up my pace, opened the trunk and put both our bags in it. Andrea climbed into the passenger seat, belted up, and then just stared straight ahead, also well on the way to crash test dummy status.

It was a long, silent twenty minutes later, and we were on the Parkway, well on our way out of town, before Andrea turned in her seat.

"Hello, George. I'm Andrea."

George jumped, prodded back into an unforgiving reality. His mouth worked soundlessly for a moment before he could make any utterance, and when it came out the meaning in it was well concealed.

"I … George … I'm very pleased … my brother … I suppose … you know…"

I glanced across quickly at Andrea. Although she can be ruthless professionally, a person or an animal in distress brings out her empathy at full wattage.

"Yes", she said through a sympathetic smile. "I'm very sorry about your brother. I hope that a few days' quiet in the country appeals to you. I always find it very refreshing." Another smile, fuller and brighter this time. I could just see part of George's face in the rear-view mirror, and a faint smile shimmered behind his features.

"We can spend some time talking when we get there, George. For now, I hope you don't mind if I doze a little. It's been a long few days for me." Without waiting for a reply, she turned to face forward again, almost immediately slid down in the seat a bit, laid her head back against the headrest, and closed her eyes. Some kind of hypnotic suggestion must have been at work, because within a few minutes I noticed George's eyelids fluttering, and soon he was asleep in the back seat.

I drove on in silence. Traffic was light, and the freeway was of no inherent interest, just a means for covering a distance.

Largs can be reached from Toronto by a number of possible routes. The one I use almost exclusively follows the freeway to its junction with Highways 115/35. From there, the car could practically drive itself. And the route from there always causes me to delve into some corner of my mental scrapbook. As it climbs away from Lake Ontario, the highway passes through a horrific strip of business slum that lines both sides of the road, something that I try to ignore. I concentrate instead on the graceful sweep of apple orchards to the left, and Lake Ontario behind, winking serenely in the sunlight. Mercifully, having the highway bypass Orono spares that lovely village from the fate of gutted congestion that has condemned many others, but for some reason, Orono always reminds me of the life and sad death of the friendliest large cat in the world, Bongo the lion. Beyond Orono, the Ganaraska Forest sleeps to the right, and almost immediately we are into glacial terrain. Here, strong memories often jump up and dance joyfully in my head, and it was all started by Mr. Talbot.

In fact, Mr. Talbot, my Grade 4 teacher, started a lot of things for me. But it was his discussion of the village of Cameron that first piqued my curiosity, giving me an interest that began when I was ten, and I'm sure will last until I draw my final breath.

Mr. Talbot said that the village of Cameron is built on a drumlin, and encouraged us to go and look at it sometime. I was mildly curious, I suppose, and at a break in the class, I asked "What's a drumlin?" That was what began it all.

It had been a long way to go, but the following Saturday, I did cycle from Largs to Cameron, and then cycled around all its streets trying to get a better impression of the place. I made some rough measurements using the odometer on my bike, and the next day I drew a map of the village and indicated on it where the high points of the land were and how it sloped away. And it is a delightful setting, sweeping gracefully down to the east where Sturgeon Lake dozes in the middle distance, and to the west looking out over a tapestry of rich farmland.

That was just the beginning.

A few weeks later, I began wondering about the old lime kilns in Coboconk, since I saw them every time I cycled there. I asked Mr. Talbot. He looked at me in a curiously interested way. We were in the middle of a geography class, and the students were all reading an assignment Mr. Talbot had just handed out, so he and I spoke in whispers.

"I'm pretty sure", he said, "that there's a connection between Coboconk and Largs. Your family probably has something on the history of Largs. You should look it up." He then walked slowly to the back of the room. I had returned to the reading assignment, but a few moments later Mr. Talbot quietly placed a book on my desk. A slip of paper marked some spot in the book. I placed the book in my satchel, and as I looked up at Mr. Talbot, he winked and smiled. Later that day, I looked at the book at home and saw immediately that something was written on the slip of paper marking Chapter 7, "The Record of the Rocks". *Some words might be difficult. Ask me. G. Talbot.* Years later, I thought of that exchange when I began learning the details of how old McCleod had constructed Largs.

Our progress toward Largs jogged other memories, images of exploration from my youth, many of them also traceable back to Mr. Talbot's hints and suggestions, but the recollections were of my own solitary explorations, recollections that were brought back vividly by aspects of the landscape drifting past outside. Not until quite late in school had it occurred to me that school and learning could possibly be anything other than fascinating.

In primary school, I was always on the quiet side. I was good at baseball, but poor at soccer. It was in Grade 5 that I learned a hard lesson about being studious. And that lesson was delivered by the dastardly Mick Ahearn. I don't know why he took a dislike to me. But he did. Maybe because school was hard for him and easy for me. I found myself being jostled for no reason that I could see, tripped unexpectedly, and checked too heavily in soccer games. Soon, I realized that whenever something like that happened, the smirking, sneering face of Mick Ahearn was not far away. I began taking great care to stay out of his way, but this seemed to make him only more determined to seek me out.

"What's wrong?" Mrs. Hastings asked me gently one morning over breakfast.

"Nothing", I mumbled. I finished my breakfast quickly, collected my things, and went out to wait for the school bus. The truth was, and I knew it, that for the first time I was reluctant to go to school, and that was a barrier damping my natural urge to satisfy my thirst to learn, something that caused me great anxiety.

I suspect that Mrs. Hastings guessed what was wrong, and that she spoke to my teachers. In the end, things only became worse. I guessed why. Ahearn must have assumed that I had snitched on him.

It was a Thursday, and I had stayed to talk to Mr. Talbot. Another boy, John, was at his desk, staying late, doing his homework, probably because it was quieter at school than at his home. I collected my things and left. The school bus had already departed, but it was only four miles to my home, and I could walk that in about an hour and a half.

Without warning, I found myself on the ground.

Ahearn.

That bastard Ahearn was now sitting astride me, grinning maliciously, and showing his rotten front tooth.

"You need to learn some manners. Real men don't snitch."

"Real men aren't bullies!" I shouted back without thinking.

Ahearn's fist caught me between mouth and nose. I could taste blood from a split lip and warm liquid began running down my cheek. I struggled to push him off me, and almost succeeded. This angered him, and he wound up for another strike. I moved my head to one side, and his fist struck the hard ground instead of my face.

"Ahhh! You little bastard!" he shouted. His face was twisted in rage as he prepared to deliver another punch.

But then, suddenly, he fell to one side. I in turn rolled well clear of him, not sure just what had happened, and sat up in time to see a large length of wood hit Ahearn on the side of the head. John stood there, holding the piece of wood, while Ahearn rolled on the ground, moaning, cupping an ear that was now torn and bleeding. John wound up for another strike, but I grabbed his arm and shook my head.

"Stay away", John said quietly to Ahearn, the threat being that much more potent because it was so softly spoken. John threw the piece of wood down onto Ahearn, and we walked off, me trying to stem the flow of blood from my nose. But my gratitude to John and the taste of victory had pinched off the urge to cry. By the time I got home, my nose was clean, so to speak. Neither John nor I ever said anything about the brawl to anyone. But I noticed afterwards that I could look Ahearn in the face and he was the one who broke eye contact first.

We had reached the junction of Highways 35 and 7, just west of Lindsay. A few kilometres further on, we passed through a rock cutting down toward the area where Sturgeon Lake peters out into swamp at its southern end. The rock cutting had significance for me, since it is part of the great limestone cliff that snakes its way through Victoria County. A few miles further on, we rode over the drumlin on which the village of Cameron sits, and I experienced, once more, that inward thrill and smile that I felt all those years ago. After a bit more winding, we passed the turning to Fenelon Falls, rose up over a stub end of the Dummer moraine, and, as always, I was elated by the sweep of Cameron Lake to the right. We passed over the bridge at Rosedale, and then, five kilometres further along, the spire of the little church at Largs came into sight, through some trees on the left.

I have never had a "normal" return to Largs, and I looked across at Andrea, who was awake, relaxed, and now smiling at my own involuntary smile of arrival. Each return was different, I found, and this time there would be the pragmatic difference of having George with us. In addition, we would meet Kate in a few hours at The Repose in Rosedale, and I could feel myself slipping once again into the welcoming embrace of Largs, this time for a two-week stay.

Whatever it was I was expecting, it didn't turn out quite that way.

Ten

The entrance to Largs from Highway 35 is to the west along Arran Street, a long curving way lined on both sides by mature maple trees, and between these trees, as a continuing legacy of Mrs. Hastings, grow irregular clumps of daffodils and lupins. In the bright sunlight of our early afternoon in June, the volume of space above Arran Street, enclosed by the maples, was a bath of delicate warm air, tinged in green by the chlorophyll in tens of thousands of leaves, and enlivened by the metallic chatter of several parliaments of sparrows. In the last quarter of its route from Highway 35, Arran Street curves more sharply round toward the left, and enters the open square in Largs from the north. The square is bounded by the little church on the west, which sits next to the lake but is elevated a couple of metres above the shoreline, by our large house on the south, by the administration building on the north, lying just west of the area where Arran Street enters the square, and on the east by a long stone trough that was at one time a horse trough. More likely than not, one would find two or three small boys playing there with model boats. The trough is still supplied by a small stream of water as a focus of attention, both aural and visual, for anyone using the three benches located just behind it. Behind the benches is a forsythia hedge, and behind the hedge sits the first of the roughly forty cottages in the village. In the middle of the square is a large circular stone pedestal, on top of which sits a block of pink granite bearing the engraved names of the two Largs men who died during WWI, and the four who died during WWII. Before this monument was erected in the early 1950s, the space was occupied by the mule-driven grain mill old McCleod had built in the mid-nineteenth century. The square is paved in granite stones, and Jimmy keeps the whole area swept and tidied.

For a village in Ontario to have this kind of central square is unexpected, very much atypical, but it works today because local nature now has tamed the place. After spending not more than a day here, one becomes accustomed, indeed strongly attached, to something that at first glance seems Old World fake. I put it down to the rather narrow local conception of how an Ontario village ought to appear. The observation that Largs grows quickly on people has been validated more than once, when some whisper of a change to the square has led to a deafening roar of outrage from permanent residents, long time visitors, and newcomers alike.

To the east of the administration building, on the east side of Arran Street as it enters the square, is a longish building of more recent construction, built in stone facing to resemble the original cottages as closely as possible. This building houses Harris' food emporium, general store, hardware store, and drug store. Somehow Wally manages to deal with the massive but relatively short-lived peak in business during the summer and the long-depressed flow of business during the rest of the year. That is Wally's picture of the reality of his business, one that isn't universally shared.

The administration building sports that grand name because McCleod used it as his office space in Largs. It sat empty for quite a few years, was used as storage space for several local businesses for about a decade, but about ten years ago, I decided to make it available for people to operate local businesses, and it now has a small dairy and ice cream shop, a dry cleaner, and a custom furniture shop.

Kelvin Place is a modified cottage sitting next to the western end of the administration building, and over the space of a couple of years it had finally decided on its role in life. Kelvin Place was already quite busy when we arrived, and at the height of summer the trade is heavy and constant. It has an attractive seating area outside that extends westward right to the edge of the lake embankment, this seating area now already filled by people in the metabolic low gear of summer. I drove around the square to the right of the central monument, pulled into the narrow lane that runs between the end of our big house and the garden in front of the first of the cottages to the east, and turned into the carport behind our house, thereby avoiding the unnecessary and unaesthetic impact of having a car parked in the square.

I looked across at Andrea and she nodded, her irritation at the beginning of the trip apparently having been mollified by two hours' passage through countryside kissed by early summer.

"Here we are, George", I said. "Let me show you where you'll be sleeping, and then you and I can take a walk around the village."

George mumbled something incomprehensible and climbed out of the car carrying his small case. Andrea and I retrieved our things from the trunk, and I unlocked the house.

The first thing evident as the door opened was the delicate touch of Gladys Nelson's housework. Gladys cleans our house every week, and she somehow manages to leave behind a fresh, scented essence in the air. As we entered, Andrea and I looked around and smiled at "essence of Gladys", and George stopped just inside the door, taking in the feeling of spacious solidity that seems to be the first impression presented to visitors by our house at Largs. I showed George his room upstairs. After making sure that he was settled and knew where things were, I walked to the other end of the house. Mild euphoria at another Largs arrival carrying me forward, I grabbed Andrea around the waist and delivered a mock passionate kiss to her neck.

"What! Wild sex in midafternoon?" she said, without even breaking her unpacking routine.

"Well", I shrugged. "It's midnight someplace."

We stood there for a moment, me clasping her about the waist, nose buried in her fragrant hair, both looking across our large second-floor bedroom and out through a generous window facing westward over the lake.

"Going to soak in the pool?" I asked, releasing my grip on her waist, and moving around so we were face to face.

"Yes", she said as she unpacked her case mechanically.

Andrea stopped, holding a blouse, then looked at me inquiringly.

"What is wrong with George? I mean, is what we see just the loss of his brother?"

"Well, as you said earlier, I don't really know him. But I think it's mostly due to the fact that he's just one of those people who've been badly equipped for life. He doesn't seem to understand people, either individually or collectively. He's possibly the nearest thing to someone who ended up on the wrong planet."

"What does he do for a living? How on earth can he possibly get by at all?"

I shrugged as preamble. "From what I know, he works in a stockroom. He probably doesn't have to talk to anyone from one day to the next. It might be that his brother was the only other human he felt comfortable with, and now that Harold is gone … well…"

Andrea stared off hopelessly into space for a moment, then slowly carried on unpacking.

"I'm going to take George for a walk around the village, try to make him feel at least somewhat at home. Then I'll go for my swim."

Andrea nodded, still distracted.

"I said that we would meet Kate at about five thirty. Is that okay for you?"

"Yes", she said, still looking absent. "Oh! Yes, Kate!" suddenly recognizing a prospect that shook off her current distraction, brought a smile to her face and gave the day new direction.

A few minutes later, George and I were strolling through the streets of Largs. We made a first ritual stop at Kelvin Place, and the proprietor, Ken Jacobsen, greeted us warmly. Ken had taken over what had been called, unenterprisingly, The Largs Café, run by one Kelvin

Garratt. Kelvin didn't really have his heart in it, and he hadn't made the connections among the name Largs, his own name, and Lord Kelvin. Ken spotted those links right away, and in a sort of double word game had renamed the restaurant Kelvin Place. In just a few short weeks, Ken had breathed new life into the joint. He had bought new and very colourful umbrellas for the lakeside patio, applied for and been granted a liquor licence, and had got my ready agreement to build a small parking area, just off Arran Street, where people coming from outside Largs could park. And very soon people did come from outside Largs because Ken had put the word out in all the local villages that Kelvin Place was open for business. Trade had jumped immediately.

Ken and I chatted for a few minutes. I bought a couple of bottles of water for George's and my walk, promised to come back later, and then George and I continued our stroll around Largs.

It was impossible to pass by the Nelsons' house without Gladys doing a "Yoohoo!" from her front door, and soon she and her husband James (who was "Jimmy" to her and only to her) and I were deep into an impromptu chat next to her glorious flower beds. Gladys and James had come to Largs about four years previously, when James was packaged out of an accounting firm, and he then turned full-time to his consuming hobby: woodcarving and woodworking. But James' woodworking was far more than just tinkering in wood. In two years, he had built a reputation for elegant pieces both large and small, and he was now working mostly on commissions booked through his website. In his "spare time", he did small jewellery boxes, book ends, chopping boards, and other items that appeared in shops all through the local area. I had commissioned a large salad bowl and individual salad dishes. I promised to come back later and have a look at his latest work that was taking shape in his workshop behind the house.

Although it was too late to think of doing it now, I still itched to ask if his middle initial, H, stood for Horatio. But he had probably been asked that a thousand times, and if he really was James Horatio, he might be reluctant to get into the whole matter.

In the middle of the village, George and I visited the school, also constructed in stone by old McCleod. It was an exceedingly attractive little building, although it hadn't been used as a school for more than forty years since students began being bused to the new regional school in Coboconk. The little school sat vacant for about four days, and then the local bridge club claimed it. Just a few years ago, there had been no schoolchildren in Largs at all, and I remembered clearly an earlier time, just after I had finished university, when, similarly, there were no children in the village. The population of Largs was greying rapidly then, and the fear at the time was that the village itself would just slide into senility along with its occupants. But then something extraordinary happened.

A man called Leslie Machacek had bought a minority interest in the Rosedale marina, and had chosen Largs as the place he wanted to live with his wife and three small children. Within a year, three more young families had bought in the village, and I had joined a group of men who decided that the rundown play area beside the little stone school needed to be brought back for use by all these children. New swings, a couple of new seesaws, a wooden carousel, and a huge new sandbox were soon in daily use. A similar initiative a few months later had installed bookcases and tables and chairs inside the little school, creating a library and indoor play area. The streets of Largs suddenly were filled once again by the laughter and chattering of children. That alone revived the place as nothing else could. I stopped near the playground and chatted to a few parents who were sitting in the sun while their children were covering themselves in sand and grass stains.

Carrying on, I waved at Harvey Wilder, a retired lawyer, a dynamo at any party, and a man who seemed to have a bottomless store of lawyer jokes. Next to Wilder lived Alexander Regan, an aspiring writer who kept handing out drafts of Chapter 1 of his novel for people to review, but as far as I was aware nobody had ever seen a Chapter 2.

Further along the same street, Beech Avenue, lived three families of salt-of-the-earth people. It had taken me a good six months to make them feel comfortable enough to join me at Kelvin Place for a beer, and now they were happy to exchange smiles and waves.

George and I walked the perimeter of the village. To the west, everything in the village is bounded, ultimately, by the shore of the lake. Apart from Arran Street, all the other streets are named after trees. Two of the streets are dead ends. At two locations in the village, two streets angle to a common intersection at a third street, one of these spots being at the southern edge of the village, the other at the eastern edge. Further south and east beyond the limits of the village are wheat fields. To the north, the village boundary, in terms of streets, is defined by Hemlock Street, and along its length it is joined at odd angles by three other streets. To the north of Hemlock Street there are three well-spaced cottages, between which are flower and vegetable gardens. Behind these cottages, further to the north, is an orchard of apple and pear trees that fills up the space between the backs of the cottages and Arran Street. To the north of Arran Street there is a narrow strip of wild grassland, the remains of a fieldstone fence, and then a dense cedar forest. Quite a lot of the land McCleod owned originally was sold off, but the fields immediately to the south and east are owned by Andrea and me, and we rent them out at a pittance to local farmers. The area to the north is also our land, and Jimmy and I prune the maples along Arran Street every autumn.

The stone cottages in the village are a good size, mostly built to a common design, and individually and collectively they are delightful. Several are covered, to varying degrees, in ivy, others sport trellises garbed in climbing roses and clematis, and one cottage has a large espalier apple that occupies almost its entire south-facing wall. At one time, there were several large elms, but they have now gone. The current population of large trees is mostly maple, although there are quite a few oaks and beeches, as well as two handsome old black locust trees, their long fronds hanging in languorous elegance, and seeming to make a statement of lushness not provided by the contrasting darker green of the maple leaves.

George had become noticeably more relaxed, and looked around in a gaze that spoke of interest rather than the fear of being hunted.

"Nice, isn't it?" I said.

George nodded. "Yes", he said, eventually.

"Where are you from, George?"

"I was … we were … Owen Sound."

"Ah! Billy Bishop country!" I said with some enthusiasm, but George's blank look indicated that he was as disconnected from the past as from the present. We walked on.

There is such a thing as a city state of mind, and it's a natural response to, perhaps partly a defence against, the speed, the noise, the tempo, and the psychic stress that can be imposed by a large city. As always happens for me after our arrival in Largs, that state of mind quickly fades and is replaced by the soft metronomic tick of Largs and the countryside. I can see it in the slow swaying of trees, of branches, in the nodding of flowers, in the waves making their slow progress across the wheat, in the quiet ripple in the sea-green canopy above me, and in the apparently happy chatter of birds safe in their perches. I couldn't detect any evident change in George that might be attributed to being in the country, but then I didn't really know him at all. He did seem to me an unhappy person, and perhaps a good dose of the peace and quiet of the country … Largs is the water, I thought, and George is the horse. I've brought him here. I can't do more.

We had reached the eastern edge of the village, where the land rises toward the end of Hemlock Street, and we looked out over the wheat field. The stalks had reached almost their full height, but the flower and seed heads were still green. We had been standing there for some time, just looking out over the wheat, which was drenched in sun, and evidently home to large populations of grasshoppers and crickets. I turned westward, and let my gaze wander over the stone cottages, jumbled happily in semi-disorder.

"You ... like it ... here?" I was surprised more by George taking the conversational initiative than by what he had said.

"I love it here, George. This is my home." I had no real knowledge of my mother, could not picture her in my mind, and knew her just as a vague presence. I had only the two photos of her, neither of them clear or flattering, and no photos of my father. Mrs. Hastings had communicated to me a great deal of her feelings, her friendship, for my mother, and it was from this that I derived some sense, not quite direct, of parental connection. There had been times when I felt twinges of regret at not having known a mother in the intimate way other boys did, but over the years my connection to Largs grew, in compensation I suppose, as the dominant link to my past. I learned to love the place deeply, at several levels. Still love it. The loss of dear Mrs. Hastings, coming relatively late and well beyond my adolescence, hadn't exactly knocked the props from beneath me, although it had been felt keenly.

"Do you remember Owen Sound, George?"

"I ... my brother ... we fished. In Georgian Bay. We had ... we built ... a tree shack. We had ... our bicycles. Yes ... I..."

George had slept almost the entire way to Largs. I think he had no real notion of where he was. There was no risk of him striking up a conversation with anybody he didn't already know, but I hoped, although I wasn't confident, that he wouldn't realize that he was on the edge of Balsam Lake, where his brother had died. Neither Andrea nor I would let on, and maybe we would get through a few days without him learning where he was.

At some point, probably early the following Monday, I would need to take him back to Toronto. Although I had alerted the lawyer, Hawley, about Harold's place being turned over, and he had said he would report it to the police, and although I had contacted Cromarty separately to let him know where we were, I still had some concerns about returning George to Toronto and leaving him there alone. But there wasn't much choice. George had a job to go to. He couldn't just hide indefinitely at Largs, and it was my hope that he would go back to

Toronto at least a bit more relaxed and a bit less anxious. In short, I was having trouble seeing how to tie off this whole George loose end thing, in either the near term or the longer term. The only option, really, was to get to the bottom of things, of Harold's "accident", as soon as possible, take the fight to the enemy, so to speak. Whoever the enemy might be.

George and I wandered back through the village, and I waved to several people out tending their lawns and gardens. I stopped to say hello to Wally Harris, rotund and pink-cheeked, the man whose food counter always had available the elements essential for cottage life: steaks, chops, chicken pieces, sausages, hamburger meat, and the usual staples: bread, milk, eggs, bacon, and coffee. As we completed our tour and approached our house, I suggested a few things George could do while he was in Largs apart from just resting, including looking through the several dozen books that were in his room, going for a swim, or just sitting or lying in the shade out behind our house. As had been Andrea's and my intention, the house, carport, shrubs, hedges, a couple of large trees, and boathouse – belonging to Andrea and me but used by Harvey Wilder – all conspired to make the grassy area behind the house entirely secluded. After a period of dithering, George said he would prefer just to sit in his room for a while. I made sure he knew where the kitchen was, and that he should just help himself, then I went to shed the constraints of my travelling clothes for the freedom of my swimming trunks. Andrea was flopped in the pool, eyes closed, well on the way to being completely unwound. The grass was cool and sweet underfoot. The gentle fingers of sun and light breeze touched my skin in a rippling caress. Small waves met the shore and spoke to me in our own private dialect.

Arrival at Largs means many things for me. But a primary ritual is to stand looking out over the lake ready for my first swim.

And once again, it didn't disappoint. Scaling the ladder down the embankment and onto the shore, I let the water wash over my feet and ankles for a few moments, then waded out before starting off on my triangular course, swimming out to the left at about forty-five degrees to the shore. This first leg would end when I could see past the promontory to my left to another point of land further along. I would then turn to the right, swimming parallel to the shore and about two hundred metres out into the lake, until I came level with the far end of the administration building. I would then turn to the right again, and aim at the ladder I had climbed down earlier. The entire circuit takes me about twenty-five minutes.

The lake always receives me in a way that is very complex: some combination of a return to the womb, the embrace of a lover, the smile of a lifelong friend, the eager greeting of a drinking partner, the laughter of a child, the challenge of an intellectual equal, the welcome of Manitou. Although this is a ritual I have done hundreds of times, it is always new. As I swam, rocks drifted by slowly about ten feet below me on the lake bed. Sunlight animated the water in large steeply angled bars that tumbled and shimmered. Water sluiced past my head, over neck and shoulders, and, along with the rhythm of crawl and breathing, converted my glide along the surface into a quiet waltz. Just me and the lake. Approaching the shore again, but still ten metres or so out, I lowered my legs and stood on silty rocks, the water about chest deep. To my right, a film of water slipped over the edge of the infinity pool and slid down the smooth concrete surface, angled slightly outward, eventually to rejoin the lake water. Directly ahead of me, the steeple of the small church rose up, a dominant feature in the –

It was just a rogue thought, and it surprised me, seeming to arise in my mind out of nowhere. Those numbers. The lawyer, Hawley. Could it be? The idea sent a small tingle throughout my body. Possibilities quickly flashed in my mind.

I could hardly wait to regain the shore, dry off quickly, and get to my laptop.

Eleven

Hair still dripping, towel over my shoulders, I took a seat at the mahogany picnic table I had constructed using perfectly serviceable wood from three pallets that had come bearing cargo from Brazil. That had been last year. I rescued them from the flames, knowing exactly what I could do with them.

Well, okay, it was Andrea who actually built the table.

In fifteen seconds, I had my laptop ready to go, and I marvelled, yet again, at how computers always seem to know when I'm in a hurry and slow down accordingly. From the side pocket of my laptop case, I drew out one of the envelopes George and I had received from the lawyer Hawley and looked again at the numbers on the sheet inside:

-0.0009	0.0199
-0.0212	0.0168
0.0113	0.0203
-0.0053	0.0392

An earlier assumption had been that these were straightforward GPS coordinates, but a moment's reflection made it clear that if that were the case, they designated spots somewhere very close to the equator. Now that my laptop had deigned to join me, I quickly confirmed that not only would they be bunched near the equator, but that they would designate four closely grouped points in the Atlantic off the coast of Ghana.

Another possibility was the one that had occurred to me after my swim, as I was preparing to climb back up the ladder. These numbers could have been derived using some reference point, and either the coordinates of the reference point were subtracted from the coordinates of the four real locations, or vice versa. Suppose that those four locations were somewhere near here. I knew that there was an often-used surveyor's benchmark in Coboconk, and that the coordinates for that point would be readily available. On Google Maps, perchance? My fingers flew over the keyboard, and then, there was the benchmark! Right next to the bridge over the Gull River, just where it should be!

Okay! If x is the desired location, and y is one of the points on the sheet in front of me, and R is the reference point, then the two possibilities are $x = R-y$ or $x = R+y$. A bit of work in Excel soon gave me two blocks of four sets of coordinates. Going back to Google Maps, I entered the coordinates, and found – nonsense. The first group of four points were all over the place: one in the middle of the village, one in the middle of the old quarry, one somewhere in a swamp, and the fourth apparently in the barn of an abandoned farm. The second set was just as ridiculously inconsistent. I tried other possibilities, using reference coordinates based on other significant local features. Same story.

I had been at it now for more than twenty minutes, had tried more than a dozen possible reference points, and my lack of success was becoming irksome. *Stop!* I said to myself. *Think back to a few minutes ago. What really was this bright idea, and how did you come upon it?*

Dutifully, I thought back. But my train of thought had hit a rut and ran stubbornly along the same track. The calculator demon in my head remained obstinately at work, casting up a clamour of other, even more distant possible reference points. I wanted to cut through this internal racket, since none of these further possibilities seemed to have that ring of truth, that –

Ring! Bell! The little church! It was indeed the most obvious spot, visible from anywhere on this part of the lake. And there was a bell in its steeple, and when it was rung it sent a sweet angelic tone rolling harmonically over the lake. I thought of Harold and his "accident".

That could be it!

My fingers tap danced across the keys as I worked the cursor over Google Maps and then worked my spreadsheet again. Taking the first set of points, I checked the map and found, once again, nothing that looked particularly rational or consistent. My earlier hope now beginning to fade, I checked the second set of points.

Take your time! Check again! I said to myself.

This time, there was no mistake.

"Aha! Gotcha! You little bastard!"

"Got who?"

As I imagined a jacklit deer would be, I was suddenly immobile, trying to identify this rough beast, this sudden intruder to my discoveries. Andrea, now recognized as the source of the interference, cast me a querying gaze from the pool, looking a bit put out at having the peace of her floatation tank so rudely disturbed.

"Nothing", I mumbled, bearing what I hoped was a suitably sheepish look.

Using the little church in Largs as my reference point, my desired points "x" were all within Balsam Lake. I quickly pulled up a map of depth contours for the lake. It took only a moment to see it.

The points were all in shallow areas, and in fact they all indicated the locations of underwater reefs.

But suddenly, the sharks of doubt were racing in, ready to tear to pieces my sleek bit of euphoria. Why shallow areas? Why reefs? Had I added 2 and 2 and come up with 6.3 masquerading as 4? Nice surprise! Nice bit of apparent consistency! But what did it mean? I had to ponder this.

I was being distracted slowly from my ponderings by a sound that began tapping insistently on the closed door of my attention. It was a faint sound, a distant drone. Gradually it became louder, closer. Suddenly a red and white float plane flashed across in front of us, barely thirty feet above the water, wings wagging madly. Then the throttle was opened, the engine roared more loudly, and the plane climbed and carried on to the south.

Andrea had leapt from the pool.

"Kate!" she shouted, as the plane disappeared behind the shore trees. "It's Kate!" she shouted again, turning toward me, smiling in anticipation.

One end result of unpacking, walking with George, looking through the house, talking to Jimmy, swimming, finding underwater reefs, and just general daydreaming, was that time had flown. My watch told me it was already quarter to five, and we were meeting Kate at The Repose at five thirty. That's where she was headed now, and Andrea and I had to get a move on.

Twelve

Rosedale is a lovely spot, and it has been able to remain quiet and peaceful because of two things: the waterway that joins Balsam Lake and Cameron Lake and the high bridge that spans this waterway. These two features quadrisect the village. As a result, there is no main street offering a track for hot rod traffic. Juvenile male drivers, in the grip of out-of-control hormones, are stymied. Their jalopies, sporting mufflers that are really little better than giant tomato-juice cans, have no stretch of road long enough to build up to that mock virile roar, a message having no specific target. In Rosedale, vehicular quiet reigns.

The Repose is located in the northwest quadrant of Rosedale, invisible from the highway, resting in seclusion on the shore of Balsam Lake behind a majestic stand of oak trees. It wasn't always called The Repose, and its proper name is still not The Repose. When it first started up, about thirty years ago, it was *Le Repos de Champlain*, named after, you know, Samuel de Champlain, that storied explorer who passed through each of Ontario's 32,000 lakes at least three times, lost several dozen astrolabes, and seemed to spend all his time carving his name on rocks. At least, that's the impression you'll get if you believe all the folklore about him. Champlain was here! Where? Doesn't matter! He was here! He doesn't deserve to be made the basis for all this local chest-thumping, because he really was a remarkable guy, and anyone who wants to get the straight goods on him will read the book *Champlain's Dream*.

But Samuel actually did pass through the waterways now surrounding the location known as Rosedale, hence the name *Le Repos de Champlain*, admittedly exuding some hyperbole. As the observant among us have noticed, English has been, in the past, a very jealous linguistic god in North America, eager to stamp out any other language that dares to raise its declensions. One has only to look at the massive French influence that was once present throughout that vast swath of North America that is now occupied by a fair bit of the US. Scattered over that area, we can find places whose names are pronounced in ways now much departed from their Gallic origins, Tare Hote and Nawlins being examples. *Grandes Fourches* has been degraded to Grand Forks, Little Rock once sported the delicate moniker *La Petite Roche*, and *Baie Verte* now sobs its way through life as Green Bay. The jealous god was hard at work in Ontario too, and a few of the early customers of *Le Repos de Champlain* started calling it Champlain's Rest. They soon found that their custom was not welcome.

The owner, Maurice, let his views be known.

"*Sacre mouchoir de la Vierge! Qu'est-ce qu'ils font, ces maudits anglais?*"

Maurice is rather given to salty expressions, *des tournures scabreuses, des expressions un peu cochonnes*, especially when he thinks that with just a bit of effort people could get things right. He wasn't having any of this Shamplane stuff in his establishment, any more than he would serve water to someone chirping "dullo", or let a person continue thinking that the utterance "doolay" would get them a glass of milk.

Câlisse!

But he was gradually convinced that the name The Repose was okay for two reasons. First of all, because "repose" is a legitimate English word, and not just a lazy bastardization of French (although it is that). Second, he was swayed by the argument that until a body has learned French, they are stuck in the single digit IQ range, are unteachable as a result, and need sympathy more than indignation. For Maurice, this notion struck the unmistakeable diapason note of truth, as clear and compelling as anything heard in St. Joseph's Oratory, or expressed in the elegant phrasing of Racine.

We drove slowly along the approach road that wound its way through the great imperious oaks, found a place to park, and entered The Repose. Maurice, clearly in charge behind the bar, waved and smiled. He is still fiery when the need arises, but now, his reputation assured and the name of his establishment protected from degradation, he rarely pumps his linguistic indignation up beyond deep red as opposed to the bright cherry volcanism he felt was demanded fifteen years ago.

There are two seating areas in The Repose. There is the "bar" for those who just want to stop for a quick beer, and then there's the *Salon de Fénelon*, a more relaxed space that looks west through a sedate stand of mature trees and out over Balsam Lake, sees some spectacular summer sunsets, and invites guests to linger. It also brings Maurice that little extra *service*, the discreet *augmentation de prix* that's applied to everything. It's worth it, and I've never hesitated to pay.

"*Bonsoir, Maurice! Ça marche?*"

"*Ah! Monsieur Vehlan!* I know you speak *le français. Aucun besoin de faire impression sur moi!*"

All spoken through friendly smiles in both directions. *Maurice était chez soi! Il avait Le Repos de Champlain en garde!* Champlain was at rest. The world was as it should be.

There were just three people in the *Salon de Fénelon* as we entered, and Andrea had made a beeline for the only woman among them. Kate. Kate rose as Andrea approached, and they hugged in true feeling. It was a delight to watch them.

Almost the same height and build, otherwise they differed in hair, eye, and skin colouring, and in occupation. But they really were sisters, kindred spirits, and when they were together, they became a fascinating amalgam: a blend of Andrea, the off-duty modern urban businesswoman, and Kate the astutely business-oriented bush pilot and truculently feminine tomboy. After their hug, they sat straight away, talking animatedly, touching each others' arms, being close but unlikely friends. Andrea wore tan slacks, sandals, and a pale yellow blouse, while Kate's outfit consisted of a blue labourer's shirt, sleeves cut off roughly at the shoulders and the name "Jim" embroidered on the pocket, faded jeans, and battered safety shoes. But despite the labourer's disguise, and without Kate having to make any effort whatever, essence of woman radiated from her form.

"Hey! Marcus! Stop impersonating Lot's wife and get over here!"

I strode over to her confidently, since Kate hates wimpiness. She clamped me in a fierce but completely ingenuous arms-around-the-neck hug, then laid on me a huge lips-to-lips smacker, her sleek black plain-cut hair tickling my cheeks.

"Better sit down now", she said, and it was true that my loins had indeed been stirred.

"Drinks!" I cried, my forced enthusiasm masking the effort to emerge from the cloud of estrogen Kate had unwittingly puffed at me.

"Can't", Kate said. "I'm flying."

"Tie the plane down", I ordered. "Stay with us tonight. I'll drive you back to it in the morning."

"Wow! There's a man in the house! Done! I'll have a Mad Tom!" Kate agreed through a huge grin. "No. Make that two Mad Toms!"

"Menus!" Kate exclaimed, turning toward the bar.

"No! We eat at our place. Barbecued chicken and Caesar salad."

"You're on. Make that three Mad Toms!"

"Tankhouse for me", this from Andrea.

"I guess it's a beer evening. I'll make mine a Cameron's Ambear, if Maurice has any", spoken back to them, half over my shoulder, as I headed for the bar. Didn't make it that far, though.

"*Hein*? Eef Maurice 'as eet? *Tu es vraiment un con, Monsieur Vehlan*", and I made a smart U-turn to accompany Maurice back to the table, our drinks, including my Cameron's Ambear, already on the tray he carried.

From that point onward, the next hour flowed, flew, on a river of conversation and laughter. Kate brought us up to date on her highly unpredictable life, and before we knew it, we had walked to Kate's plane where she secured it to Maurice's dock, and were in my car and headed back to Largs. On the way, I briefed Kate about our house guest. But at the back of my mind, all the way to Largs, I wondered about one of the men who had been sitting in The Repose. I had caught his eye once and there was a flicker of something, but that was what I half expected because I was sure I knew him from way back in my life. If he was who I thought he was, I would have to seek him out at some point. Some point soon.

We entered the house, making the clamour of a gathering that was already in full swing. Andrea disappeared to climb into party fatigues. Kate's shoes were kicked into a corner, and she whipped off her jeans revealing what looked like cycling shorts underneath. I handed Kate a couple of bottles of wine, it being understood that we would reassemble in the back garden. The chicken was prepared and ready to go, the romaine cleaned and ready to be shredded, the homemade Caesar dressing made, and the garlic bread wrapped in foil and ready to be heated. I retrieved it all from the fridge, and Kate and I descended the few steps to the garden. It was still late afternoon, a good two hours to the beginning of a spectacular sunset, and consequently the mosquitoes hadn't yet formed their evening attack squadrons. We placed wine and salad on the table, and chicken and garlic bread ready for the barbecue. I collected the needed wine glasses from our outdoor cabinet, got the barbecue going, and then went to sit with Kate for a moment before Andrea emerged.

We got the ritual of cheers, clink, and first sip out of the way.

"Have you had a chance to look for the canoe?"

"Looked for and found", Kate said economically.

"Where was it?"

"Strange place. On the west side of Indian Point, a good kilometre up into North Bay."

I pondered this for a moment. Not just strange, I thought. Impossible.

"Could you take me there tomorrow? Can you land the plane nearby?"

"Is this a business deal?"

"It can be."

"No. Just joking. Yes, we can go there."

I smiled at Kate and raised my glass to her once more, then went back inside to collect the condiments and to coax George to join us.

I didn't know what to expect when George appeared, but given the other members of the group I needn't have worried.

Thirteen

It took several minutes to coax George to join us for dinner. Even then he was far from convinced that it was a good idea and was nervous and jumpy. But he did come down.

"Kate", I said in a calm and quiet voice, "this is George, a client of mine going through a rough patch and staying with us for a good dose of country relaxation." Kate and Andrea rose from the table, smiling brightly.

"Come, George", I said. "Come over and have a seat", and I laid a friendly arm across his shoulders.

"Please sit here, George", Andrea said, indicating the centre of the seat facing the lake, and she walked over and took his arm. They moved slowly to the table and George was enfolded by the two women, one on each side of him, who proceeded to set up a quiet, continuous flow of talk about the lake (not named), our house, Largs, the countryside, the weather, and how pleasant it was in the country in summer. No questions were posed. The choice of things to drink (beer, wine, Sprite, and mineral water) was given, and George quietly selected a can of Sprite. I drifted off to attend to the barbecue. The soft, unchallenging patter continued behind me. I heated the garlic bread, cooked and sliced the chicken, brought it to the table, and we put together our meals.

The short version is that we ate, George saying not a word while we all chowed down, but he smiled a few times in apparent acknowledgement that he was following the discussion.

I poured more wine for Andrea, Kate, and myself, waved a second can of Sprite at George, which he accepted with a smile, and we all just sat in silence watching the sun descend toward the western shore of the lake.

"Thank you", George said at length. "That was … yes … very good. But … I … it's time for me to…" and he waved vaguely toward the house.

"By all means, George", Andrea said. "If you want to retire, please do. And thank you for your company."

I rose, placed a hand on George's shoulder, and said that I would see him back to his room. He nodded, smiled faintly, said "Good night" to the company in general, and then turned toward the house.

After I had rejoined the two women, Kate asked a few questions about George, and I filled in some details without really getting into the case. There was a short lull that was broken by Andrea.

"Tomorrow I want to look at Number 6 White Pine Lane. Part of the floor needs replacing, and I think it's the simplest job of all the possibilities", she said.

"Ah!" I said brightly. "I forgot about that one. Good! Count me in!" I knew that the first task would be to come up with a list of what needed doing, what materials, tools, and supplies would be required, and then ordering them and having them delivered.

Andrea was aware of the need to look at the canoe Kate had spotted. "We can do that right after breakfast", I said.

"I don't do breakfast", Kate stated bluntly. "Waste of time. Besides, I have four jobs on tomorrow."

"Oh! Do you want to reschedule the hop over to look at the canoe?"

"No", Kate said, waving her hand dismissively. "It's less than five minutes flying time to the canoe. The whole trip should take less than a half-hour. What time? Seven thirty?"

"Can we make it seven, Kate? Then I can be back here well before eight, and Andrea and I can get stuck into the White Pine Lane job."

"Suits me."

The bugs were now beginning to become a nuisance, so we collected the dinner things and the wine and wine glasses, carried them all inside, and settled down for one last good glug of wine.

I finished first, and rose to start washing plates and cutlery.

"Let me help", Kate said, rising to come to the sink.

"No. My job. Ask Andrea. You two shove off to bed."

Several unspoken messages flashed back and forth between Kate and Andrea, they said goodnight, and left me chained to my sink.

The plane coughed to life the next morning at five minutes past seven, after Kate had untied the moorings, and completed a few checks, and after I had pushed the plane around until it was parallel to Maurice's dock. I climbed in, then we chugged out into the lake as quietly as possible, which really wasn't all that quiet. But it was a hell of a lot quieter than it became when we were a quarter mile offshore and Kate opened it up. I made to speak to Kate, but she pointed to the headset, I put it on, and the noise level dropped by a factor of ten.

"Noisy little bugger", Kate said over the intercom.

This needed no reply, so I just nodded.

In a surprisingly short time, we lifted off from the lake surface, and I was doubly surprised at how quickly we climbed, even after Kate had throttled back a bit. We levelled off at about eight hundred feet, and headed toward the north end of Grand Island.

"Can you fly me over these four points?" I asked Kate, handing her a single sheet of paper showing the coordinates. She gave me an inquiring look.

"Sure", she said at length, leaving an unspoken "why" in the air.

"I'll explain later", I said.

"You want to do that first?"

"Yes. Then go and look at the canoe."

The lake was still very calm, and if there was anything to see at these four locations, I wanted to have the best chance of seeing it, which meant the least waves and surface disturbance. I pulled out a notebook and pen.

Kate had evidently decided to cover the four points in a counter-clockwise pattern, starting at the most distant one. I looked down. Shapes drifted past below, patterns on the bottom of the lake, and I was surprised at how clear things were, or how shallow the water appeared, or maybe both. Occasionally, I could see well-defined rock formations below the surface. I thought I knew the lake well, but here were features I hadn't guessed at. But then I had never been able to drive my canoe over the surface at seventy miles an hour nor get this kind of perspective.

"The first spot is coming up", Kate said. "And it's directly below right – now", and as she said this Kate took the little plane into a tight turn to make one complete circuit of the location. Below us, a line of rocks was very clear against an undifferentiated featureless background. The depth to these rocks couldn't have been more than about two metres. Apart from two strange, faint, straight lines, there was nothing below me that was recognizable as anything other than rocks.

"No", I said. "Nothing of interest. Next location."

"You've really got me curious."

"Later", I said.

Two minutes passed, then we were over the second location. This was a large broad lump of rock beneath the surface, even shallower, perhaps only a metre deep, but I could see nothing below apart from random rock shapes.

The third location was much more interesting. The depth was maybe two metres, and there was definitely something down there. I made a note in my book.

"Last location."

We were there in under three minutes. A complex set of jagged rocks drifted past below me, and Kate went into her turn. At that point, we were about a hundred metres above the water, and a bit more than a hundred metres from the shore of Indian Point, not quite two kilometres north of the tip. I looked up briefly and was surprised to see the steeple of the Largs church less than a kilometre away and slightly to my right, but I dragged my attention back to the point we were circling below.

"Can you go around once more, Kate?"

We were circling clockwise around the spot and taking twelve o'clock as north I noticed as we rounded nine o'clock that there was a small flash of green below, on the bottom. By the time we reached twelve o'clock, the flash had disappeared.

"One more circuit please, Kate?"

The green flash reappeared at about seven o'clock and disappeared once more at about eleven o'clock.

"Okay. On to the canoe."

We headed south along the east shore of Indian Point, rounded the tip, and then Kate pulled out somewhat further over the lake as she swung north along the western shore of the point.

"There it is", she said. "About four hundred metres ahead."

"Got it!" I responded, my excitement evident.

Kate made several passes along the shore to the north and south of the canoe.

"Rocks. Deadheads. Can't be too careful. Okay. We're going in", she announced. Two minutes later, the floats touched the water as we made a direct approach perpendicular to the shore.

"I'm assuming you want to take a close look."

"Damned right", I said.

"Then you're going to have to get wet. I can't drive the plane up onto the rocks."

The little plane chugged slowly across the final few hundred metres of water, then Kate turned the plane's nose out into the lake when we were twenty metres from shore, stabilized the position, and cut the engine.

I was wearing old pull-on walking shoes, and I slid them off, stripped off my socks and shirt, then tackled the harder task of removing my pants in the cramped space. Finally, I pulled my shoes on again. By this time, Kate wore an interested grin.

"I won't tell if you don't", I offered.

"Hah!" she barked, looking around the cabin. "You might be a contortionist, but I'm not!"

I pulled my cellphone from my pants pocket, opened the door, climbed down onto the starboard float, set the cellphone onto a flat float surface ahead of me, then slipped into the water. It was too deep to touch bottom. Floating on my back, I picked the cellphone from the pontoon, held it clear of the water, and did an awkward three-limbed backstroke toward the shore. Three feet from the shore, the water was about knee deep above a rocky bottom.

The canoe was resting at about a thirty-degree bow-up angle perpendicular to the shore. None of the canoe was in water. In fact, the stern was at least three feet up from the water's edge, and the forward half of the canoe was almost covered by scrub willow and other small shore shrubs. I took about twenty pictures, walking along the water's edge to get as many angles as possible, but not going ashore in order to avoid any possible future accusations of contaminating a scene. With a little difficulty, I was able to mark the GPS coordinates using my cellphone. I then e-mailed all this material to myself so I could examine it more carefully on my computer back in Largs, but also as assurance. It would have been stupid and embarrassing to turn the whole exercise into a waste if I happened to drop my phone into the lake.

Getting back to the plane was just the reverse exercise, and I was soon standing on the float again, where I could reach the door and toss my phone onto the seat. I stripped off my wet underwear, wrung them out, and tossed them inside on the floor. By this time Kate had restarted the engine. I hurriedly pulled off my shoes, tossed them in on the floor as well, and then climbed buck-naked back into the plane. Irrationally, I put on the headset first. Perhaps a tiny lingering thread of puritanism insisted that I should be wearing something, anything.

"This would make a great publicity photo", Kate commented wryly. "Might allow me to crack a whole new closed market among the kinky crowd."

"Go ahead. My rates are reasonable", but actually I was struggling to drag my pants back on over naked wet lower limbs and abdomen.

We chugged some distance out from the shore, then Kate opened the throttle, and we roared out into the lake, lifted off, and made a graceful climbing turn back toward Rosedale and Maurice's dock. The specific tasks of the morning now being out of the way, I took the opportunity to gaze over the lake – my mentor, my protector, my muse. God, but it is so beautiful! I'm sure that my face was sporting a huge grin and that Kate noticed it. She climbed to about two thousand feet, put the plane into a shallow starboard turn, and began making a circle, about a kilometre wide, out over the lake.

Kate's voice crackled over my headset.

"Go ahead. Take a good look. It really is gorgeous."

Long silence.

"This is what the country really is all about, Mark. Lakes and forests and rivers, and being raised here puts that feeling in one's blood."

After a few more minutes of serene silence, I spoke into the microphone again.

"I might need your help again, Kate, and next time it will be a business deal. But there's background you need to know, and I'd like to fill you in on it over a beer whenever you have time, but as soon as possible."

"The rest of today and the next two days I'm busy. I'll e-mail you."

I sensed that she was pondering the need to keep this little nude aviation caper from Andrea, but I wasn't worried about that. In fact, I was looking forward to telling Andrea myself because I knew it would have her rolling helplessly on the floor.

Fourteen

It was going to be a hot and cloudless day. I told George what Andrea and I would be doing for a fair part of the day, but George was now much more relaxed compared to yesterday, and said he wanted to lie outside in the shade. The quiet and the medicinal air of Largs were at work. I made sure that he had enough for a decent lunch.

Andrea and I let ourselves into Number 6 White Pine Lane and opened windows to drive out the stuffiness. Although this cottage was generally in good shape, the number of things needing attention was large enough to make it not rentable. We had seen over the previous two years an increased number of rental inquiries, in some cases for the entire summer. Full summer rentals represented a large income opportunity.

Of the twelve cottages we owned, only three were in prime condition. Another four were marginal, and we let them occasionally, but only for a week at a time, and at a very low rate. We definitely didn't want people starting to grumble about us charging premium rates for slum properties. The remaining five cottages were run down to varying degrees. Jimmy was splitting his time between the marginals and the unusable properties, doing his best to upgrade marginal to prime, and to drag the unusables out of their swamp. Of these five unusables, Number 6 White Pine Lane was the one nearest to being clear of the swamp.

It took us less than an hour to determine what needed to be done to bring the underfloor to the point where a permanent hardwood covering would be a sound investment, and where its feel on bare feet would generate unrestrained summer holiday smiles.

I had produced a spreadsheet where we could list and cost the elements needed, and consulting this spreadsheet, combined with a quick look around the inside and outside of Number 6, indicated that we had a good shot at bringing this cottage to the point where it could be rented next season. We both grinned at the prospect of seeing a clear end in sight for the work on this cottage, and it was more than evident that Andrea was impatient to get on with it.

By eleven o'clock, we had a list of materials, and we headed off to Fenelon Falls to the best local building supplies merchant. We selected what we needed, and then bullied him into delivering it to us by the end of the day before paying.

Back in Largs, I suggested that we take a look at two other properties that were in only slightly worse shape than Number 6 – Number 3 Ash Grove and Number 7 Poplar Street. We finished that by two thirty, and at a first estimate it looked like we might also be able to do the windows at Number 3 in the present year, maybe even during the next two weeks, and that all three cottages could be brought to rental status by the end of the following year. The project was beginning to take shape, especially for Andrea who had slid into her new role effortlessly. It also hinted at the notion of Jimmy dropping any focus on the unusables and putting all his time into one or two marginals. At three thirty, the building supplies dealer called to say his delivery truck was on the way to us, and Andrea suggested that I go check on George, that she could deal with the delivery. I agreed, not because a lot of time needed to be spent with George, but because my new role meant that I had to start getting the evening meal organized. When I got back to our house, I found George stretched out on a lounge chair in the back garden, sleeping in the shade, a dog best left lying.

I decided quickly enough that for dinner we would have assorted olives and stuffed vine leaves to start, pork tenderloin in port, onions, bacon, and capers for the main course, and watermelon for dessert. It took an hour to find and buy the ingredients, at five o'clock I had a quick shower, and then I began to prepare the tenderloin.

I answered my cellphone. The display told me it was Cromarty.

"Where are you?" he asked without preamble.

"And a good day to you too, Bent."

"Ah! Sorry. Yes. Hello."

"Hello, Bent. Nice of you to call. What can I do for you?"

"I'm following up on Harold's apartment, trying to determine what they were looking for."

"Not sure I can help you, Bent. If you've seen the place, you know as much about it as I do."

"You didn't go in? Look around?"

"Come on, Bent! Give me some credit! No, I didn't go in and look around, and I'm sure Hawley told you that."

"Yes, but he's a lawyer."

"You have a point there, I admit. But really, Bent, there's no way I can help you. I never met Harold, knew nothing about him. I met George only two days ago, and I know precious little about him."

"What about the Balsam Lake connection? Surely you won't deny that."

I knew that Cromarty was fishing, and it was starting to get on my wick.

"Oh? Do tell, Bent. And just what evidence do you have that links the tossing of Harold's place to his body being found in Balsam Lake, hmmm? I assume that's what you're referring to as the connection."

"Well, you have to admit that it's – "

"I don't have to admit anything, Bent. I have no admission to make. I don't even have to agree with your presumed connection until I see some convincing evidence."

There was a silence here.

"Look, Bent. Why don't you just come out with it and tell me what you're trying to get at?"

"I'll get back to you", he said curtly, and then broke the connection.

Andrea would do her usual thing and work in White Pine Lane until well after six. I expected she would be measuring, cutting planks, getting everything ready to put together. And it wouldn't surprise me at all if she also went to Number 3 Ash Grove and started measuring windows. The windows in place there would almost certainly be non-standard, and we would have to rip out the existing frames and build new ones to fit decent standard windows, something else we would be able to start sourcing once we knew more about what was in place. What I was really waiting to see was her mood when she eventually came home. If she was pumped and enthusiastic, then it would be full steam ahead. If she was frustrated and down, then that might be a sign that the whole project of Andrea Clifton, journeyperson carpenter, was in doubt.

But I needed to think more about this after dinner. For the moment, I put it all aside and jumped into the details of preparing dinner, something that immediately sent the mood of Mark Whelan, master chef, toward the stratosphere.

Andrea burst through the door at just after six thirty, flush from a day of activity that changed the physical state of a small part of the universe, and full of plans for the next few days. She trailed a monologue description of her day on the way to the shower, of measuring, cutting, fitting –

But then the bathroom door had closed.

Fifteen

Dinner was a laid-back affair. George was more relaxed but excused himself again for an early night, despite apparently having slept most of the day in the back garden. Andrea and I cleared things away, sat down to look at her measurements from the day, put them into the spreadsheet that I had produced, and set out a list of things to do over the next two days. First thing in the morning, we would look at windows, and hope that the sizes we needed would be available as stock items. Completing the floor at Number 6 White Pine Lane now seemed to be mostly an assembly job, and we could put that on hold for a day or two. Rebuilding the window frames for Number 3 Ash Grove now looked to be the priority, and that would definitely be the case if decent replacement windows were available. So Andrea and I produced some notes and rough drawings for window frames. That meant more lumber, which we could buy when we went in search of windows, and with luck we could have lumber delivered immediately and windows a short time later. I suggested that the inevitable lull tomorrow while we waited for our lumber could be filled by inspecting Number 7 Poplar Street for windows and wiring, both of which needed work, but just how much wasn't clear. Andrea's response to this was a metaphorical rubbing together of hands in anticipation.

"What are you going to do tomorrow?" she asked, suppressing a yawn.

"Well, I can help you, but if you're happy working alone I could also do an inspection of the area where George's brother's body was found."

"You don't think the police would have covered everything well enough?"

"Probably, yes. But I'd still like to make sure, check for myself."

"Okay. Go. I can manage fine on my own. And I think, actually, that this sort of work is easier for one person than two."

"You're sure?"

"Yes. Go."

"All right. I'll have my cellphone with me, so just call if you need help."

"Thanks", Andrea said, stifling another yawn.

"Go to bed", I said, putting an arm around her shoulders.

"The dishes – "

"Are my job", I said, completing her sentence. "Go. You've had a longish day."

Andrea gave me a tired peck on the cheek and headed off to the bedroom.

Being addicted to playing in water from the age of two, I spurned the dishwasher and did the few dinner things by hand, dried them, put them away, and hung up the tea towel.

Now, I said to myself, taking a seat in the den, it's time to walk through this whole business right from the start. I lined up the points in my mind, jotting them down on a notepad as I went.

First point. The starting event was that first discussion with Cromarty. If he had asked me why I had reservations about Harold's death being an "accident", I would have told him, but I was damned if I was going do his job for him. The propeller marks on Harold's back told me what was likely the real story. A power boat passing over someone at speed would have left gashes in the body separated much more widely than was the case for Harold's body. In fact, his back looked more like badly made hamburger meat. Something that I would expect if the boat had been positioned over the body, then accelerated away from a standing start. Deliberately. In other words, murder. Well, maybe. Might the intention have been not to kill Harold, but to take him alive and then grind out of him what his attackers were after? In trying to immobilize him, did somebody use too much force, recognize that Harold's injury was mortal, that he was not going to recover, and then try to cover up by making it look like a boating accident?

Second point. One of the blows to Harold's head could have occurred as a result of the body being pushed against the rocks by waves, and here I recalled the note e-mailed to me by Cromarty. But to me that seemed unlikely because of its location on his head and more probably resulted from a blow delivered by hand. At that stage, the poor bugger would have been unconscious and easy to line up with the propeller when and if they found they had to improvise.

Third point. The canoe Kate and I found was in a very odd location, separated from Harold's body by almost two kilometres of Indian Point shoreline. Suppose first that the canoe had started off somewhere near where Harold's body had been found. There was no way it could have drifted to where it ended up, given the currents in the lake. Suppose that whatever Harold had been doing, he was doing it near where we found the canoe. But then, once again given the lake currents, there's no way that his body could have ended up where it was found. Was it Harold who took the canoe to the spot where we found it? There was no reason I could see why Harold would park his car where he did, then lug a canoe more than a kilometre overland, or take it somewhere close to where his body was eventually found and then paddle the canoe two kilometres to where we found it, from where he would then have to walk back or swim back. If the "accident" occurred reasonably close to where his body had been found, a simpler explanation was that the canoe was originally there too, and somebody had tried to hide it, probably to delay the time until Harold's body came to light. An empty drifting canoe would be spotted and reported quickly. It might be days before a body, partly submerged along a remote piece of shoreline, would be found.

Fourth point. Cromarty was probably wondering whether there really was any connection between Harold's death and the break-in at his place, but he wasn't going to face the displeasure of his superiors by raising that speculation as an excuse to spend more time on the closed Harold Barbour case. No. He wanted to see whether I had anything that he didn't, and that's why he called me earlier in the day, but I wasn't going to take that bait.

Fifth point. The break-in at Harold's place was very unlikely to have been just coincidence. Somebody was looking for something, and it might well have been something connected to Harold being present in the lake off Indian Point.

Sixth point. It appears that Harold was indeed looking for something in the lake. Cromarty's note indicated that he was found wearing one diver's fin, a good quality one. But he was found along an unused stretch of Indian Point: no cottages, no campsites, no fire pits, nothing.

Seventh point. It appears as though whoever interrupted Harold would not assume that he had come there by car, given the canoe nearby. According to information obtained from the police, the marks on the ground indicated that only one person had passed between the car and the shore, a distance of about two hundred metres. Given where the police said they found Harold's car, I confirmed that it wouldn't have been visible from the shore. If Harold's attackers had found his car, what would they have been likely to do? I could think of a few possibilities, but just leaving it where it was is an option that's hard to explain. So I concluded that they didn't see it.

Eighth point. And this is the strongest and most tantalizing piece of information: the sheet that Harold passed to George via the attorney Hawley. On that sheet was information that had led Kate and me, independently of any other information, to a spot very close to where Harold's body had been found. There were three other locations given by that sheet, and I had still to try to find out what significance those locations had, if any. It also occurred to me that George should take steps to engage Hawley as his lawyer to keep all this confidential.

I sat pondering this, looking over the page of notes I had made, trying to see whether I had missed anything, had misrepresented anything. It might have seemed to some that this could be considered evidence, that some theory might be built based on it and then tested. But I was convinced that these pieces of information covered too wide a canvas, that they didn't point unambiguously to just one theory, but hinted vaguely at two, three, or more possible theories.

There were still several avenues left to travel, but given all this material, it now seemed prudent to go down any of those avenues very carefully. Something was afoot out there.

I'm not sure how or why it came to me, but I became aware that I had indeed missed something. On the face of it, Harold Barbour was a total unknown. And yet he had become involved in something that was neither simple nor easily explained, nor, it seemed, had well-defined boundaries.

So.

Just who was Harold Barbour?

Time to find out.

A quick e-mail to my long-standing contact James Hazlitt got the ball rolling.

Sixteen

Saturday was a blur when I looked back on it. We all had an early breakfast. George was looking more relaxed than I had seen him so far. He came close to saying that he was really enjoying his stay with us and said he was more than happy just to rest in the back garden again.

We left him to it. Andrea and I went off to look at Poplar Street and spent another hour at the building supplies merchant, then went our separate ways for a short time – Andrea back to Poplar Street, me back to our house. As expected, James Hazlitt, who sported the nickname "Jocko" for no reason that anyone could remember, had e-mailed back a number of questions. I called him.

"Jocko, got a few minutes to talk?"

"Make it snappy", he barked. "I've got a full order book, creditors that were Komodo dragons before someone tamed them, a case of head yeast, and a rumbly gut. I've got – "

"Jocko! It's me, Whelan. I've heard it all before. Let me get a word in edgewise."

Like distant thunder, the moaning faded but never really ceased. I explained what I wanted.

"How much time you want to spend on it?"

"I think it won't be complicated, Jocko. Give it a day, and then let me know what you've got. We'll take it from there."

The rumbling surged a bit, then faded once more. I had used Jocko quite a few times before. He was tenacious to a fault, and I was pretty sure that I would have a much clearer picture of just who Harold was by Monday afternoon.

"Thanks, Jocko."

"Yeah, yeah", he muttered dismissively, sneezed wetly, declared "Fuck!" to whatever miscreant had given him this snotty horror and broke the connection.

Nice to know that there remain some constants in the world.

Those arrangements completed, I hurried back to Poplar Street, helped Andrea with the window and electrical inspection, and then we returned to White Pine Lane. On entering, I stopped and looked around. Cut planks were stacked against one wall in an order that obviously matched how they would be set in place. Offcuts were piled neatly against another wall.

"Andrea, dearest! Look what thou hast wrought! Fantastic!"

She blushed in pleasure, but also gave me a shoulder push, implying that I should stop this foolishness. Over her objections, I set aside my plan for a close quartering of the suspect area on Indian Point, and decided then and there that we would complete this job together.

We worked until almost six, finishing laying the planks that replaced the rotted section of underfloor we had removed earlier. They fitted like a glove, and when the last piece slid neatly into place and was nailed down, I gave my wife a huge hug. We briefly discussed next steps for this cottage. Our plan was to have the floor finished in hardwood, but we would use a flooring company to complete that part of the job. Drywall needed replacing in a couple of areas, and we estimated that three panels of drywall would be enough. An examination of the toilet bowl and tank revealed chipping and incipient cracks that would only become worse, leading to the conclusion that both tank and bowl should be retired to that great WC in the sky. We made it back to the building supplies place just before it closed to order the sheets of drywall and a new toilet.

Having skipped lunch, we were ready for something quick but substantial, so we dropped in to Wally's place. Wally greeted us,

Pickwickian cheeks aglow. He made a pitch for virtually everything in his food counter, but laughed happily when we chose three generous steaks and some nice crispy broccoli, and he gave a broad smile of approval upon learning that to accompany his comestibles I planned to whip up portions of penne in oil, garlic, and a pinch of chili flakes.

Over dinner, I raised with George the arrangements for taking him back to Toronto on Monday, and saw a cloud pass over his features. I said nothing, recognizing that he knew his stay here really was an evasive manoeuvre and that there was still psychological music to be faced. But I hoped that at least those few days had given him some additional reserves to draw on during the coming week.

Once again, George excused himself at nine thirty, saying he felt tired. Andrea and I wished him a pleasant night, said that the agenda for tomorrow was wide open, and that we would see him at breakfast. George slunk away, and as I followed his retreating back I had to acknowledge his acutely painful current plight, his chronically out-of-focus life, and my long-standing sympathy for people like him.

"Armagnac?" I suggested to Andrea.

"You've read my mind", she said, sliding down into the sofa, feet up on our coffee table, which was made by Jimmy from a section through a huge elm log and bearing all the character of its origins.

Interesting comment, because I always felt that Andrea was the only mind reader in the family. (But then for anyone having antennae as good as Andrea has, I might as well be a large-print book.) I passed her the globe of amber liquid and then settled down with my own portion in the big plush armchair, which was my favourite seat in our "cottage" living area. Glancing surreptitiously at Andrea, I recognized, once again, what I hoped I would keep on seeing for the rest of our lives: a complex girl-woman. She gazed at the glass, and the picture before me was the look of a young girl seeing a perfectly formed daisy for the first time, but also a mature woman recalling the experience of many past social occasions infused by Armagnac and trying to make this one do more than any of its predecessors: draw that extra bit of essence out of the moment. Was she thinking about the work done today? About the dinner we had just finished? About some past event? About her work?

"You're looking pretty smug", she said, bringing me roughly out of my reverie.

"I admit", I began, "that my expressions of dreaminess and stupidity are almost identical."

"Never mind", she said, dismissing my frivolity, "I used to marvel at how keen you were to come up here, but the work that I've done, that we've done, over the past two days gives me a new perspective on why this village is so attractive."

I took a slow sip of Armagnac. "I feel we made good progress today. What do you think? I was thinking also that we'll need to revisit our projections of cost and income from Largs soon. I think both will jump next year."

From her expression, Andrea wasn't quite sure how I managed that topic switch, but we spent the next few minutes talking about what we could accomplish during the coming week. Even looking at it from the slightly pessimistic side of realistic, it seemed to me that we would be able to lift three cottages to the point where Jimmy could complete all the final cosmetic touches on them by the end of September. Thanksgiving sometimes produced a nice spike in demand, and maybe we could have three more units in place ready to meet a similar spike this year.

There was a long pleasant silence, then Andrea drained her glass, gave a sigh of approval, and placed the glass silently on the coffee table. Mine was also empty, and I moved to collect hers and take them to the kitchen.

"That can wait", Andrea said.

I knew that languid look.

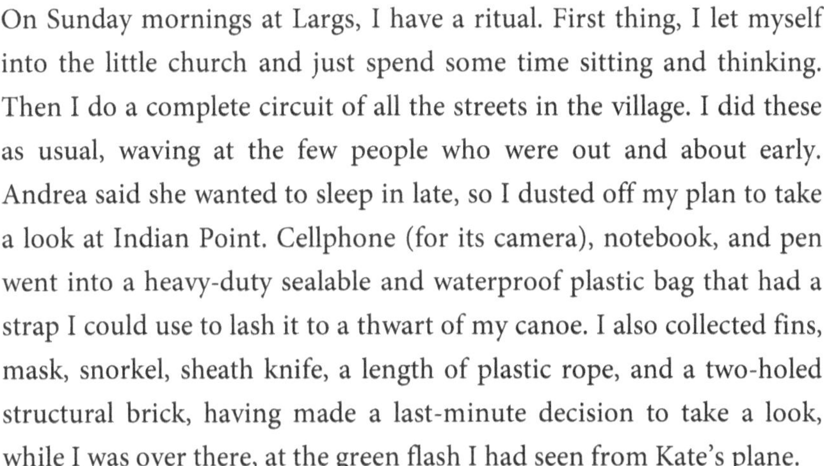

On Sunday mornings at Largs, I have a ritual. First thing, I let myself into the little church and just spend some time sitting and thinking. Then I do a complete circuit of all the streets in the village. I did these as usual, waving at the few people who were out and about early. Andrea said she wanted to sleep in late, so I dusted off my plan to take a look at Indian Point. Cellphone (for its camera), notebook, and pen went into a heavy-duty sealable and waterproof plastic bag that had a strap I could use to lash it to a thwart of my canoe. I also collected fins, mask, snorkel, sheath knife, a length of plastic rope, and a two-holed structural brick, having made a last-minute decision to take a look, while I was over there, at the green flash I had seen from Kate's plane.

The morning was warm, so I set off in my canoe wearing just my swimming trunks, a T-shirt, and a pair of rubber sandals. It took little time to reach Indian Point. I pulled my canoe up onto the shore, and then walked back and forth along the shore until I found the spot where somebody had been walking toward or away from the water's edge. The way the grass and weeds were broken down indicated clearly that there really had been just a single person who had moved one way – toward the shore. That must have been Harold. To one side, a couple of metres away, there was an area where the grass was more trampled than broken down. This had probably been done by the police, and I recalled the notes in Cromarty's e-mailed report. I then took a close look at the bottom near the shoreline. Nothing. Finally, I spent about twenty minutes examining all the rocks that were just out of the water along the shore. What I found was one small shred of black plastic foam hooked onto a sharp edge of rock, and I put this piece of foam into the sealed plastic bag that held phone, notebook, and pen.

I tied the brick to one end of the rope, tied the other end of the rope to the front thwart, dragged the canoe back into the water, climbed in, and set off. It took me almost half an hour to find the underwater rock formation I had seen from the plane, and once I had done that, I dropped the brick into the water as an anchor. Looking at the shore of Indian Point, and at the little church on the opposite shore to make sure of my bearings, I noticed also a power boat carrying three or four fishermen that had parked a few hundred metres to the north of me, just off shore. The water lapped happily. The sun shone benevolently. It was just another lazy Sunday. I slithered over the stern of the canoe into the water, then put on fins, mask, and snorkel.

Four dives gave me a good picture of the size and shape of the reef. I did a complete tour around the reef, snorkelling on the surface, and then I saw the green flash again. It was to the Indian Point side of the reef, in somewhat deeper water, beside what seemed to be a jumble of largish boulders. Diving down once more, I aimed at the green flash, and when I was about a couple of metres from it, I recognized that it was a diver's fin partly covered in silt. I was pretty sure that this would prove to be Harold's other fin.

There have been a few times in my life when a sixth sense spoke to me. It spoke to me now. I was swimming close to the bottom, countering the buoyancy that would have carried me up naturally, and I turned to look up just in time to see a scuba diver, about five feet away, coming quickly toward me. I headed off as fast as I could at right angles to his direction, but then found my legs clamped in a tight grip. I struggled but couldn't free either of my feet. There was a moment of confusion. This must be a mistake, a misunderstanding. But then I came to the cold realization that there was no misunderstanding. Someone was doing this quite deliberately. He was simply going to hang onto me until I had to breathe. He was trying to drown me.

In a situation like that, it's impossible not to be afraid, but it is possible to keep a lid on panic. I started going through the facts of my situation. I had been down about fifteen seconds and probably could not hold my breath more than about another twenty seconds. I was in roughly twelve to fifteen feet of water. The guy who had hold of me was strong. The situation was not good, and as the seconds passed it was rapidly getting much worse.

Despite my efforts, the black thoughts of panic were pressing in. The urge to breathe was becoming very strong. My lungs were now on fire and my heart rate was climbing. I glanced up briefly, and I could see the bottom of my canoe, looking small, forlorn, and distant on the surface. But at least the other boat, which was probably where this bugger had started out from, had not moved in. Things were not all that clear in a visual sense either, because our thrashing about dispersed his exhaled air into many small bubbles, and I was very much aware of these bubbles moving past me, over all my skin. This in itself alarmed me even more because the fact of me spending any effort recording that detail signalled distraction, dissociation, and loss of focus. I tried giving one more kick to free at least one leg. Nothing.

Come on, Whelan! Pull it together! You haven't much time now! Andrea would not be impressed!

Andrea.

Rather than straining in panic to reach the surface, which is what the guy below me was almost certainly expecting, I doubled down, smashed the faceplate of his mask, then sliced through the heavy rubber tube that brought air from his regulator to his mouthpiece. Thank heaven for sharp knives. Never go anywhere without a knife.

Things changed quite a bit then. All at once, there was a lot more thrashing, and my legs were suddenly freed. I raced to the surface, burst through to the atmosphere, ripped off my face mask, and took in huge lungsful of air. Beautiful, sweet, life-charged air. Balsam Lake air. In my hand was my knife, the haft of which I had used on the diver's mask. In my youth, a knife carried while I was swimming would have been used to pry open a treasure chest, and I had been convinced back then that dozens of them probably awaited discovery at the bottom of Balsam Lake. But as a matter of practicality, it is surprisingly easy to become entangled in something when underwater, and a knife can be one's best friend in that circumstance.

I make it all sound very calm, but it was nothing of the sort, more like five or six action movies playing at the same time. My immediate need for oxygen satisfied, my fear quickly turned now to cold anger. I pulled on my mask again and looked down. The man below was struggling, but he knew not to panic as well. He had evidently hit the release on his weight belt, which had been counteracting the buoyancy of his wet suit, and was surfacing while undoing his scuba harness. I watched as his tank fell away and joined his weights on the bottom.

Okay, you bastard, I thought. The tables had turned, and that was confirmed when he broke the surface coughing and spluttering desperately. In his condition, it would have been quite possible for me to come at him from below, grab his legs, and pull him under.

But I had a better idea.

He had his coughing almost under control and had begun swimming along the surface toward the "fishing" boat, not making good time because of the water he was still trying to clear from his lungs. That boat would almost certainly begin coming to pick him up. I took several deep breaths, submerged, and then approached him from below.

Even underwater I could hear his scream, and it was much louder than I expected.

The sharp metallic underwater sound of the "fishing" boat's motor starting up came to me immediately, and still submerged, I swam back to the canoe and surfaced on the side of it facing away from them. Moving to the front of the canoe, and peering around, I could see that my attacker had resumed a slow swim to his mother ship, which was now coming toward him quickly. The question now was, could I do it.

Reaching into the canoe, I cut through the strap that held my waterproof plastic bag to the front thwart, took four or five very deep breaths, and submerged again. The fins I was wearing were the best quality, and they drove me through the water at a speed I found hard to believe. But on the other hand, it was a hell of a long way to go.

Stop thinking! Just swim!

To this day, I think it was Stan Rogers who came to my rescue. Because, looking back, all I can now recall is my legs pumping to the beat of "The Mary Ellen Carter" and the indomitable message of that song rising again and again in my head. It surprised me when one of my knees struck a rock painfully, signalling that I had reached the shore of Indian Point. I turned under water toward the way I had come and slowly raised my face above the surface, breathing heavily. The swimmer, my would-be executioner, was almost at the boat; hands were reaching down to grab him.

Thinking that nobody would be looking for me just then along the shore of Indian Point, I quickly sat on the bottom, tore open the waterproof bag, fumbled out my cellphone, and began taking picture after picture. I had no idea of the quality of what I was getting, or what use the images might be, but better something than nothing. Two or three of these pictures were shot when one or more of the men on the boat had his head raised and was looking out over the water.

I quickly stuffed the cellphone back in the bag, sealed it, took a few more deep breaths, and struck off again underwater southward along the shore of Indian Point, looking for one of the numerous spots where large rocks offered a good place where I could hide, concealed from the gaze of the swine on that boat, who might cruise down the shore to try to find me, or just scan the shore using good binoculars. Whatever their mode of search, I wanted to have disappeared before they began it.

In my mind, there was doubt that they would come looking for me, or perhaps hope that they wouldn't, not when one of their number had a deep knife gash in his left calf, at about the point where the calf muscle, the gastrocnemius, tapers down to become the Achilles tendon.

"I'm going to find you, you bastards, and there will definitely be payback. Count on it."

As I had hoped, less than a minute after the casualty had been dragged into the boat, it roared off to the north. They wouldn't go to a population centre like Coboconk. They would likely land at some cottage, get their guy into a car, and take him to a doctor who didn't ask too many questions. I waited about half an hour, in case they off-loaded their guy, then came back. But it was just a quiet Sunday. I swam back to my canoe and made the crossing back to Largs in record time.

There were two important things left to do. Harvey Wilder kept a modest power boat in our boathouse. When I asked him, he said sure, that I should go ahead and use it. Soon I had retrieved the scuba tank and weight belt, before their owners could recover them, and had safely stored them in the lock-up Jimmy used for his gardening tools.

And it was time to speak to Mike.

Seventeen

On Monday morning, I awoke in a quandary. And not a trivial one.

Would I tell Andrea about yesterday's adventure? My immediate instinct was to tell her everything, since secrets can be corrosive to all involved, even the information, revealed later, that a secret had been kept. It wasn't clear whether the guys who attacked me knew who I was. If they did, might they come after Andrea? Would knowing about yesterday's incident be an advantage to her if they did?

But she would certainly have questions. Who are these guys? What were they trying to do? What is causing all this? And I had no answers to these questions. I was almost completely in the dark. So would telling Andrea just cause her to worry about something that, at the moment, neither of us could do anything to combat? Far from this line of thinking being just an idiotic rationale for doing nothing, I was acutely aware that I had to understand and neutralize this threat, no matter what. And I had to do it very soon. The thought of Andrea being at any risk, no matter how slight the possibility or how unlikely the thought, was something that left me deeply uncomfortable.

It seemed unlikely to me that they had come after me because they thought I knew something and they wanted to get it out of me. Drowning me wouldn't do that, and even if that hadn't been their objective, an elaborate underwater kidnapping would be just about the most awkward way imaginable of doing whatever they wanted to do.

Much easier to try to nab me somewhere off the street. No. An underwater snatch was too improbable to consider any further. There was a much more likely theory.

They had seen me nosing around that reef yesterday, or that section of shoreline, so I was a loose end that had to be tied off. The implication of this was that they had been keeping at least an intermittent watch on the place, which implied in turn that they were trying to protect something there, or keep something secret. The fact that Harold had been snooping in the same area, and that he had suffered the fate that almost befell me, made this theory hard to rebut. But if my theory about Harold was correct, that his death really was to cover up an abduction gone wrong, then they must have thought that Harold knew something they didn't, and that they believed I knew something as well.

This train of thought led immediately to some decisions. And these decisions all meant that I could no longer afford to be passive about what was going on. I had to get my ass in gear.

I needed to make a trip to Toronto to take George home, but now I would be doing several other things while I was there: speaking to Jocko face to face, taking a look in Harold's safety deposit box, paying a visit to an old colleague from the police, Mike Jefferson, now also a private investigator. And one other thing: I wanted to visit the offices of the company where my one-time trustee, now deceased, had worked.

In preparation for all this, I had sent out the e-mails first thing requesting these meetings.

There was one final important decision. I wasn't going to say anything to Andrea. Not just yet.

George would probably make a delayed appearance, putting off the time when he would need to be on the way back to Toronto. It was flattering the way he had taken to Largs, but I had told him that we had to be on the road by eight o'clock at the latest. Glancing at my watch, I saw that it was still only six thirty, but I got the coffee going while I waited for Andrea, then opened my laptop to update my notes and the electronic diary I keep. I had been working on my laptop for about an hour when my phone rang.

"Mark, you old bastard! Got your e-mail." It was Mike Jefferson.

"Mike! Good to hear your mellow tones."

This brought a short burst of abuse.

"What's going on there? I couldn't believe your e-mail message. Almost impossible to imagine something like that happening up in coma-land? What have you set up in the way of physical security for yourself? For Andrea? And how is my favourite water nymph?"

"We're both fine, Mike. It was the physical security bit, along with other stuff, that I wanted to talk to you about."

"So. Let me guess. You have no security in place yet. What are you doing, Mark? You're not invincible! It's time old Jefferson got in there on your behalf. I can be at your place by just before eight."

"Just before eight! This morning? Got your own helicopter, Mike?"

"No. Just my trusty Volvo. Which I'm in now. Just north of Lindsay. Why don't you fill me in while I drive?"

It took me a second to overcome my surprise and to hold off the obvious questions until later, so my immediate response was just an odd whine.

"Isn't that illegal, Mike?"

"Oh, yeah, you're right! Wait, though. There's a Catholic church just ahead. I'll stop there and confess. Come on, Mark! Ditch the puritan prick act!"

"Okay, Mike. But understand that this is a business deal. No favours."

"You're preaching to the converted, Bub. I've got a mouth to feed, rent to pay, and at least three local pubs to support."

So I spent about ten minutes bringing Mike up to date.

"And that's the thumbnail sketch of things", I said in conclusion.

"Okay! Great talking to you, kid. We likely won't see each other for another fifteen minutes."

"Who was that?"

Andrea had made a soundless entrance, surprising me, but her question was just idle interest as she headed for the refrigerator to get a yogurt.

"That was Mike Jefferson. He's going to help in the Harold Barbour case and some other stuff. He'll be here in twenty minutes or so." I was digging myself a hole here but, at least in my own mind, I felt it couldn't be helped.

"What do you plan to do today", I asked, trying to change the subject.

"I'm going to do a first inspection of the remaining four unusables. Get some idea of the scope of work that will be needed."

"You're really getting stuck into this", I said, genuinely pleased that she had latched onto these projects with such enthusiasm.

"Well, it doesn't beat lying in the pool, but it does avoid attacks of Protestant guilt."

I smiled and nodded, it being evident that Andrea's case of mild workaholism was just surfacing in a different guise.

"The drywalling is probably shot in those four cottages, so I'll expose as much of the wiring as I can and we can take a look at it later."

"Well", I said, "it will really be only a second opinion. I'm not an electrician."

"You know what to look for though. But, you're right. Neither of us is an electrician, and we probably should have someone else check it."

I nodded. "We'll take it as it comes."

We sat in silence for a few moments, Andrea slowly spooning out her yogurt, me scanning the day's news. I looked up once and observed, with pleasure, the little smile of anticipation on Andrea's lips, almost certainly reflecting her eagerness to get started on her survey of the unusables. As I switched off and closed my laptop, my cellphone vibrated.

"Whelan."

It was Jocko, and he had some information to send me.

"Do you have it in a state you can send it right now, Jocko?"

He did.

"Okay. Please e-mail it to me. I'll have a look at it before I leave. Will you have time to get together at, say, noon today?"

He would.

"Perfect. Thanks, Jocko. Could we meet at C'est What?"

We could.

As soon as Andrea recognized the call was business, she retired to the sitting room. I restarted my laptop and found Jocko's e-mail. I opened the attachment and began to read, but it turned out to be surprise after surprise. I hadn't got even halfway through the material when there was a shave-and-a-haircut knock at the door.

Mike.

He blew into the house in the only way Mike knows, in friendly authority and irresistible bullish charm.

"There she is! How's my favourite little heartbreaker?" and he headed for Andrea in what appeared to be rugby-tackle mode.

"Hold it, Mike! Hands up! Hands where I can see them!"

"Aw, now, Andrea! You don't think that I'd…", but he broke off partway through and turned to me.

"Mark! What does a weary traveller have to do to get a cup of coffee?"

Mike had been my mentor in the police, and is not quite fifteen years my senior. He's a powerfully built man. At just shy of six feet and 210 pounds, everything about him pulses out the warning "Don't mess with me, you asshole!" He has buzzed blond hair, brilliant blue eyes, hands as large as dinner plates and as strong as bolt cutters, surprisingly fine features, and a mobile face that can radiate anything from the sympathy of maudlin tears to the grimace of barbarian cruelty. Needless to say, he's a fearsome interrogator, pursues his cases with pitbull tenacity, and is someone you don't want to face in a street fight, not even if you're backed by five friends, strong and true. Mike and I are close professional confidants, and we share drinks regularly, but beyond that I know little about him. Mike evidently keeps his private life very private.

"Let's go outside and have our coffee there, Mike. Is that okay with you, Andrea?"

'That's fine. Go. Go."

Once we were seated at the picnic table, Mike was all business.

"How many of them were there?"

"Four, including the diver."

"What was the boat?"

"Couldn't tell."

"Did you get the registration number?"

"No. It was covered up."

"What about the motor?"

"It was a Mercury. Looked like ninety horse. But look, Mike, I did manage to take thirty-four pictures using my cellphone. The boat was more than fifty metres away when I took those shots, and I don't know what quality I got, but there were at least six pictures taken when one or more of the three guys in the boat had their heads up and looking vaguely in my direction."

As I was answering this last question, I pulled up the photos on my laptop, and we both examined them for the first time. Some were simply too blurry, but at least half of them were quite clear.

"I'll send these to you, Mike. You might be able to blow them up, get enhanced images. One other thing."

"What?"

"I got the guy's scuba tank and weight belt. I'll show you where I've stashed them. I'd be grateful if you could take them away. I'm worried about Andrea getting anxious."

"The tank! Great! We might be able to get somewhere using the tank's serial number."

We sat there briefly, both thinking.

"Let's plan the day", Mike said at length. "I'm going to put the word out here locally that we're onto these charlies, and that any further threat against you or yours will be nipped in the bud, or maybe a bit lower. I'm going to follow up on medical treatment first, then on the scuba tank. Do you know where there are tank charging stations?"

"There's one in Fenelon Falls, one in Bobcaygeon, and one in Lindsay."

"Good. Give me a list of the places you'll be during the day. I'm going to be spending a lot of time here close to Largs to watch for any snoopers. Are you going straight to Toronto?"

"Was planning to."

"See if you can find four or five plausible reasons for detours, so you can look for tails. If you think you're being tailed, call me."

"And you'll come running?"

"Someone will."

Mike had taken about two pages of notes as we talked. From the house we heard voices, indicating that George was up.

"Okay, Mike. Time to go and collect my charge. You'll stay here tonight?"

"I will indeed!"

"Good. See you this afternoon."

A quick check of my e-mail confirmed Jocko's commitment to meet me and that I should drop in to the office where my former trustee worked "at a time convenient for me".

Eighteen

Rather than go straight to my car, George and I did a quick walk around Largs, giving me the chance to say again how lovely the place was, that I hoped he had enjoyed his few days here, and that he was welcome to come back any time. Only then, after George managed a small spontaneous smile and some head nodding, indicating that he had enjoyed the visit, only then did I make my way to the car, open it, place a small briefcase on the back seat, and climb into the driver's seat. George dallied over the job of taking the passenger seat.

"Okay, George?"

A noncommittal nod.

"Then we're off."

George had relaxed sufficiently during his time with us in Largs that his faltering speech patterns had become a bit more fluid. I had also learned to ask him questions that required "yes" or "no" answers or short responses of less than five words. But I noticed as we made our right turn from Arran Street south on Highway 35, marking definitively the return to Toronto, that George's agitation had returned to its normal state. It was another gorgeous day, fair weather cumulus clouds dotting the sky, a warm wind fanning the wheat and oats in the fields to ripeness, and through occasional breaks in the trees to our right, I caught glimpses of the lake, giving me its private unspoken reassurance "It's okay, I'm here". George and I spoke in a desultory way for the first twenty minutes or so, me asking my harmless questions and George supplying monosyllabic responses. When it was clear that he was as relaxed as he was likely to be about the trip back, I lapsed into silence and gave the appearance of just concentrating on my driving.

And although I was concentrating on driving, I was also keeping an eye out behind for "followers" and ruminating on what Jocko had passed to me.

Harold had spent time in prison for both breaking and entering and robbery. That was one of the things Jocko had uncovered. Did George know this or not? Better not to make any assumptions, but in either case, implications could and should be drawn. Harold also had been charged at one point with computer fraud, but the charge was dropped due to lack of evidence. Jocko's information noted the break-in and tossing of Harold's apartment, but there were no written details apart from notes made by the officers who investigated. There were a few pictures, and they coincided with my recollection of the scene, although that recollection was based on not much more than a fifteen-second glance. All this just confirmed my need to take a look at Harold's safety deposit box. The lawyer, Hawley, had filed the paperwork needed for George to be able to gain legal access to the box. But George had asked me to hang onto Harold's keys; he still appeared reluctant to go very far in admitting that Harold was no longer with us, or perhaps he was just reluctant to take on any personal responsibility in the matter in order to keep his world as simple as possible. So I still had Harold's keys, including the key to the safety deposit box, and it looked as though they would be staying with me for the foreseeable future.

The thought also occurred to me that I would have to take the lead in cleaning up Harold's apartment, selling his furniture, and either subletting the place or arranging for the rental lease to be terminated. This all placed responsibilities on me, and I made a note to have George sign a standard contract making it clear that actions taken by me were done on George's behalf and at his request. It's not that I had any fear of George turning on me somehow, but the whole case had become strange and conceivably could lurch sideways at any moment.

At the turning near Lindsay, instead of crossing Highway 7 and carrying on to the south, I turned left into Lindsay itself, drove straight down Kent Street, then did some back street work to arrive at a Tim Horton's, where I turned in to the drive through.

"Coffee, George?"

A "yes" was eventually forthcoming.

"Anything to eat, George? I'm getting a sandwich."

George surprised me by asking right away for some Timbits.

Could be the country air, I thought.

Our order came back through the window, and I started the car and drove out into the parking area. We sipped our coffee, George smiled at me, and then attacked his little box of Timbits with more enthusiasm than I had seen him apply to anything.

The sugar hit seemed to enliven George, since he joined in my conversation about spring, the weather, and how Lindsay was changing.

Coffee gulped and Timbits scarfed, we struck out again, doing some ridiculous weaving through more back streets to arrive eventually at Highway 35. We carried on to the south. About fifteen miles south of Lindsay, I said to George, as if taken by a sudden enthusiasm, that I wanted to revisit a familiar spot, where one could get a good panoramic view to the south from a nice lookout point. I drove to the lookout point and, as expected, it was as popular as usual, ten or fifteen cars already parked there.

"Nice, isn't it?" I commented, and George nodded, retrieving a last flake of sugar from the corner of his mouth. I said I was getting out for a moment to take a look, but George indicated he was happy to remain in the car. He was now looking less buoyant, the effect perhaps of falling blood sugar levels.

Walking to the edge of the lookout, I drew out my cellphone and made as though I were taking a series of pictures.

"Mike. It's Whelan."

"Where are you?"

I explained exactly where I was, and gave a description of the car that had been following us all through Lindsay to here, all while holding the phone up in front of me as though aiming and clicking.

"Can you stay there for fifteen minutes?"

"Yes. No problem. What am I waiting for?"

"Never mind about that", Mike rumbled ominously. "Wait fifteen minutes. If I haven't called you back by then, wait another ten minutes then carry on to Toronto. Don't look at any of the cars around you. Got that?"

"You're my man, Mike!"

"You got that right, Mark, my boy. If you don't hear from me in fifteen minutes, I'll call you later."

Returning to the car, I had a quick word with George, grabbed my sandwich, and went back to perusing the wonders of nature. Fifteen minutes came and went. No call from Mike. At twenty minutes, I wolfed the rest of my sandwich, tossed the wrapper into a waste container, hopped in the car, and drove away sporting the smile of one who was freshly in the thrall of nature's glories.

At the point where Highways 35 and 115 intersect the expressway, I picked up the pace, wanting to get into town, do what needed to be done, and return to Largs.

"I think we should go to the bank, George, and take a look in Harold's safety deposit box. Is that okay with you? It won't take long."

George flinched nervously, and managed to indicate his agreement.

"Good. After that, I'll take you back to your place. Is there anything I can help you with while I'm in town?"

"No … I'm fine … thanks."

We found the bank, where I introduced us and said what we wanted to do. I produced the documentation authorizing George to act on behalf of his brother, and we were ushered into a small room where our two keys soon had the safety deposit box sitting on a table in front of us. George eyed it doubtfully, a sleeping animal that would become vicious the moment it awakened.

I opened the box and took out everything it contained, placing the contents in little piles on the table. An insurance policy, documents related to his car, all things to be expected. Then a birth certificate and a passport. Some heavy cord held together an assortment of correspondence, most on the letterheads of lawyers and accountants, some appearing to be personal. Two small government bonds, a few years short of maturity. Then there were the more interesting items: four large notebooks, a sealed envelope marked *Photos*, and what looked like a small leather change purse that had a zip closure. George was evidently curious, but stood back about four feet, well out of contact range.

"Do you mind if I take all this material away and have a close look at it, George?"

"No", George said quickly, shaking his head, appearing eager to disown it all.

"I'm going to make an inventory. I'll pass that on to you, and you can have all the contents whenever you want them."

There was more unequivocal head shaking. "No. It's okay."

I placed all the material in my briefcase, closed the box, and then called the bank employee.

We returned to my car, I drove George to his place, went with him up to his apartment just to make sure that there would be no sudden panic attacks, and asked if he could get me a drink of water.

Faced by something practical, George seemed to relax, got me a glass of water, and then we chatted some more while I drank it slowly. George managed to tell me that he was not expected at his workplace until tomorrow morning, but thought he would probably turn up that afternoon, which meant likely in about two hours, since it was now almost eleven thirty.

I asked George several times if he was sure he would be all right. He nodded, said yes, and then surprised me.

"It was ... the last few days ... at Largs ... thank you, Mr. Whelan. Thank you very much."

I gave him several copies of my card. "You're welcome back any time, George. You can reach me on my cell number at any time, and if you need to talk please just call me. It doesn't matter if it's the middle of the night. Okay?"

"Yes. Thank … thank you."

We shook hands warmly, and then I left.

Back in my car, I realized that I would need to hurry to meet Jocko at the appointed time, but I found a place to park and made my way to C'est What? with a few minutes to spare. Being late at a Jocko appointment would bring out a contradictory and self-defeating harangue, something that might go on for fifteen minutes, about how little time he had and that now some of that precious time had been wasted.

My discussion with Jocko added a few more details to the material he had e-mailed me, but made no substantive difference. I thanked Jocko, said that I had enough information for now, and that he was to send me his invoice, but that I might want more help later, probably on short notice.

"Yeah, yeah! You and every other mother I do work for! Okay! Piss off! I'm up to my eyeballs! Shit on the left, shit on the right, here shit, there shit, everywhere shit, shit…"

I closed the pub door against his emerging rant, and smiled at seeing Jocko so happy with life.

The next and final stop was the firm of Clarence and Donaldson, a venerable institution where Gary (his preferred short form of Garfield) Aldred, my trustee turned portfolio manager, had worked. I had remained in fairly close contact with him until his death at the age of ninety-eight, just a little more than a year ago. But right up to the end he had been clear-minded and able to tap his first-class memory.

His last letter to me had asked after my health, wanted me to pass on his regards to Andrea, and requested a meeting. We had met a few weeks later; he was lively but did give the impression that he was failing and knew it. Nevertheless we shared an excellent wine, and he insisted on me bringing him up to date on what I was up to. Just as I was getting ready to leave, he passed me a folder of what he called "notes". When I got home, I filed that folder of notes, the bittersweet confusion I felt at the end of our meeting having left me unwilling and indeed unable to examine them. I had been pretty sure that he and I had just had our last meeting, and that turned out to be the case.

It was only about a week ago, when I had taken to heart the marriage counsellor's suggestion, and turned a corner in my own mind on how Andrea and I should approach dealing with Largs, that I recalled Mr. Aldred's folder of "notes". As I made my way now to the offices of Clarence and Donaldson, I turned over in my mind what I had learned on reading the "notes", which was what prompted the meeting that was about to take place.

On entering the offices, I was met by a smartly dressed man in his thirties who introduced himself as James Donaldson, the nephew of the senior partner in the firm, Arthur Donaldson. He welcomed me, and once he had learned my reason for calling in, we chatted for a few minutes before he offered to lead me to my appointment. I was shown into the office of Arthur Donaldson and the younger Donaldson left and closed the door.

Arthur Donaldson set aside some papers and rose from his desk.

"Mr. Whelan! Good to see you again." We had met a few times, always in conjunction with one of my review sessions with Gary Aldred, after Mr. Aldred had formally retired. Despite being retired, he continued acting for me as a kind of portfolio manager, but even though I had visited his offices many times, Donaldson and I didn't really know each other at all.

"Yes. Good to see you again, Mr. Donaldson. I'll come straight to the point. I wanted to hand this to you in person", and I passed him a sealed envelope.

He looked at it quickly, then opened it. It was a single sheet of paper, signed by me, and the message in it was simple. It was a formal request, prepared after I had understood some of the subtleties in Mr. Aldred's "notes", for Clarence and Donaldson to hand over to me a number of exactly specified files, which was in fact all the documentation held by Clarence and Donaldson on The McCleod Foundation.

"Give me a moment please, Mr. Whelan", and he left the room. He was back less than ten minutes later carrying a large banker's box, and an eleven-page letter that included a sign-off page. It took me almost twenty minutes to read through the letter, and I had several questions that Donaldson answered readily. We then signed and shook hands.

"Thank you, Mr. Whelan. I have to say that this concludes the longest-running contractual agreement our firm has ever had. And I want to assure you that if you have any further questions, I will be willing to deal with them at any time."

I thanked him and left.

I knew I would have to read through everything in the banker's box. But at the moment my main interest was in getting back to Largs to help Andrea and to have another discussion with Mike.

The trip home was smooth and quick. All the way, I thought about various things, the chief one being the contents of Harold's safety deposit box and the need to examine those contents, now sleeping in my briefcase on the back seat.

The banker's box from Clarence and Donaldson, and its unknown cargo of papers, was also sleeping back there.

It wasn't clear to me what all that paperwork might mean.

I was soon to find out.

Nineteen

By midafternoon, I was approaching Rosedale again from the south and my first glimpse of Balsam Lake, resting in its hollow, was as good as a whispered "Welcome home". I carried on to Largs, drove down the long inviting *allée* of Arran Street, parked the car behind our house, as usual, and then carried briefcase and banker's box into our common room, where I locked them away in the secure filing cabinet. I called Mike, leaving a message and the time, indicating I was back, that I was about to check on how Andrea was doing, and that I wanted to speak to him. Only then did I go out again in search of Andrea. I found her, flushed from a day's work and apparent success, at Number 2 Cedar Grove. She was making liberal use of a laser distance measuring tool, a camera, a notebook, and her iPad.

She had done what looked like extraordinary surveys on three of the four unusables, and the closed, relatively airless spaces she had been working in had given her face an attractive glow of exertion. I went over to her and gave her a huge hug. She responded but then quickly pulled away, saying that she wanted to finish, that it was all going *so* well. "I'm on a roll so I can't stop to explain, and best if you just let me finish alone." That was okay for me, because I wanted to spend some time with Mike, and I remained aware of my role as provisioner and cook. Andrea insisted, through a beaming smile of satisfaction, that she really did want to explain it all, but later, after a shower, and over a glass of wine. This easily served the end I expect it was meant for – to neutralize any inferred sting at being shunted roughly out of the way of the real work.

"I'm off to see Mike. Then I'll bend my mind to dinner. I'll aim for seven o'clock."

"Perfect!" she said, already bent over her iPad once more.

"Mike! Where are you?" I said into my cellphone once I was outside again.

"On my way back", Mike said, and I could hear car noises in the background. "I'll be at the house in less than five minutes. See you then. We have a lot to discuss." I would have replied but Mike had signed off immediately. His more than usual brusqueness indicated that he did indeed have things to tell me. I walked quickly back toward the house, and just as I arrived Mike came around the village square at speed and pulled up next to my car behind the house. He climbed out of his car with his always surprising large man's grace and speed.

"Inside", he commanded.

We went straight into the living area.

"Got a cold beer? Need an antidote to both thirst and bullshit."

I got us four beers, flipped the caps off all of them, and Mike drained three-quarters of his first one at a single glug.

"So. You go first, Mike. What did you find?"

"Made some headway. First, I cleaned up your pictures, and we've now got reasonable shots of two of our guys, and a blurry one of a third. What do you know about the diver?" Mike placed three prints on the table.

"I would guess about five feet, nine inches, but that's just a guess, stocky build, medium-length brown hair, that's it."

"They might not have been thinking straight when they headed north after you stuck the diver in the leg. They can't take a boat any further up the Gull River than Coboconk. So I checked all the rental cabins looking for the boat and as many of the regular cottages as I could. Nothing. But they had to put in somewhere between here and the dam in Coboconk."

I was already on my phone. There was no answer, so I left a message for Kate.

"What was that?" Mike demanded, in his usual rough way.

"Float plane. We'll scan for the boat."

Mike nodded, then resumed his report.

"They wouldn't have taken their guy to a hospital, and there are only five doctors in the area. I doubt they would take him to any of those either. They all have their offices in towns or villages. Pretty hard to disguise a guy who limps from a knife wound to the leg. And all the doctors are well known. Not easy for any of them to make a house call without the risk of somebody seeing when and where. So, I think they've taken Diver Dan to some isolated spot and got a tame quack to come in. Anyway, he'll be patched up and invalided out. Probably done by now. But he won't be doing any more diving for a few weeks."

"What else?" I asked.

Mike was waving his hand impatiently.

"Beer break, man! Back off!"

I waited until Mike had drained half another bottle, but then looked at my watch pointedly.

Mike's bottle hit the table with a thud. "Ahhh! Man, that's good!"

Looking up at me, he went back into business mode.

"I've asked a few contacts if they can identify the two clear-image clowns. I also tacked up a few posters in Coboconk."

"Posters? What kind of posters?"

"Panic posters. Pictures of these two charlies and a message saying that they have been reported missing and are believed to be vacationing in the Coboconk area and if anyone sees them they should contact the police."

"Shit, Mike! That's illegal!"

"Yeah! Nice, isn't it", Mike chirped and beamed like a cherub. "If those guys or any of their watchers see that, they'll become scarce very quickly."

My cellphone buzzed, I pulled it out, and answered.

"Kate! Yes! Can you do a half-hour of contract flying for us? Right now. No, not me and Andrea, a friend of mine called Mike. Yes, standard conditions. Yes, payment at the end of the flight. Twenty minutes in front of the Largs church? Excellent! Thanks, Kate. See you shortly."

I looked at Mike. "You're going for a plane ride, Mike."

"Looking for a boat, right?"

"That's it."

"What are you going to do?"

"Oh, I thought I'd trim my toenails, have a nap – "

"I know it's hard for you, Mark, but try not to be an asshole."

"Okay. I'm going to make dinner for the three of us, maybe four, if Kate wants to stay."

I turned back to the relatively clear pictures of two of the guys in the boat.

"When do you think you might hear from your contact on who these guys might be?" I asked.

"Probably late this afternoon, or early evening."

"What will we do if we get names for them?"

"Well, that depends", Mike said. "If I know them, then we'll know right away whether they're big fish or little fish and what they've done with their lives up to now. If I don't know them, then I'll take steps to find out all that information. If they really are bad asses, then maybe we'll need some support."

"Anything more on whoever was following me earlier today on the way to Toronto?"

"Nothing yet", Mike said. "Patience. Things comes to them buggers as waits."

We sat looking at the photos a bit longer. And I thought again about George, and how he had been caught up in all this mess, in something that was foreign to his life. My ongoing concern for George was that he would discover unpleasant things about his brother Harold, the only person who appeared to matter in his life, and I wondered how he would handle that. I resolved pretty much on the spot to invite George to Largs again for the coming weekend.

I turned my head, listened, then stood.

"Time to get ready, Mike. Your flight is about to leave", and I saw that he then recognized the distant buzz that signalled Kate's approach. Walking to the desk in our family room, I retrieved a small set of powerful binoculars.

"These might come in handy, Mike." He took them and just as we both went outside and headed toward the lake, we heard the whoosh as the floats touched the water. Kate pulled up next to the small dock, floats squeaking against the tire bumpers, nose pointed out toward the lake. Mike opened the passenger side door, I introduced them, and he climbed in.

"Usual hourly rate, Kate?" I asked, practically shouting to be heard over the rough engine idle.

She nodded.

I pulled $300 from my wallet and handed it to Mike.

"Too much", Kate shouted back, frowning and shaking her head.

"Okay. Go now", I responded. "No time to waste. This young fellow has to be back in time for dinner and early to bed."

Mike shut the door, the plane chugged out into the lake, turned, and then roared off to the south.

It took me half an hour to get everything I needed for a dinner of pad thai, and at five thirty, as I began getting things ready in the kitchen, I heard the plane returning. Having forgotten to ask Kate if she wanted to stay for dinner, I hoped that Mike remembered to do so. The sound of the plane's engine being shut down after the approach to the dock and after a few moments of idling indicated that he had and that both Kate and Mike would be coming in through the back door any second.

Bringing up Andrea's number on my cellphone, I called.

"Hi, what's up?" she answered.

"We're having pad thai for dinner. I hope that's okay. Kate's here and she'll be eating with us."

"Kate! Really? Good! I'll finish up here and be home in fifteen minutes."

Mike and Kate blew in through the back door, Kate carried on to the loo to clean up for dinner, and I took Mike aside.

"There's a good chance that sometime during the evening we'll be talking about what you and I have been doing today to identify the guys we think were involved with Harold, but keep it general, and say nothing about the attack on me. Okay?"

"Got it, kid. I'll take my lead from you."

"Good. Andrea will be back soon, and when Kate rejoins us, I'll be taking orders for drinks."

"I think we found the boat." As he was saying this, Mike unfolded a large-scale map. "It's sitting just here", Mike said, as he jabbed a stubby finger at the map unforgivingly.

I looked at the spot he indicated. "Those are Stinson's cottages."

"You know the guy?"

"Yeah. He looks and sounds pleasant enough on the outside, but he'd sell his mother's glass eye for a buck. We can have a rough word with him tomorrow. But in his world, it's a matter of "ask me no questions and I'll tell you no lies". There's probably a good chance that the only thing he knows about those guys is the colour of their money."

Mike smiled grimly, and I almost felt sorry for old Rick Stinson. Almost.

Kate rejoined us, Mike went off for his pre-prandial ablutions, and I invited Kate into the kitchen to watch me cook.

I always look forward to dinner with Andrea, and having Kate along made it just that much better. But looking beyond dinner, I knew that it would be a long night.

Twenty

Dinner was a surprise combination of urbanity, entertainment, and hilarity.

Kate and Mike had evidently hit it off from the get-go, Kate talking about flying, Mike talking about detecting.

"What do you do to relax, Mike?" Kate asked, after fifteen minutes of their accounts of derring-do. "Do you read?"

"Nah. Not much."

"What then?"

"I like music. That's relaxing."

Kate kept digging, asking for details. Eventually, we got there.

"Opera!" Kate cried, surprised and delighted.

"Yeah, yeah, I know", Mike rumbled, looking a bit ruffled, uncertain. "Gumshoe, Grade 8 education. Spends his days in life's sewers. Beats people senseless for diversion. Likes Verdi and Puccini. Doesn't fit, does it?"

Nobody bought Mike's low-grade description of himself, least of all me since I was aware of his degree in criminology. But the operatic interest was something that not even I knew about, and Mike had our full attention now, as our voices rose in rebuke at his rough and one-dimensional self-characterization.

"I don't know", Mike said, in response to more questions. "Favourites? Very hard to choose. So much good stuff."

But we didn't let up, and eventually Mike stood. His fine, rich tenor delivered an excellent version of "Nessun Dorma". Mike held the last high "Vincero" perfectly, and there was complete silence from his audience of three. But then enthusiastic applause erupted immediately, followed by another round of questions.

The evening broke up when Kate excused herself, saying that she wanted to arrive home before official sunset. We all went out with her to her plane and said our warm goodbyes, then watched as she fired up the bird, moved slowly out into the lake, turned the plane to face north, then roared off into the evening.

"How long will it take her to get home?" Mike asked.

"About ten minutes", Andrea said.

We stood looking out over the lake, listening to the wavelets lap the shore, hearing the occasional night bird, and following the sound of the plane as it faded away.

"Okay", I said suddenly as I was attacked by a mosquito, "everybody inside for digestifs while I clean up", holding up my hands to decline the offers of assistance in the kitchen.

Everyone flopped in the sitting room, and after glasses of sambuca were distributed I repaired to the kitchen to do the last bits of cleanup. When I rejoined Andrea and Mike, Andrea had sipped about half her sambuca, but the drooping eyelids and nodding head demonstrated clearly enough that she had run out of steam. Mike's glass was empty and he was at work on his cellphone.

"I have some antisocial work to do, if you'll excuse me", he said, and without waiting for a response he rose and headed for his room, uttering a "sleep tight" over his shoulder as he rounded the corner. I sat down next to Andrea and draped an arm over her sagging shoulders.

"Time for beddy-byes." She nodded and mumbled something, I helped her to her feet, and led her off to our bedroom.

Back in our family room, I retrieved the cloth carrier bag and the banker's box from the filing cabinet, unpacked the contents of Harold's safety deposit box from the carrier bag and the files from the banker's box, and laid them all out on the large coffee table.

Placing a pile of cushions on the floor, and retrieving a fresh note pad, I set to work.

The small leather change purse had my attention first, simply because it seemed so out of the ordinary. Opening it, I found four memory sticks. Thinking back, I tried to reconstruct the details of Harold's apartment in my mind. I had seen it for less than thirty seconds, although my gaze had swept around the main room systematically, following my police training, which I find resurfaces regularly and usefully. What I recalled was what one might expect. There had been a dreary grey sofa awaiting its own post-mortem, a threadbare armchair from which some of the stuffing was making good its escape, a scarred coffee table, a cheap kitchen table and three chrome and plastic chairs, a tottery four-shelf bookcase, and a desk and swivel chair. The floor had been covered in scattered papers, the few books had been riffled and were in disarray on the floor, what looked like it had once been a decent rose-coloured vase was in pieces, all three drawers of the desk had been pulled out roughly, one of them destructively, and lay empty to one side, their contents evidently strewn about.

There was a power bar on the desk, but no computer.

I recalled being able to see partway through the doorway into the kitchen. There was no evidence that I could see of anyone having searched for something hidden in flour bags, cereal boxes, or sugar bowls.

Someone accused of computer fraud would have had a computer. So it was a safe bet that whoever had been there trashing the place had taken a computer, probably a laptop. What they might have found among Harold's paperwork was impossible to guess.

It took me the best part of an hour and a half to look through and list the contents of Harold's four memory sticks. The first one I chose appeared to be records of his personal financial affairs, which indicated that he had smallish savings accounts in four separate banks. The total in all these accounts came to a bit more than $26,000, and based on the files in this memory stick there had been very little activity in these accounts over a period of months, either as deposits or withdrawals.

I moved quickly through the remaining memory sticks, which contained a lot of personal correspondence, and some snippets of history that Harold had evidently collected. Voltaire's dismissive description of "our home and native land" as "*quelques arpents de neige*" – a few acres of snow – had caught Harold's attention because he had included two papers just on that comment. I flipped quickly through a surprisingly voluminous collection of papers and copied bits of reports on the period 1759 to 1763. But I spent a good amount of time on one of Harold's memory sticks, which included more than a hundred files of local history for villages and areas centred on the Balsam Lake area. The name George Laidlaw was associated with many of these files.

So, Harold was an amateur historian! Interesting…

One file that did catch my eye described the long withdrawal after the French defeat at the Plains of Abraham. There were French settled thinly in what later became Upper Canada. Some decided to depart, others were determined to remain, and some of them would become part of a founding stream of the Métis. There were isolated groups of Jesuits who had set about trying to convert the native people to Christianity. Some met the essential precondition for this task – they survived. But after 1763, some of them stayed since the church's work went on. Those who left made the long trek from spots on the upper Great Lakes, through the traditional routes down to Lake Ontario, and thence to Montreal, either to remain in Quebec or to find passage back to France. At the same time, there was an influx of soldiers and settlers from England. Not huge, but very much noticeable. Despite the fact that the English wanted peaceful accommodation with their conquered French population, inevitably there were some clashes between the departing French and the arriving English, since the Seven Years' War had only sharpened the mutual antagonisms between ancestral enemies.

As it happened, it was the fourth and last memory stick that held the real pay dirt, although I didn't realize this right away. The files on this stick were identified by date only, the dates going back almost fifteen years, and the most recent dates being just a year ago. It looked as though this was a record of at least some of Harold's research.

Seven of the files on this stick, copies of reports and newspaper items, all bore dates from between six to ten years earlier. I dipped into some of them. There were dry compilations of waterborne traffic on Balsam Lake, Cameron Lake, and Sturgeon Lake in the mid-nineteenth century. A long newspaper article excerpted at length from the memoir of a late-nineteenth-century log driver, recounting stories of booms, jams, sluices, and being caught in rapids. The facts behind it might have been few and doubtful, but it certainly wasn't boring. There were several pictures of steamboats, grainy images of people in their finery waving at the camera. It was the story of a world now gone.

Then I found an article written by Harold himself, seemingly just to document things. He had tabulated boats, lakes, years, cargoes, and numbers of passengers. But the article just ended in mid-air.

I was ready to conclude that it was all just hurriedly thrown together, having little internal logic, when I found a two-page note. The note gave details on nine boats that had been lost due to boiler explosions, fire, or being holed by water hazards.

Opening six of Harold's files, I began taking notes. Some of the timings were inconsistent. But where there were firm dates, they seemed all to be in the ten years between the mid-1850s and mid-1860s. This was up to fifteen years before the railway came to Coboconk and transport by water was really the only way to go. Two of the reports in Harold's files emphasized that there were no real roads, just tracks, and even those were rough and scarcely passable at the best of times, becoming totally unusable, due to deep, thick mud in spring or any time after heavy rains.

Lawlessness.

It was mentioned a couple of times in two of the articles. And that tweaked a thought.

What about highwaymen?

Looking back through Harold's articles, I found no mention of this. A few internet searches revealed a cache of likely sources, and I soon learned that there wasn't much trouble from highwaymen in Upper Canada at that time, although they were around. There were scattered accounts, the basis for which wasn't evident, of highwaymen operating between larger centres, such as Lindsay and Peterborough, probably in the wake of the extending network of railways. But this was likely just some initiative by local young bucks, hardly the stuff of Butch Cassidy and Jesse James mythology.

At eleven thirty, needing a break, I walked outside, and was bathed in the glory of the firmament: thousands of visible stars, and untold millions of invisible ones, in a silent, constant holding pattern above me, these stars speaking a language of collective turmoil and violence beyond the conceivable. This was a deeply burnt image of my childhood and early youth – the night sky at Balsam Lake, the great stardust sash of the Milky Way.

The night sky has always inspired and relaxed me, and it didn't fail to do so now.

Returning to the den, I popped in a CD, pulled on headphones, and my night was suddenly full of the wonderful haunting tones of BWV 974. For a few therapeutic minutes, I was afloat with Bach, the music eventually slowed to its conclusion, and the sound faded to that restless silent potential of an empty CD track, the Biblical Void prior to the First Day.

Returning to my pile of cushions, I savoured what was now a clear and refreshed mind, a mental reboot. Into the clarity, a name arose.

Harold.

Harold had been a very pragmatic man and evidently not heavily burdened by ethics or morals. He wasn't here at Balsam Lake looking at nature, gazing at the stars, or snorkelling just for pleasure. Nor was he engaged in some sort of Jim Hawkins adventure. Harold did things for reasons. Pragmatic reasons. Very self-interested reasons. Reasons that held out the promise of immediate payback.

What had he been looking for?

Whatever it was, it would be valuable in the monetary sense. My recently contemplated treasure of learning had led me to the notion of physical treasure.

Was Harold looking for natural mineral wealth, treasure of an antique nature somewhere at the bottom of Balsam Lake, artefacts that would be of value to collectors? Was he looking for treasure that had more of a historical character? Or was he looking for something that he, Harold Barbour, could immediately take to the bank, so to speak?

One could pretty well rule out mineral wealth, I thought. It wasn't a quick fix. So it very likely wasn't Harold.

I knew of possible treasure of an antique nature, but this derived from a persistent myth that reappeared regularly. The lost treasure of Ghost Island.

What about the other two possibilities? Treasure having mostly or only historical value. Treasure that was antique in nature, or that otherwise could be turned immediately into cash.

Blank.

Thinking about it a bit longer, I realized that the treasure categories of most interest to me were linked to people, to individuals. Things of value that people had lost very recently, say during the past twenty or so years, could be ruled out. Those people would have some idea where they had lost their valuables, and given the search methods and equipment available now, anything of any real value would be recovered to high probability. In the middle of the nineteenth century, which was where the documents on Harold's memory sticks were pointing, there were few Europeans in the Balsam Lake area, and none of them was wealthy. As a group, they would gradually accrue some wealth, through their labour and the properties they built, and there would be some physical exchanges of money as part of everyday life. Money would need to be transferred, if only in small quantities, and the only practical means to travel had been by water. So, one might expect that some of the old steamboats, on occasion, would be carrying people who in turn would be carrying some money. The only way this could translate into "treasure" was if and when some of these boats capsized or sank for other reasons.

This line of reasoning led me back to Harold's files, and I spent another forty-five minutes reading them more closely. Boats lost on the lake were a clue, and Harold's notes did spend some time on boats that had gone down. But it seemed to be just an indiscriminate listing of sunken boats with no attempt to connect any of these to something valuable being lost. Had Harold been making some assumptions about this, assumptions that he hadn't bothered to write down? Or had he documented them and they were now lost? Or was this something I had missed? I had to fall back on the old reality check that nothing is that easy. It wasn't going to be just handed to me on a plate.

I looked through the list of steamboats again. There were surprisingly many of them, forty-three. Some were evidently just rinky-dink operations and didn't last long. They all consumed firewood voraciously, so would have been expensive to keep going, and therefore would have needed a regular and high-volume supply of cargo or passenger traffic to justify their continued operation. One of the boats in this list caught my attention, not because of its name, the *Coboconk*, but because of its relatively short service life. It had caught fire and sunk somewhere off Rosedale.

Niggle, niggle.

Why was this sounding familiar somehow?

I pulled out a large-scale roadmap of the Victoria County area, focused on Balsam Lake, and located Rosedale easily.

Could it be? Could it really be?

I found the list of locations that Kate had flown me over in her plane two days ago, the list that the lawyer, Hawley, had passed to George under Harold's instructions. Turning to my laptop, I brought up Google Earth, and moved the cursor over the four points in Harold's list. The easternmost point of the four was in the lake just west of Rosedale.

I sat back in near disbelief.

Could this have been the trail that Harold was following? Nineteenth-century steamboat wrecks?

Twenty-one

Despite the late night, I was up by seven thirty the next morning and found Mike settled in the kitchen, enjoying coffee, eggs, and toast.

"Ah! Good morning, Rip!" he said past a mouthful of egg. "Pull up a pew. Let me fry you a couple of eggs", and before I could say anything, Mike was on his feet, had the gas lit, and had broken two eggs into the pan.

"Coffee?" he asked, redundantly, as he handed me a mug of very black liquid. I just had time to take in the partly overcast morning and the lake already well in ripple before the sound of the toast popping up announced the full scope of my breakfast. No better idea on what to do or say having occurred to me, I sat down.

"Sleep well, Mike?"

"Like a baby, my boy, especially after reading the information I received about our argonauts."

I looked at Mike questioningly.

"We now know who the two lads are you took clear pictures of. Both fairly low-level villains from Toronto. So they might be working for someone higher up, but I suspect not."

"Why?"

"Well, because it's all just too messy, too sloppy, even for a semi-professional bunch. I think we're seeing a bit of private initiative."

"But the bigger piece of information", Mike continued after taking a slug of coffee, "is that I think we now know where Diver Dan is lying low."

"Oh? Really!" My increased interest must have been evident.

"Yes. A guy I hired for the day intercepted your tail when you were taking George back to Toronto. Your tail followed you to that lookout point and parked six or seven cars along. My man Chuck pulled in tight behind him, then got out and set about having a piss. He said a couple of women looked away in disgust and a couple looked on in interest. Odd ploy, but he said he couldn't think of anything better and had to piss anyhow. Well, Tommy the Tail got a tad anxious because he could see you were leaving, and began to berate Chuck because he couldn't move his car any more than a couple of inches. 'In a minute man, in a minute', Chuck said to him. 'You can see I'm busy.' Wish I'd been there", Mike said through a smile, then gave a good belly laugh. "I can just hear Chuck saying something like that. Anyway, it took a while for Chuck to empty the piss barrel and Tommy the Tail was dancing about like it was him whose back teeth were floating. Chuck got his car out of the way, Tommy jumped in and drove back to the highway, but he couldn't see you anywhere by then."

Mike took another swig of coffee and scratched his groin contentedly.

"And then?" I prodded.

"Oh, yeah. And then Chuck followed Tommy, but it looked as though Tommy was so anxious that he forgot to check on whether he was being tailed. I've seen it before. Tails don't seem to think that anybody would ever tail them. Anyroad, Tommy decided to go right at the exit from the lookout point, which is the way you actually had gone, but because of the way the lookout parking lot slopes away from the road, he had no sightline, so he was just guessing, even though the shortest way back to the main road was to the left. I'm sure he expected that you were heading for Toronto. But I think he thought that you might have been concerned about being followed, so would take the least obvious route from the lookout point. But he was screwed in any case. Chuck said that Tommy drove like a madman, probably hoping to catch sight of you somewhere. He stopped at one point and talked on a cellphone while he seemed to be looking at a map. Then he set out again and eventually stopped at a seedy motel just south of Lindsay. My guy got some pictures of Tommy talking to another guy just before they went into one of the units."

After a few seconds of Mike's smug silence, I prodded him again impatiently.

"Yeah. I have copies of the pictures here. But the good news is that the guy Tommy met was limping, favouring his left leg."

"The diver!" I exclaimed.

"Very likely", Mike said through a happy smile.

"So", I said, thinking my way through this. "Our diver is something of a sitting duck, at least for now, since he probably can't drive himself. So I expect you'll be paying him a visit at his hotel today."

"Bingo! That's my boy! Right on the money. In fact, now that I've finished my coffee, that's what I'm about to do."

I laid down my knife and fork, and Mike took our plates and coffee mugs to the sink, then turned to look at me.

"And what about you?"

"I'm going to do some more paper chasing. You remember me telling you about the four coordinates that Harold's lawyer passed on to George?"

A nod.

"Well, I think they're the sites of old steamboat wrecks."

"No! Surely not! We're not after a bunch of treasure hunters, are we?"

"I don't think it's that simple. But I really don't know just what they're up to. I'd like to find out just how long they've been looking. Old Rick will know."

"Okay. I'll do that first, make a call on Stinson, then pay a visit to Diver Dan."

The day's agenda having been settled, I moved to the sink and began to clean up. Mike and I agreed to be in fairly regular phone contact during the day. Then he grabbed his notebook and laptop, checked that he had his phone, clapped me on the shoulder, and went out to his car.

Andrea rose just before nine o'clock, stiff and sore, but clear-eyed, rested, and eager to get back at it again. She had a minimal breakfast, and I kept her company with a second cup of coffee, then I walked with her back to the last of the unusables. She had done a stunning amount of work, and now had a table of project elements, listed by cottage, that we could cost out and put in a sensible order for completion, one that would lead to most units being brought to prime condition in the shortest time. We talked for a few minutes about her day's work, then she showed me the door, diplomatically.

Back in the den, I carried on reading from where I had left off in the wee hours of that morning. An hour's work was enough to identify steamboat names that could conceivably be associated with three of the four points in Harold's list of coordinates. The one point I could find no matching name for was the most interesting: the one opposite Largs and just offshore from Indian Point, the place where the diver had tried to drown me.

I puzzled over this, then pouted for a while at my lack of success for that location before I completed detailed notes on what I had done yesterday and today, and then turned to the material in the Clarence and Donaldson banker's box. I had barely begun to get into this when my cellphone buzzed. It was Mike.

"What's up, Mike?"

"What's up? Well, if I could lick my own ass, I'm sure the taste in my mouth would be ambrosia compared to what's there now. Rick Stinson. Gangrene soup could hardly be less appealing."

"I did warn you. What did you get?"

"Well, nothing contagious, I hope. But our boatmen have been there in his ramshackle cabin only three days. And he tells me that they've been out in their boat only twice."

"Do you know where they got the boat?"

"Rancid Rick tells me they brought it with them. I got the registration number, and I've traced it to a rental shop in Lindsay, so I'll check that when I've finished with Diver Dan."

"I take it that our boatmen weren't there."

"No", Mike replied. "Stinson said they left this morning about half an hour before I arrived. Didn't know where they were going."

"Did you get a look in their cabin?"

"Just a peek through the windows. Nothing there. Looks almost as though they might have left."

"And just abandoned the boat?"

"Why not? It's not their boat."

"Did you get their car licence number?"

"No. But I might be able to get that from the boat-rental place in Lindsay."

We talked a bit more about Mike's exchanges with Stinson.

"I'm surprised you got that much out of him. How can you be sure he isn't stringing you along for some reason?"

"Tsk! Tsk! Oh ye of little faith! You've forgotten, evidently, that old Mike has great powers of persuasion. And when you hint to most people the personal consequences of aiding and abetting in a murder, they tend suddenly to see the happy side of cooperation. I think what I got is bankable."

"So you're off to see the diver now?"

"On my way as we speak. I'll call you when he and I have had our little chat."

I went back to my files. Having made some notes from my conversation with Mike, I returned to the Clarence and Donaldson banker's box. I had previously added to its contents the file I had obtained from my former trustee, Mr. Aldred, on the occasion of our last meeting. I took everything out of the box now.

Aldred's file contained his own handwritten notes, and there were more than seventy pages of them. I flicked through a little more than half of them quickly, but nothing that I didn't already know caught my eye, so I set the file aside.

The remaining contents of the box consisted of four relatively thick files.

One of these files contained mostly very old documents, browned from age and looking decidedly brittle along the edges. Somebody, probably Aldred himself, had placed each of the individual sheets of these old documents into high-quality onion-skin paper, folded so that each of the sheets was completely covered. I presumed that this was done to preserve the old paper. Most of the text was legible through the onion skin. A quick perusal indicated that these sheets documented how old McCleod had tried to prevent his legacy and his fortune from being dissipated by his no-good offspring. I would need to have this document copied carefully in order to read it closely without damaging the original.

The second file contained a detailed set of financial accounts for Largs, by year, documenting separately the capital put into the initial construction of the place, the rents charged to tenants who took up residence in the cottages, and, starting some years later, the commercial income McCleod realized once his lake boats began operating.

The remaining files contained McCleod's own projections, indicating which potential lines of business might bring in how much income over the years.

I was about to return to Aldred's file when my cellphone buzzed again. It was Mike.

"So, what did you find, Mike", I began somewhat enthusiastically.

"I'm on my way back, Mark", Mike said in a very strange, flat, and oddly expressionless voice. "We'll talk when I arrive."

"Sure, Mike, but what did you…"

I realized then that I was speaking to a dead line.

About twenty minutes later, I heard Mike's car pull in, and then he tumbled through the door and sat heavily in an easy chair. I had made some coffee and moved to get a cup.

"Cup of coff – " I began.

"Is Andrea here?" Same flat voice that I heard over the phone.

"No, she's … what's wrong, Mike?"

"Triple scotch first", and without waiting for me to get it for him, Mike moved to the liquor cabinet, poured what was at least a triple, and downed a third of it.

"Got to the motel, knew the unit number from the photo Chuck had sent me, knocked on the door, no answer, nobody around, picked the lock, found Diver Dan."

Mike drained half of what remained in his glass.

"Somebody had shot him once through the head."

Twenty-two

For a few seconds I just sat there, getting my head around what Mike had said.

"We need to do a couple of things right away, Mike."

Mike was nodding.

"I've already done the first of them. I called Chuck and asked him to send in a tip from a public pay phone, and that he needed to use wiped coins and gloves, and make sure nobody saw him. By now, the police probably have already found the diver's body."

Now I was nodding.

"And the second thing", I began, but was interrupted as Mike held up one hand and pulled out his cellphone.

"Jefferson."

Long silence as Mike listened.

"Okay. Thanks, Chuck."

"Developments?" I asked.

"You could say that. The police have found something. In a stand of poplars about a quarter-mile from Diver Dan's motel. In the corner of a field. Three bodies. The men from Diver Dan's boat. All executed."

We just looked at each other for a moment.

"You were saying something?" Mike asked.

"Yes. I was about to say that it's time for us to rethink this whole business. But that seems a little redundant now. This thing really has gone lethal. There are professionals out there, and we're right in the middle of it, whatever it is."

Mike was nodding again.

I got up, went to the liquor cabinet, poured myself a generous scotch, and took a good swig. Then Mike and I sat down and went through everything we knew about this operation.

At the end of an hour, we had a new perspective on what we were facing. There was something valuable out there that somebody wanted very badly. It looked as though the diver had become a liability, possibly had said that he wanted out, and very quickly demonstrated that he might be by far the weakest link in their operation, risking them all. But it was more likely that the professionals had just eliminated the amateurs. Well, Diver Dan was a risk no longer, nor were his colleagues, but there would now be another much higher profile police investigation taking place that might hinder the work of whoever was after the prize, whatever it was.

"I don't think any of us is at immediate risk", Mike said, "at least not while we aren't in their way. But let's think through our actions here. I want to go over our physical security and what exactly we should be trying to protect ourselves from. You need to find out what these goons are after. Chances are that we won't be caught in any police dragnet, but there's at least one loose end I can think of – Rancid Rick. I need a story for why I was talking to him."

"There's one other link", I said, "and I expect it to connect any time now."

"What's that?"

"Bent Cromarty."

"But it's out of his jurisdiction. This has nothing to do with Toronto. This will be picked up by the OPP."

"He won't come at us, or at least at me, officially. He'll just make an inquiry. The Harold Barbour case was snatched away from him by higher-ups who could see no path forward and wanted to reduce the number of open cases on the books. For some reason, Bent has got his teeth into this one, and I'm sure he thinks I know more about it than the police but that I've been holding back."

"Tough!" Mike barked. "Unless he can show interference in an investigation, fuck 'im!"

"Fuck 'im indeed. He can't show interference, because there's no investigation to interfere in. But he won't let go easily. My approach to him is easier. I'll plead ignorance. I'm just a PI taking a couple of weeks' well-deserved vacation in the company of my old friend Mike. But I agree with you that you need a story, and maybe you can work this holiday angle into it."

"Let's get to it, then", Mike said, rising in new resolve and heading for his room. But he turned back almost immediately.

"Where's Andrea?"

I felt a jolt of concern, until I realized he wasn't sounding an alarm but just wanted to have everything covered. Andrea wasn't at risk, but now that Mike had raised the subject I had to make extra sure that our security net covered all of us all the time.

"That's a good call. She's at Number 3 Cedar Grove today. I'll take her some water and spend the rest of the day working there with her."

"No, Mark. You need to stay here and do our paper sleuthing. I'll take the water. Where's the best place to keep an eye on Number 3?"

"From Number 2, where she was working yesterday. But it really should be me – "

"Goddammit Mark! We need to find out what the fuck's going on here! You're the only one who can do that! So hop to it! Nothing's going to happen to Andrea!" He pulled six bottles of water from the fridge and stuffed them into a plastic bag.

I could see Mike's point, but not taking direct steps myself to look after my own family made me feel totally inadequate and irresponsible.

"Well, okay. But you call me if there's even a suggestion that you might need help."

Mike gave me a severe dose of the bent eye.

"The only way I'm likely to need help is in carrying the plates with the heads of whoever the buggers are behind all this."

He turned to leave, signalling the end of the discussion.

"Wait!" I said. "Here's the key to Number 2", and I tossed it to him.

Once Mike had left, I dived into the paperwork. Almost all the material in the banker's box had to do with commercial matters in one way or another. I identified and set aside all the arrangements old McCleod had with other businesses in Toronto. Likewise, I ignored all his commercial accounts and banking details. Without having a clear idea why, I homed in on his shipping accounts. These covered warehousing details in Toronto, transfers between businesses within Toronto, and shipment of goods to and from Toronto by ship and railways. I soon located the details of shipments to, from, and within the hinterland areas. Fortunately, McCleod's records were broken down by area.

My eye gravitated naturally toward old McCleod's two steamboats that had operated on Balsam and Cameron Lakes. There were statements summarizing hundreds of bills of lading for the cargoes carried by these boats. There were also records showing that McCleod shipped goods from Toronto to Fenelon Falls in stages, first via lake ship from Toronto to Port Hope, by rail from there to Lindsay, and then by boat to Fenelon Falls. The two Balsam and Cameron Lake boats, the *Jackson* and the *Daniella*, were busy almost all the time from spring thaw to winter freeze up, and over a period of ten years it looked as though McCleod made a tidy profit from these operations, at least from the *Jackson*. Records of the *Daniella* disappeared about 1860 and another boat, the *Damsel May*, began appearing in the records a year or so later. The *Jackson* and *Daniella* were built and launched at Fenelon Falls in 1857; the *Damsel May* was also built at Fenelon Falls, but no date was given. They were all steamboats, each capable of carrying about sixty passengers or about seven tons of freight.

McCleod owned land. Lots of it. He owned properties in Toronto, Port Hope, and Cobourg, and he bought and sold land over the years in Coboconk, Fenelon Falls, Lindsay, and of course he owned Largs. There were also records of land he owned in Hastings County, quite a bit of land, land he had bought during a one-year period, held for a short time, then sold within about four months. Most of these records simply named the properties, or in some cases just the lot numbers. The financial transactions, I guessed, were all consolidated in his corporate accounts, and the records of all this had all been moved into the files of The McCleod Foundation a few years before he died. He died of natural causes, and it seems he spent his last years reading, socializing in Toronto, and looking after a few investments. I recalled from a conversation with Mr. Aldred many years earlier that McCleod had an elaborate management scheme for The McCleod Foundation, that he had placed it all in the hands of a few trusted bankers, and that his plan for maintaining it over the years was very conservative. When everybody else was speculating like idiots, McCleod's foundation would go ultra-conservative, in some cases converting all his assets to gold until it was clear that the financial turbulence had passed. So he or his operations came out of almost every downturn and recession better off or at least as well off as when they went into it.

The business about The McCleod Foundation fluttered around in my mind but refused to be netted. There was way too much material here to start thinking about very specific items, and I recognized that I was assuming that something about The McCleod Foundation, some specific insight, would leap out at me. There was something here I couldn't put my finger on. I made a note in the small notebook where I kept a record of stray thoughts and possibly good ideas, rather than in the pages and pages of jottings I was making on the material I had brought back from Toronto, where I'd never find it again. Despite all this, something said to me that I should take some time right now to get a better handle on what it was that was niggling.

But there was no time.

I went through Aldred's onion-skin file, but this time I carefully perused all of it. It was pretty uninspiring financial detail. As well as the goods destined for Lindsay and beyond, McCleod shipped an even greater quantity of stuff to Peterborough, and the areas surrounding it, goods that were needed by farmers, by merchants who served the communities, and even some goods required by the few fledgling industries that were springing up. One of these industries was mining. An item in this file that I hadn't seen on my previous skim, because I had stopped before I reached it, was one of the very few interviews McCleod had ever given and which was printed in an issue of the *Toronto Leader*. In the article, the reporter quoted McCleod as saying that it was hard enough getting goods out to outlying centres, but it was just as hard or harder to bring the receipts from the sale of these goods back to Toronto. "Whenever I could", McCleod was quoted, "I relied on my own boats to carry these receipts under armed guard. On only one occasion, that dreadful August 17, was I struck by disaster in the course of one of these shipments."

By three thirty that afternoon, I had made almost forty pages of notes, and I began entering them into a spreadsheet so that I could move blocks of my notes and data around, rearrange them, and look for any patterns. But the only pattern that appeared to emerge was the fact that the information relating to McCleod's activities showed that most of these activities were far from Balsam Lake, and I could find nothing to explain the interest of whoever we were up against. The one persistent idea that resurfaced again and again, sometimes in correspondence, sometimes in news articles, involved the Ghost Island treasure. But the idea of anyone seriously looking for the Ghost Island treasure was ridiculous. People had been hunting for it for more than two hundred years, with never the merest hint of success. Any rational person, wanting to invest resources and expecting a return, would not turn to the Ghost Island treasure even as a last resort.

So these people, the boatmen or whoever was behind them, what had they been after, who had killed them, and why?

An idea occurred to me suddenly. I went through it all again quickly, looking more closely at the rather anomalous collection of

McCleod's properties in Hastings County. They were all just lot numbers. When he sold them, a few had been sold to individuals whose occupations were given as "farmer", some were designated as "businessman", but for many of them, the buyer was just a name with no occupation. But the key point here, it seemed to me, was that McLeod had bought and sold more than a hundred and fifty properties over the space of less than two years. It seemed to me that this was not typical of McCleod and I suspected that I was onto something.

It was now after four o'clock, and I had to think about the evening meal. I decided on something simple, beef souvlaki. Wally had closed for a family wedding, but I could find what I needed for our meal easily enough. I called Mike on his cell to say that I was off to get the wherewithal for dinner and that I would be back in half an hour. He asked me how it was going, and I mumbled something noncommittal.

"Take heart, my boy", he said encouragingly. "I know you. You don't give up easily, and we both know that gold is where you find it."

I drove into Coboconk, got what I needed, said hello to five or six people, and headed back toward Largs. I was about halfway home when the notion of treasure suddenly flashed a different face at my mind's eye, and I literally jumped at the surge of excitement it delivered.

Twenty-three

Luckily there were no radar traps on the highway that day because I raced along at well above the speed limit all the way back to Largs. Navigating the village impatiently, I parked and galloped into the house. Instead of giving in to the huge temptation to go straight to the den, I hurriedly put together the souvlaki skewers, peeled some potatoes, roughly shredded lettuce for a salad, then made a beeline for my notes.

It took me an hour to go through all the paperwork again looking for those items that might confirm the hunch that had occurred to me back there on the highway.

And I found them.

McCleod was not unidimensional. He had interests outside his businesses. He had hobbies. He collected things. Specifically, he collected indigenous artefacts. I recalled that Aldred had mentioned that in passing somewhere in his notes.

For the next twenty minutes, I sat there flipping through and reading documents, thinking, and noting points on my writing pad.

Was it conceivable? Yes.

Did it make sense from McCleod's point of view? Very much so.

Was it credible today? Yes.

Did it explain the activity and the intent we had seen thus far? Yes.

Did it provide me the basis for a counter-strategy? Yes.

I went through my points again, checked them against what I had found in the banker's box files, and did another reality check. It all held together. I couldn't see any assumptions that might have converted something meaningless or ridiculous into what I believed now lay before me. McCleod had built up a substantial collection of indigenous artefacts at Largs. He had planned to move it all to Toronto where it would be more secure. McCleod never did anything by halves, so although without an inventory I had no way of knowing his collection's value, it would now be more than 150 years old.

So, valuable.

Most likely very valuable, both then and now.

It was now almost six o'clock. I called Andrea.

"*Ciao, Bellissima!* How's it going?

"Oh! What time is it? It's going fine."

"It's six o'clock. I'm making beef souvlaki for dinner, with Greek potatoes and a Greek salad. I've got the beef ready for the barbecue."

"Well, I've got at least another two hours here, so I'll start wrapping it up for today. Be back in twenty minutes."

"Okay. *Ciao!*"

Then I called Mike.

"Mike, Andrea's packing up now and says she'll be back here in about twenty minutes."

"Great! I'm getting peckish. How's the sleuthing going?"

"I think I've got it, Mike. If you can get back here in five minutes, I'll brief you quickly before Andrea returns."

"I'm leaving now. Open me a cold beer."

"Oh! And Mike. I'm going to let Andrea in on things tonight. I don't want to keep her in the dark any longer."

"Roger", Mike said, and by the sound of his voice he was already pounding the streets at a fast walk back to our house.

As usual, Mike's first beer enjoyed a gleeful freefall into a black hole. He listened intently while I gave him a two-minute summary of my findings.

"You think that's what's out there in the lake?"

"Everything fits."

"So, old McCleod was a collector. And he kept a collection of something here at Largs."

"It looks that way", I said.

"And you think that maybe he was moving his collection to Toronto and somehow it was lost here in the lake? But what could he collect here?" Mike continued. "What was there of value?"

"He had several collections. He had a collection of musical instruments in Toronto, but in his will he bequeathed that collection to the museum. You're right that at that time there wasn't much to collect here, and he probably just collected stuff that interested him."

"What kind of stuff?"

"Well, Aldred mentioned somewhere that McCleod had a collection of arrowheads. I would bet that he also had a collection of other aboriginal artefacts."

"But", Mike began.

"Yes, I know. They would have had no value then, except to McCleod for whatever was the reason he collected them. But think about today. Depending on what might have been in the collection, there are people who would love to have what might now be a unique assortment of Ojibway artefacts."

"What kind of artefacts?"

"Well, there could have been bows, lances, ceremonial pipes, all sorts of personal decorations."

"Would all that stuff survive?"

"Some of it certainly would", I said. "Wood can last a long time if it has some sort of protection, even if it's submerged. And there could be other things not subject to decay."

"Oh? Such as?"

"The local people, the Anishinaabe, were good at identifying deposits of clay that could be used to make pots. These would be reasonably durable."

Mike looked at me doubtfully.

"The thing about many indigenous peoples is that they didn't leave a lot behind. In terms of living with the land, they were very sophisticated compared to wastrels like us. They had no written records, so everything about them has to be deduced from their own oral tradition and from physical objects that have survived. These things would have great anthropological value today, so a decent collection of artefacts, in good condition, might be worth a lot to a dedicated private collector. If the clowns we're facing have been contracted by such a collector to deliver something like that, a complete set, ... well..."

Mike was silent, but I knew he was holding things up to the light in his mind, turning them this way and that, looking for anything not right. I could tell that he wasn't convinced.

"Whatever it is, it has value to somebody", I said. "That much is pretty obvious. If our treasure hunters are working on contract, they'll earn nothing unless they deliver, and that means that if they don't find what they're looking for they'll most likely think that I've found it, and then they'll come after me."

Mike was nodding, indicating that he agreed at least with that part. He then turned to focus on me.

"Let them come. We'll sort out the sods."

At that point, I was very grateful indeed to have Mike in my corner because he's smart, fearless, and has one of the quickest minds of anybody I know. But bravado has always made me nervous. By focusing on "beating them to a pulp" as a response, one runs the risk of underestimating the situation by assuming a favourable outcome. This can lead to the unconscious conviction that the problem has been solved even before one begins to grapple with it. Dangerous.

I had put the potatoes on to boil just before Andrea came in, flushed from another day of personal success, but not looking quite so tired as she had late afternoon yesterday.

"Just going to have a quick shower and change", she said in passing, but slowing down enough to take a look at my colourful souvlaki skewers. "Back in fifteen minutes."

"Your wine and a chunk of garlic bread will be waiting."

Andrea's riposte "I could get used to living like this", came to me just as she kicked off her boots and began climbing the stairs.

"Anything I can do?" Mike asked, as I began preparing the remaining ingredients for our Greek salad.

"Help yourself to more beer, if you want. There's a bottle of sauvignon blanc in the fridge that you could open. Get a tray from the cupboard up there, second from the right end, three glasses from the cabinet in the next room, and take it all outside. And get on the horn to your contacts and have the swine who's behind all our aggro delivered trussed at the front door in fifteen minutes. Think you can manage all that?"

Mike mumbled something about "smartass" but set about his tasks.

Andrea reappeared and we all trooped outside. The barbecue was fired up and the garlic bread was heating, lemon and parsley wafted powerfully from the potatoes, and the *composé* elements of the salad – romaine, tomatoes, cucumber, yellow pepper, chopped onion, olives, plenty of rich dark olive oil, a generous pinch of dried oregano, and crumbled feta cheese – looked like they simply could not wait to be combined.

Dinner was an utterly relaxed affair. Our surroundings looked on in approval. Filaments of conversation and discussion floated out over the lake at irregular intervals.

Then Mike offered to clear the table. Andrea rose to help, but he waved her down again, piled everything onto a tray, and trundled off to the kitchen. Time for my heart-to-heart.

I explained to Andrea the situation as we understood it, but leaving out everything related to my encounter with the diver two days earlier. She began asking questions, and I went through how we considered this was all linked to Harold's death. The matter of the strange "treasure" came up, and I walked Andrea through the details of what I had dug up during the day, connected it back to my visit to Clarence and Donaldson, and then related to her the flash of insight I had had in the car driving back this afternoon from my shopping expedition to Coboconk.

As it all sank in, Andrea became sombre, then shocked, and when she began to grasp the implications and the naked criminality of the whole thing, her anger flared, at whom exactly I wasn't sure. But it's a natural enough reaction when this kind of black slime oozes its way into one's life. It was clear that she had grasped the realization that this was something having the potential to engulf both of us.

"How did Harold find out about all this?" Andrea demanded.

"I don't know. That's one of the things I want to determine."

"And these other people, whoever they are…?"

"I don't know that either."

"So how do we…? Are we just going to sit around and…?"

"Andrea, I don't like this any more than you do. I asked Mike to come here and help specifically because I have no intention of just sitting around."

"But, but … the police!"

"The police have already closed the investigation into Harold's death because they have no evidence and no expectation they will turn up any evidence. And since Harold's death is viewed as an isolated accident case in the eyes of the police, then that's it. There was no crime here."

"So far, but…"

"Yes. So far. What I've just told you is my best speculation at what's going on behind the scenes, and the police won't turn up to look into anything unless there's more than just speculation at play."

"Speculation? What use is speculation then?"

I took Andrea's hands in mine, looked at her for a few moments, hoping to avoid any further rise in temperature.

"Whoever killed Harold did it for a reason. It isn't just that they might have wanted him out of the way, because death by outboard motor would be a truly bizarre assassination method. But at the same time everything I've seen tells me that it wasn't just an accident. The information that Harold passed along to George through his attorney, and the fact that Harold's body was found where it was, just at the coordinates of one of the four points in Harold's information, is not a coincidence. So, my first assumption is that there's something near where Harold's body was found that somebody else wants. My digging today through the paperwork from Clarence and Donaldson gave me one theory."

I related this theory to her and the reasons why I thought it was credible. She sat ruminating.

"Try as I might", I continued, "I've not been able to come up with any other theory that's anywhere near as convincing. If I can determine what these people are looking for and why, then Mike and I have a much better chance of protecting us all."

"Yes", Andrea said slowly in a resigned tone, but one that failed to cover the underlying anger and feeling of offence. "I can see, I think, that you're doing all you have to do. But this really worries me. Are you sure there's no other way?"

We talked more. There were questions. It was painfully clear that I didn't have all, or even most of, the answers. There were some long silences.

Andrea is not in the least fatalistic or given to throwing in the towel early. She fixed me in a long look. Her hesitation and deep concern were clear. But the determination that I knew of old was back in her eyes once more.

"What's our next move?"

"Well", I began, "the more we know, the better off we are, so one activity is to dig like hell to find out more details of just who's behind all this. If we have enough background information, it could be possible to go public with it and make it next to impossible for these clowns to continue operating under cover of a general lack of information. And if we can find the right kinds of information, then we can look for ways to drag the police back into things."

There was another long silence.

"I'm sorry about all this. I didn't want, or expect, any of this to happen, and now I just want to find a way to make it all go away."

She nodded.

"What can I do?" she asked at length.

I nodded in turn.

"I'll be working on this again tonight. Can you work with me?"

"Yes. Absolutely."

I squeezed Andrea's hand, smiled at her, and she smiled back weakly.

Rising suddenly, I shouted "Mike! More wine."

There was an ursine rumble from somewhere within the house, then Mike tripped down the stairs carrying our partly consumed bottle of sauvignon blanc and a replacement bottle.

I looked at Andrea.

"Which lamp do you suppose this genie came out of?" I asked, inclining my head toward Mike.

Mike rumbled again, almost suppressed a belch, and plunked himself down at the table.

"Drink up chill'un. Even though we have a problem to solve, it's summertime, and the livin' should be easy."

There were a couple of snorts from Andrea and me, and then we set to work on replenished glasses and watched Balsam Lake preparing to put itself to bed.

Twenty-four

Andrea and I sat together in our family room, and I walked her through my notes, referring to the Clarence and Donaldson files as I came to an important item. Although I knew the material intimately, Andrea didn't. So I stepped through it all systematically in order to lay out for her a detailed picture of what I thought was going on and why I thought it. But I knew before an hour was up that Andrea was struggling. The effects of a long day of sustained physical activity, a good meal, a couple of glasses of wine, and the effort of having to put up with Mike's and my company made the extra mental concentration she was trying to call forth now just a bit too much. Andrea struggled against her weariness, but when her eyelids fluttered a second time, I called off the exercise.

"You're beat, Andrea. You need to go to bed."

She wanted to argue. I know she was annoyed at not being able to muster the energy needed. She wanted to stay, I'm sure. I did need her help, and it really was energizing having her working next to me, but it wasn't going to happen and she knew it.

"I'm sorry", she said. "You're right. I just can't do this", and she rose to leave.

"Don't stay up too late", she said, then headed off wearily to bed.

I sat there thinking about things for five minutes. I was feeling guilty, impatient, and frustrated, but I forced myself to go back to my notes.

What more could I find out in all this?' I asked myself. When it came right down to it, my rather vague speculations about a collection of aboriginal artefacts had unconvincing aspects, and the more I thought about it the less convincing it became. It felt like I was missing something.

How else could I approach this? The question practically posed itself to me.

Well, Whelan, my alter ego replied to me caustically, *you could start thinking more incisively about all this nebulous treasure nonsense. What was McCleod really up to? Maybe he wasn't the kind of artsy-fartsy flake you seem happy to assume he was. You could work on that for a start. Is it just possible that real money is behind it all? He couldn't just transfer his money or his valuables around electronically like you can today. So how did he get his returns converted to something that was bankable, and how did he get all those somethings back to Toronto and to the bank?*

I thought about this for a while. McCleod had ships, and he shipped things in them.

Bravo, Whelan! my evil alter ego muttered in the background. *Not even Einstein would have been able to work that out!*

There was a sort of internal standoff at that point, an exchange of rough expletives at fifty paces between me and my alter ego. I won.

So, ships were no real problem. McCleod or his agents would be paid in Toronto or at various points along the north shore of Lake Ontario as goods were either loaded onto or off the ships. Then there would be – what? Transfers of money or gold back to Toronto in the ships' safes or strong boxes? But what about things that were then to be carried further by rail? The same thing? Payment at the ports or payment at the end stations? Then how would the money come back? In strong boxes on railway carriages?

But McCleod also had boats where there were no railways, where the only means back and forth were his own boats. Presumably he would set up arrangements similar to those for his rail shipments.

And in all these cases, we wouldn't be talking about fortunes that had to be shipped back to Toronto. There would be dozens, probably hundreds, of small payments that had to be organized. So what if he lost one or two of these small consignments? We'd be talking about just a few thousand dollars in today's money, hardly incentive enough to have driven everything we had seen. It seemed as though all this was a non-problem. The only fortune, the real treasure, would be what had accumulated in McCleod's banks in Toronto.

I dropped my pencil and gazed off into space for a moment. Snippets of text that I had come across in the files fluttered through my mind. I recalled more than one occasion where there was a note about money being shipped with care and under guard on a boat or ship. So presumably sometimes there were larger amounts of cash or gold that needed extra attention. Other lines and notes also came to mind. I recalled the item saying that McCleod had a serious setback – no, what had he called it, a disaster – during one of these shipments. Nothing new emerged. Could the disaster have been the loss of one of his collections of artefacts? He might well have considered something like that to be a disaster.

Not being willing to admit that I was looking for something that wasn't there, I had no option but to go back over the whole thing again from the top.

Time check. Almost ten thirty. I would be here until well after midnight. But there was no other way, so I turned to a clean page on my note pad and prepared to root through it all again. Once more, with feeling.

My cellphone vibrated. The display was just a number, a local number, but I had no idea whose.

"Hello?"

"Hello, Mark. This is John Woodhouse."

There was a long delay here.

"Hello? Are you there, Mark?"

"Yes. Are you the John Woodhouse I went to primary school with? And were you sitting in The Repose four nights ago?"

"Yes and yes."

"But … why? How?"

"We should get together, Mark."

"When? Now?"

"I'm in The Repose at the moment. Maurice will likely stay open for at least another hour. Come on down."

And then the line went dead. Just like that.

I was mystified and annoyed but intrigued. Of course I would go and meet him.

I let Mike know where I would be, picked up my keys, went out to the car, and headed off to Rosedale.

There was no traffic. I didn't meet even one car during the short five-minute drive, but when I arrived at The Repose I was slightly surprised to see at least ten cars parked among the oaks in front of Maurice's place.

I locked the car and went in. Maurice smiled from behind the bar, gave his signature friendly wave, then pointed toward the *Salon Fénelon*. I could see John, the same figure I had spotted when Andrea, Kate, and I were there, seated now on his own near the windows. He gave a wave of greeting and began to rise when I was about six feet from his table.

We shook hands warmly, and looking at him closely I could see the face of the boy who had helped me overcome my problem with the dreaded Mick Ahearn all those years ago.

"Have a seat", John said, and just before sitting down himself, he waved to Maurice and pointed at his own glass of beer then at me.

"How did you find me? And what made you want to get in touch after all this time?"

"Not difficult, Mark. When I saw you here the other night, I made a promise to myself to get in touch. On my way here to The Repose, I suddenly thought on a whim that it was as good a time as any to contact you. So here I am. How are you?"

I brought him up to date on the past twenty years. We talked in a roundabout way about Rosedale, Largs, and Coboconk, and then John filled me in on his story.

He had studied at the University of Toronto, first modern languages, then law. He had passed his exams, met all the requirements for practising law in Ontario, and hung out a shingle in Toronto. He did well. But then someone local to Rosedale had heard that he was a practising lawyer and got in touch. There was a problem this individual wanted help on, and more out of curiosity than anything John agreed to take on the case.

"It wasn't much of a case. Some personal gripe. I contacted the other guy's lawyer and we worked out an agreement. It took a while, but we convinced those two grumpy old sods that they weren't going to get anything better. They signed."

Here John stopped. Fifteen seconds passed but he still just sat there.

"And how does all that connect to you and me being here now?" I asked.

John shrugged. "The other guy was a First Nations chap from Curve Lake. We talked. He told me there was history. Referred to a 'document'. I dug out the background. Started reading it. Found out things."

By then I realized that John was a man of few words. I waited for him to go on. Then I made some "and then?" hand motions.

"Just whispers, at first. Found some odd gaps in a few of the records. Came across a name."

John stopped again. He seemed to be collecting his thoughts, so I didn't prod him.

"All just handwritten notes. Then a pattern. Irregularities. It had to do with a young girl. I dug further. Two days more serious research. Found the same patterns but different cases. One of them was the last thing I expected."

John took a sip of his beer, set the glass down, looked at his hands, then fixed me in a steady gaze.

"I'm Anishinaabe. Taken from my parents when I was one year old. Raised by Alf and Margery Woodhouse. I don't know why or how this happened. You can guess the rest."

"Well…, no, I can't, John. Is that all you know?"

"There aren't many facts, Mark. There's a lot of rumour and insinuation."

I was beginning to guess that this was hard for John. In his own time, I thought.

"The story is that my natural parents were both "drunk Indians". There's no evidence for that, of course. My adoptive parents were good people. I can't complain about my upbringing. Alf and Margery truly did love me and I have nothing but fond memories of them. But this information, well … it taints everything. Alf and Margery are both dead now. They left no records about me, so … no easy way to clear this up."

John had been looking off into the distance, but then he focused on me.

"But then I said to myself, 'You're a lawyer, for God's sake'. I started digging. Systematically. Appalling record keeping, almost non-existent. Connected the few dots I did have. Dredged up what I could. There was a birth certificate, for a boy. Born to Joseph and Amanda Longfeather. The date was my birthday. Joseph and Amanda are both dead now, far as I can tell. Found one more tatty record. Joseph and Amanda's baby taken into protective care on May 18, 1980. Just a few weeks before I was adopted by Alf and Margery. The baby had a birthmark, just here, on the left side of his neck", and as John spoke he pulled down his shirt collar to show me a birthmark at that location.

There was a longish silence here.

"I don't know what to say", I offered feebly.

"Well, try on my shoes."

"Are you still looking?"

John nodded.

"I arranged for my practice to be looked after while I took three months off work. To research who I am."

"Wow! I still don't know what to say." But this time I didn't know what to say because I still didn't know how to ask him why this had anything to do with me.

"I'm glad you took the trouble to look me up", I said, if only as a means of trying to limp toward the light and some kind of understanding on just what was going on here.

"Not getting ready to leave, are you, Mark? Because this will be a two-pint evening at least", and here he waved again at Maurice, giving the universal signal for another round.

To break another lengthening silence, I asked John where he was looking.

"Pretty much anywhere I can think of, Mark. It's a blank space, but it's well contained. I'm still who I am. Still a lawyer. Still somebody who grew up here. Don't know where I came from, that's all."

John shook his head. "Very strange words: *don't know where I came from, that's all.*"

John drained his glass. "The really odd thing about it is that once I began to get used to the shock, come to terms with it, I started to be curious. Got a lot more interested in the research. I have a fairly good idea of what I'll find in general. It's a story that's been told before."

Maurice brought two more pints. By this time John had my full attention. I was beginning to have an inkling of what impact this was having on him and had become engrossed in his account to an extent that surprised me.

I think John recognized that I was beginning to connect with what he had told me. We raised our new pints, clinked them together, held eye contact for a few seconds, and just before taking a sip I sensed that an old boyhood friendship had reignited.

"I'm not sure what I could do to help in this, John. But if there is anything, just say the word."

John nodded in acknowledgement.

"There is a word. Two words, actually. 'Sounding board'. I'd like to be able to walk you through what I know at some stage", he said. "Another view would help."

John stopped here and looked at me for a moment.

"I wasn't sure how you might take this", he said. "Thought maybe you might just say 'very interesting, John', then walk away."

I made to object, but John held up his hand. I recognized his slow smile.

"Just wanted to check that I could still get your goat."

There was another pause here. I then made some blunt comments on my own outrage at realizing, finally, what had happened to First Nations peoples and the scarcely believable stances taken by successive governments. "It just beggars belief", I concluded lamely.

John nodded, and I could almost sense his relief. His manner then changed subtly, and he took a longer draw on his pint. He wiped his mouth on the back of his hand, set his glass down with exaggerated care, then directed at me a piercing gaze.

"At this point", he said, in a careful and deliberate way, "I think I'm likely to be more help to you than the other way round."

"Oh?"

"Yes. There are other people out there digging as well. Digging into old First Nations records and into a lot of historical stuff from the nineteenth century."

I was beginning to have an uneasy feeling.

"And some of the questions they've been asking have been about you."

Twenty-five

My deer-caught-in-the-headlights look probably lasted only a second or two.

"About me?"

John nodded.

"Why? I don't … I can understand people looking for gossip. My connection to Largs has always been a favourite topic, but I've got used to that. But you seem … you're saying that you've come across some sort of reference … some current reference to me in some pretty serious research that you've been doing? Can you give me details?"

John explained it all in what struck me as the clear, logical thinking of a lawyer. Over a period of just a few weeks, he had come across a few pieces of paper that had revealed an unknown past. His father was a member of the Curve Lake First Nation; the status of his mother was not known. John's father had been in and out of trouble with the law most of his life, but the experience of recent decades left ample room for doubt about police bias that might have been involved in these judgments. In John's mind, the situation surrounding his parents might well have been somewhat chaotic, but his reading over the past months had left him in no doubt about the damage caused to the native culture and to individual lives, left crippled and rudderless by a century and a half of deliberate and systematic suppression. The effects would have been profoundly negative. And it was clear that John was seeing this now in a directly personal way.

A mere four pieces of paper were the only result of the weeks of John's searching. There was a birth certificate bearing the name John Longfeather, a statement documenting that John Longfeather had been taken into protective care by county authorities when he was thirteen months old, adoption papers granting the care of John Longfeather to Alfred and Margery Woodhouse dated one month after the protective care order, and a legal change of name from John Longfeather to John Woodhouse.

In the process of locating this material, John had found many documents relating to the Curve Lake First Nation, to the Anishinaabe and Ojibway in general, and to the interactions of these peoples with the French, later with the English, and much later with the Canadians. Things were blurry here, and it was something of a mug's game to be too specific in assigning "responsibility" for what had happened. But over a period of more than a century, actions had been taken, some of them quite sanctimoniously, that resulted in suppression of indigenous peoples, if not a slow long-term genocide. John had read about the Iroquois wars, the French missions in Huronia, and especially the Sulpician mission established by Francois Fénelon at the Bay of Quinte. From that base, missionaries, including Fénelon himself, travelled along what is now the Trent waterway and the Kawartha Lakes trying to bring Christianity to the Iroquois and others. John noted that he became very interested in this "French connection", especially the link between Fénelon the missionary and Chateau Fénelon in Périgord, and to Fénelon's much better-known younger brother of the same name, who remained in France and gained renown as a theologian, poet, and writer.

"The younger Fénelon wrote *Les Aventures de Telemaque*, or *The Adventures of Telemachus*", and while this somewhat off-the-wall statement by John sailed right over my head, I was greatly impressed by his French pronunciation, until I remembered the modern languages course he pursued as an undergraduate.

John caught me smiling at him.

"I know", he said, slightly defensively. "Self-indulgent. But I was always interested in history", something I hadn't known or hadn't remembered. Then a connection occurred to me.

"Is this particular angle of history a recent interest?"

"You should have been a lawyer", he said drily. "No. But many of the links going back to First Nations have suddenly become of interest. You know about the mound near Balsam Lake along the shore of South Bay? There's clear evidence that it had been there probably centuries before the French came to North America. Got me thinking about what those French found, what they thought, back then. Began looking for information on local natives. Found out things. Lots of things. Those people, the First Nations, they'd been here a long, long time. Thousands of years. I found I was left with a very odd feeling, learning that they considered this area, the Kawartha Lakes, to be special."

It was a struggle not to let my impatience show. But it seemed that I might have to wait some time to hear about how my name popped up in John's researches.

"You're probably wondering when I'll get to you", John said, as if reading my mind.

John related how his reading gradually led him to that time when New France was handed over to England after France's defeat at the Plains of Abraham.

"You have to dig for it", he said, "but things happened as the French learned that the place was under new management. The English were coming in. There were clashes. Some of the French decided to leave. Some dropped everything, made a dash for Montreal. There were patrols of redcoats coming in. Many of the French who met English regulars were stripped of anything valuable. After all, they were the losers and ancestral enemies to boot. There were long-time missionaries in Huronia. Been there ages. All along the shore of Georgian Bay. There was a story that they had built up some wealth. Hard to believe, in my view. There's a story that lives on. The story is that some of these guys took their wealth with them, golden church artefacts, so the tale goes. No idea where they might have got the gold."

John continued his account. Some of the missionaries made it safely to Montreal. But one group narrowly escaped detection by redcoats, and they decided to bury their gold and attempt to come back for it later. And the story is that they buried it here, on Ghost Island, in Balsam Lake.

"Lots of people have looked for this gold. Nobody has ever found any. The whole story is likely preposterous, an impossible fabrication. But the rumours are still around after more than two and a half centuries."

John shook his head, a wry expression on his face.

"Believe it or not, I went looking for details of this. Found that I had to start making phone calls. I spoke to people who just repeated the Ghost Island myth, but when I asked them specific questions it was clear that they knew nothing. A couple of people seemed well-informed. One of them, a man named Jacobs, indicated how surprised he had been when he had to field two similar and apparently serious inquiries in the same week. I asked Jacobs about this. He went into details on the other inquiry. Said the guy had asked him about Ghost Island. But also about Largs and men called McCleod and Whelan. I then asked Jacobs who had been making the inquiries. Might help me if I contacted this fellow, I said. Jacobs said he had already probed that angle, out of his own interest. The guy just waved the question off, said that he was inquiring on behalf of a client. Couldn't tell Jacobs who or why. The inquirer then asked if any written information was available. Jacobs told him that over the years several local historical societies had collected the speculations and the few crumbs of fact that were available. It had all been consolidated into a book. Happened that Jacobs was offering this book for sale as a private publication. The inquirer said he would take a copy." John paused here.

"That's when the inquirer did something odd: he paid for the book by credit card."

John drained his beer glass, looked at me inquiringly, but I indicated that two was enough.

"It took some coaxing. But I got Jacobs to give me the man's credit card number", and at that point John passed a slip of paper to me.

"Do you mind if I make a call?" I asked.

John waved me his permission, so I called Mike and passed on a short version of what I had just heard, along with the credit card number.

Laying my cellphone on the table, I smiled across at John.

"Don't ask", I said.

John shook his head. "No intention."

Maurice came by with our beer and a big smile, and we both took long swigs. I looked at John in what must have seemed to him a speculative manner.

"I hope we can have more conversations, John. I would very much like to do a lot of catching up. I hope you would like to do so as well."

"I would. Very much."

"I'd also like to talk to you about this, what should I call it, change in identity."

"Gladly", John said.

The fact was that I had become aware of another connection we now had, something different, a link that went "back to the land" in a way, back to something primeval.

John smiled, and it seemed that he knew what I was thinking.

He looked at me levelly and said, "Let's travel this road together."

Twenty-six

It was almost midnight when I got home again to Largs. I was buoyed up by the discussion I had had with John, who was beginning to feel like a new old friend. But I was also encouraged by the possibility that the credit card number he had given me would provide a way into whatever operation it was that I had run afoul of over the past days.

Mike was sitting at the kitchen table when I came in.

"Sit!" he ordered, and when I did that without question or comment, Mike explained to me briefly that he had called a colleague and told him to get onto this business pronto, and that there would be a fat bonus if he really hit the deck running and got results.

Mike had just received those results.

"The credit card was in the name of a company, but that didn't stop my guy. We have a name and an address now."

I knew better than to ask how.

"I've sent another guy around to have a chat with Mr. Credit Card."

"Another guy?" I asked, a little perplexed.

"Some people are good at digging and some people are good at persuading. They aren't necessarily the same people."

"What happens now?" I asked.

"We wait."

"How long do you think it will take?"

Mike made to answer, but just then his cellphone vibrated. It was a text message.

"Okay. My guy is at our chap's place, a rather grubby spot near Dufferin and St. Clair."

"What will he do now?"

"I leave that up to the guy on the scene."

Mike put down his phone. He had the air of someone who was content to wait, since he didn't expect to have to wait long.

"Just out of curiosity", Mike said, "give me a bit of background on how John got this information."

I filled him in quickly, but we both glanced at his cellphone every few seconds.

"Hard to believe that the guy would use a credit card. I'm sensing a gene pool that's short on water", Mike commented drily.

"Or overconfidence, feeling that nobody would ever find out about their little game", I added.

"Or both", Mike concluded.

We both looked at the cellphone again.

"It sounds", Mike mused, "as though the competition is some way behind, that they're still thrashing around trying to get a better fix on where they should be looking."

"Maybe", I said. "But in fact they might be ahead of us in this. Somewhere they've got hold of what they consider credible information that whatever it is that's worth having really does exist. They also seem to think that they know approximately where it is. 'Some way behind' doesn't seem to me to fit that description very well."

"And?"

"What do you mean 'and'?" I said. "That means that probably nothing I say or do would convince them that there's nothing to be had. So, if they don't find it themselves, there's every chance they would suspect that I might know more, and come after me to tell them. What we seem to be looking at is something between a serious nuisance and a dangerous threat."

"What makes you think there's nothing to be had?" Mike asked.

"When you're grubbing around the bottom of a lake for something that you think is valuable, you're basically treasure hunting. All but the most serious of these ventures are just based on delusions. Given the number of divers, snorkellers, and people who just like to look for stuff, and given the numbers of those people who have spent time on Balsam Lake over I don't know how many decades, I think that anything bigger than a change purse would have been found already."

"I'm sure you realize that I really don't buy this business of a collection of artefacts. In fact, I'm very vague on just what this 'valuable something' might be", Mike said, leaning back in his chair.

"That makes two of us, Mike. But let's take the one bit of factual information we have: somebody thinks there is something valuable there for some reason. Maybe it's an assembly of old artefacts, as I've speculated. But maybe it's something else. Maybe it's something closer to the strike-it-rich idea at the core of the old romantic notion of treasure. When I look at it from that point of view, the first thing I come across is the lost treasure of Ghost Island. It almost certainly doesn't exist. Then there are wrecks of old steamboats and what might have gone down with them. Finding these wrecks is the first step. One was found near Peterborough a couple of years back when they drained part of the canal system there to do some repairs. There it was, one morning, the skeleton of an old boat poking out of the water. Some people seem to think that every steamboat on the lakes around here was full of Mississippi gamblers, high rollers carrying wads of cash and bags of gold, and that any steamboat wreck is likely hiding its own fortune. Worse than delusional. Sheer invention. Then there's the question of those boats' cargoes. People seem to think – "

Mike was paying attention through only one ear. But when I stopped speaking, he looked over at me in some amusement and found me staring off into space.

"People seem to think … what, Mark?"

Mike sat up.

"Hey! Mark! People seem to think what?"

"Sorry, Mike, but I've just come up with something that can't wait."

I rose quickly.

"I've got to work it out."

Mike made to say something.

"No, Mike. No talking. I mean I have to work it out right now."

And I walked out of the room into the den, leaving Mike to wonder and wait.

After an hour and a half, I had three variants that made sense. I went over the eighty pages or so of notes that I had accumulated from my reading over the past two days and found something that narrowed the three variants to two. I wrote out narratives for both of them, then sat looking at the page of text for each. They were a little rough, and there were some small gaps, but I could find no fatal errors, no fundamental idiocies. I went over them both several times more. The pages seemed almost to blend into one another, but the story was clear enough that I could actually picture a typical McCleod steamboat. It was sitting at the Largs landing stage taking on passengers. Wood smoke was rising in a vertical column from its single stack. The captain gave a toot on the whistle. There was a damp musty smell of steam in the air. Men were shouting and cursing at a load of cargo. I could now smell the woodsmoke. It was resiny, resiny and … and…

"Mark!"

Someone shouting, shouting at me … from the dock?

"Mark!"

I was suddenly being jostled in a crowd.

"Mark! Wake up!"

I raised my head. Mike still had his hand on my shoulder where he had been shaking me. A sheet of paper was stuck to my right cheek.

"We've got some information now!" Mike said. "The guy in charge is someone called Carl Dickson."

"Who is he?" I asked.

"Don't have the foggiest."

"Probably not his real name anyhow."

I was fully awake now, and Mike explained to me the few other shreds his man had passed on to him.

"What's your guy going to do now? He can't just walk away and leave Dickson's stooge on his own. The stooge will warn Dickson and then our surprise will be lost."

"What surprise?" Mike growled. "We might know Dickson's name, but we have no idea just where he is, even though I suspect he's somewhere very near. Besides, when he tries to contact his stooge again, which he's bound to do, he'll become suspicious right away when the stooge doesn't answer."

"Why wouldn't the stooge answer?"

"Because my guy convinced him to take a few sleeping pills. Don't worry, they won't kill him. But he won't wake up for about eighteen hours."

So we had a few hours in hand. We smiled at each other. It was just before three o'clock in the morning and we decided that there was time for two hours' sleep.

Twenty-seven

At ten past six, I awoke gritty-eyed and grumpy. Sometimes just a little sleep is worse than none at all. The face that looked back at me from the mirror was ghastly. I tried to cheer myself up by feeling sorry for it. It had eye bags that hadn't been there the day before. Its skin was a grey-green-yellow blend, a colour that I imagined, if the world had any fairness to it, would be reserved exclusively for a slurry of mustard, tapenade, and elephant dung. Even though I felt sorry for it, I looked at it impassively. "Tough break, Dorian", I muttered to it cruelly. "You're the image. I'm the reality", and I walked out, leaving it to despair alone.

The image's electroshocked mop had caused me to run my hands through my own hair, and I could only hope that its gritty eyes were worse than mine. Mike, in contrast, when I met him in the kitchen, looked brushed and combed, as cheery and happy as a six-year-old after fifteen hours' sleep. Sometimes I hate Mike. Sometimes I hate the world.

"So!" Mike said, rubbing his hands together in enthusiasm. "Some elixir of life, and then we plan the day. Lots to do."

I grumbled miserably that I didn't want any coffee.

"Who said anything about coffee", Mike exclaimed in surprise, while brandishing a flask of Talisker. Without delay or awaiting a reply from me, he immediately poured us each a two-ounce measure.

I downed my Talisker in two glugs and almost right away it began giving the Sandman a good duffing up. Mike and I reached our views on the day's chores at almost the same time, and we both looked up and opened our mouths to speak.

"Go ahead", I said.

"I want to go into Coboconk and float some inquiries about our Carl Dickson. I'm going to call the three dive shops and drop his name there as well. And while I'm at that, I'm going to call my man in Toronto and ask him to do more rooting around on Dickson. We need to know more, as much as we can find."

"And I'm going to stay here", I said. "I'll keep a close eye on Andrea and go through my notes once more."

"You think you've missed something?"

"Don't know. But a lot of new information has come into play in the past twenty-four hours, and new information can sometimes make you see something in old information that you missed on the previous round."

Mike nodded. "Let's keep in contact. You call me every half-hour, or whenever something important comes up. If I'm on a call, leave a message." And without waiting for me to reply, Mike went out the back door to his car.

It was now quarter to seven and Andrea would be stirring soon. I went into the den, picked up a notepad, pen, and my notes, which now were distributed across four folders, and the laptop, and brought it all out to the breakfast table.

Over the past two days, my listing of significant data items and happenings had expanded and their time sequence had needed multiple reorderings. Looking at the notes I had jotted down based on my discussion with John last night, I went through the current time sequence again. There were also notes on background material and these were even more extensive than the listing of time sequence events. I was in the middle of this when someone bit my earlobe. I hadn't heard Andrea enter the room because of the noise of a motorboat going past outside.

"Oh! Hello there, *ma petite!*"

"Hello, handsome! Where's Mike?"

"Off to Coboconk to troll some gutters again. You going to be able to finish at Number 3 today?"

"Easily", Andrea said. "Then, I think, there's only one more to assess and make a list of things to be done."

She had gone over to the fridge and picked a yogurt, then brought it back to the table and began spooning it into her mouth in that deliberate way that I enjoyed watching surreptitiously.

"What are you doing today?"

"I'm slogging away at my notes and files, and I need to think about what I learned from John last night."

"John?" she asked, and I realized that she was unaware I had met John last night, that she knew nothing about the personal history he had related to me in The Repose, and that almost certainly she wouldn't relate any current individual 'John' to the schoolboy friend I had mentioned to her several times in passing. So I explained it all to her at length now. After five minutes, during which time Andrea seemed to have been frozen in attention, spoon partway to her mouth, she began asking questions.

"You're not making this up, are you?"

"Not at all. But it really does sound like a first-rate yarn, doesn't it."

"It's absolutely stunning. When can I meet him?"

"Whenever you'd like. I'll find out when he has time free."

Andrea's spoon of yogurt finished its journey at long last, but it was clear that she was pondering what she had just heard.

"How does John feel about it all?"

"Hard to imagine", I said. "But I doubt that he's really got his own head around it yet."

"Indeed!"

Andrea finished her yogurt and went off to find her work boots. In ten minutes she had everything she needed for the day, and waved as she left for Number 3 Ash Grove. I gave it a few minutes, then took my notes and papers back to the den, grabbed my laptop, and headed off toward Number 2 Ash Grove. I had no intention of letting Andrea out of my sight.

The morning seemed to pass very slowly. At about eleven o'clock, I heard Andrea leave Number 3, and watched as she crossed the street at an angle and let herself in to Number 6 Ash Grove, the last of the unusables. From Number 2, I had a good view of Number 6 as well, and the day carried on.

As we had arranged, I had called Mike every half-hour. He sounded increasingly hot and frustrated as the day wore on, and I suspected that his inquiries were leading nowhere useful. At four o'clock I called him again and asked if he could wrap it up and come back to Largs and meet me at Number 2 Ash Grove, since I had to go off and buy what we needed for dinner.

"What feast are you planning for tonight?" he asked.

"I thought we'd have coronation chicken."

"What? Never heard of it."

"Well, you don't need to have it, if you'd prefer Kraft Dinner instead."

His reply used the word "smartass" with emphasis.

"Don't worry, Mike. It's a quite simple dish, and it really is delicious. You'll like it. In fact, I'm prepared to wager that you'll love it."

I told him that I was in Number 2, and twenty minutes later he tapped on the door. I told him where Andrea was, said how long I'd be gone, and left. Wally Harris' food counter was unlikely to include a good mango, so a brief shopping expedition to Coboconk netted me the ingredients I wanted. Half an hour later, it was me who tapped on the door of Number 2. I told Mike I was going to the house to start putting the grub together, and that I'd call both him and Andrea when their attendance was required. It took little time to get the dish prepared, and I stuck it in the fridge to cool for twenty minutes. As I waited, I leafed through what I had accomplished during the day, and had to conclude that it was essentially nothing.

Putting my notes away, I called Andrea and Mike. Andrea arrived first and Mike about five minutes later. They went off to clean up and came back to large glasses of an excellent dry riesling. At the first taste of the coronation chicken, Mike looked up in astonishment.

"Good God, Mark! This stuff is too good to be real!"

Mike went back for "a bit more" several times, we talked in relaxed disconnection about the unusables, about John, about books, about the weather, forgetting, for the time being, a situation worthy of the most serious unease. We chatted and laughed, and three smiling faces glided down the slope of an evening, gently lubricated by glasses of a very good Pear Williams, into a happy space that could not have been beaten by The Teddy Bears' Picnic.

Twenty-eight

It was Wednesday morning. I had slept more deeply during the night than any time within the past week, and felt good for it, physically. Mentally, well, that was another story. Today Mike would be picking up George from the bus station in Lindsay at about noon, Andrea would be trying to finish off at Number 6, and apart from being eager to throw myself at the paperwork, I had no real idea what I would be trying to do. It was that unsettled and directionless feeling that bothered me. A vague but oddly nagging sense of the calm before the storm seemed to hover somewhere, and try as I might I couldn't see why that feeling persisted or where it was coming from.

The three of us had a leisurely breakfast, Mike disappeared to do his inevitable "paperwork", Andrea headed off to Number 6 at about eight thirty, and a few minutes later I walked to Number 2 with my files, notebook, and laptop. It was another sunny day, refreshingly cool, and in no time I was installed at the table in Number 2. The walk seemed miraculously to drive away the cloud that was hanging over me, leaving just a fresh outlook, and my life force felt restored by a good night's sleep. Energy bubbled up from somewhere within, and I tackled my paperwork once again (once more with feeling), this time starting at Aldred's files. Bringing a tight and penetrating focus to the material, something that had been a difficult chore on previous occasions, now became natural and relatively effortless. The documented landscape was familiar, and looking back and forth from Aldred's notes to my own point-form summary showed that there was no irregularity, no deviation between them. This in itself was satisfying.

Aldred's file, and my own notes, recorded what was really a compressed story of old McCleod's business career. In connection with significant changes in McCleod's approach on how he directed his business, Aldred had noted several times that the old man was exceedingly secretive, that he went sometimes to extraordinary measures to make sure that his decisions, and his reasons behind them, remained opaque to the outside world. Aldred recorded significant instances of such business ventures: the three expansions of McCleod's fleet of lake ships, his measures to redirect his business focus in adjusting to the new reality of an expanding railway network, his success in convincing Gooderham that he could provide a reliable means for shipping grain to Gooderham's distillery in Toronto, his expansion into land ownership in Hastings County, and his decision to wind down that investment over what was really a short period, just a few months. It seemed evident that Aldred had done a great deal of digging to be able to paint such a detailed picture. He was able to do this specifically because he had access to all the files by virtue of his work at Clarence and Donaldson, one aspect of which was looking after The McCleod Foundation. He had been completely dedicated to McCleod, and he carried on working on the McCleod Foundation files out of personal interest and on his own time during the middle decades of the twentieth century.

Aldred also had documented how McCleod wound down his business interests in the years before his death. McCleod had divided his operations into packages which he sold off separately. The lake ships were sold as a separate going concern. His warehousing operations in Toronto were handled similarly. His contracting business for managing the collection, storage, and delivery of goods by rail to inland centres north of Lake Ontario was also sold off as a unit. I had recorded all this, but was now able to add details that I had missed on earlier passes through Aldred's notes.

McCleod's two steamboats on Balsam Lake and Cameron Lake, the *Jackson* and the *Damsel May*, were sold as a pair and as a going-concern business. I stopped here for a moment, pondering. Somewhere else in his notes, Aldred had mentioned these two steamboats, and I began leafing back through the pages to locate that spot, mostly out of curiosity. It took only a few minutes to find Aldred's note that the two boats were the *Jackson* and the *Daniella*. Hmmm. Returning to Aldred's later note, I could see that he was definitely referring to the *Damsel May* and not the *Daniella*. I shrugged and moved on.

About five pages later, Aldred appeared to be making a point of documenting how McCleod had undertaken moving on from a life in business to the leisure of a retired man. He travelled less and less frequently to Largs as he grew older, and this seemed to be a situation he accepted very reluctantly. Apparently, during his prime business years McCleod had taken to going on cruises on Balsam Lake whenever he was there, especially in the *Daniella*, which appeared to be by far his favourite boat. And then there was a particular note made by Aldred: "McCleod was especially aggrieved at the loss of the *Daniella*, which developed a serious steam leak the day before she was scheduled to make an important trip, and then foundered on rocks and sank as the crew was taking her to Fenelon Falls for repairs. These events seemed to have particular and oddly unexplained weight for McCleod."

Odd indeed. I spent some time thinking about this. There was no way of knowing, at this remove, why McCleod might have recorded these things, or if indeed this was just Aldred's conclusion from what was evidently his own close and careful examination of the events of McCleod's life. If this had been Aldred's reading of things, there was still no way of knowing why the records of these events in the files had made such an impression on Aldred that he felt the need to document them here in his own notes. They were details that seemed strangely out of place in an otherwise broad-brush overview of my great-great-grandfather's extraordinary life. And once again I couldn't shake the feeling that Aldred's account had been written very specifically with me, or someone like me, in mind as the only reader.

Aldred's account had some information on the order in which McCleod had terminated his businesses, liquidated their value, and assigned almost all of the proceeds to The McCleod Foundation. He retained some capital separately and this supplied him a generous stream of what would now be called retirement income. Aldred also noted that McCleod had weeded his companies' files down to a manageable size and had them transferred to a storage space in a smallish building McCleod had owned and which was given over for use by The McCleod Foundation. At McCleod's direction, the Foundation took on a philanthropic role, and some of the Foundation's capital was distributed in this way. Then, in a three-line note that was easy to miss, since it was half on one page and half on the next, Aldred wrote: "In 1957, seventy years after McCleod's death, The McCleod Foundation donated Mr. McCleod's weeded files to the City of Toronto Archives, for their potential historical value."

How had I missed this until now?

In no time, I found the City of Toronto Archives website. The amount of information stored there is huge, as would be expected. After about a half-hour of digging, I managed to find references to the McCleod files and I gave a sigh of relief to find that they had all been digitized.

Searching the electronic files was not hard, and I soon found what I wanted. There was a lot of detail, more than I expected, and I skimmed it impatiently. I was stopped by three entries: "Valuable shipment carried by *Jackson* on August 15, 1860, to Fenelon Falls, eventually delivered safely to Toronto." "*Daniella* partially crippled by boiler-steam leak on August 14, 1860. Attempted trip to Fenelon Falls for repairs under ad hoc fix and reduced steam pressure." And then: "My dear old *Daniella* was lost, August 17, 1860, after striking a reef off Largs."

There it was.

But there was something not quite right here and I couldn't pinpoint it. I was pretty sure that I had noted the "something" somewhere, but the volume of my notes had mounted continuously, and finding that reference would likely take up to an hour. Despite all this, I had a feeling that I had made real progress during the morning.

There was a knock on the door. Opening it, I was met by Mike's smiling puss and the hunted face of George, who relaxed immediately on seeing me. I could just imagine how intimidating Mike must have seemed to him during the trip from Lindsay to Largs. Mike delivered George to my charge, saying that he was going off to the dive shop in Fenelon Falls, something he hadn't got round to earlier, and then he headed back to his car. I walked with George from Number 2 Ash Grove to our house, told him he would be in the same room as before, made sure he had everything he needed, then left and went back to Number 2. Andrea had taken some lunch with her to Number 6, but I imagined that she was hard at it making sure she could finish before the end of the day. I settled down once more to my notes. I had worked for about twenty minutes when my cellphone buzzed. Andrea, I thought right away, but then noticed that the display said Unknown Caller.

"Hello."

"Good afternoon, Mr. Whelan." A man's voice. One I didn't recognize.

"Your wife has decided to keep me company for a little while."

All the blood drained from my body and my veins were suddenly full of dry ice.

Andrea. They had Andrea.

"I know that you might be momentarily in shock, Mr. Whelan, so let me just say a few things. First, don't bother asking to speak to your wife. That's not going to happen. Second, please don't call the police. Your wife is very lovely and I'm sure you want her to stay that way. Third, some friends of mine will be visiting you very shortly. You are going to help them get what I want. I want to have it before the end of the day today. When I have it, you can have your wife back and we can all go our separate ways. I'm pleased that you haven't objected to any of this. I appreciate your cooperation very much. Goodbye for now."

And just like that, the line was dead.

Twenty-nine

I looked outside. The door to Number 6 Ash Grove stood open.

I was shaking. What had I done? Where … Andrea? I had lost … Oh, Andrea!

Leaned against the wall. Wracked by a huge sob. Gulped. Wrestled with image after horrific image.

This was all my fault.

But then the familiar inner voice came back to me.

Stop this bullshit and do something! You haven't much time! Andrea would not be impressed at all!

Despite my shaking hands, I managed to call Mike.

"Mark, how's – "

"Mike. They've got Andrea. Dickson's goons are on their way to get me. They're going to force me to help them find whatever they're looking for. I'll have to go with them. I need to try to find a way out of this. I'm not – okay, they're here, Mike. Three of them."

I cut Mike off, pocketed my cellphone, and waited.

They didn't knock, just walked straight in. They knew exactly where I would be, had been ahead of me the whole way. Seeing them there made everything ten times worse. Their presence showed me the physical reality of the situation, that a nightmare too black ever to imagine was not a nightmare at all. It was the real thing. It meant that I might never see Andrea alive again. For the first time in my life, I knew deep, deep despair.

The largest one of them, blond hair, about forty, blank expression, looked strong, came up to me. The other two stood behind and on either side of him.

"Cellphone", he said.

I handed over my phone.

"The boss called you, you know why we're here, so let's go." They bound my hands behind me using a short length of rope, and then led me out to a car parked in front of Number 2. The leader stuffed my cellphone into his back pocket, then climbed in behind the wheel. I was bundled quickly into the rear seat, one of the other two on either side of me.

We drove out of Largs, turned south on Highway 35, then turned right onto a dirt track that I knew led to about eight down-at-heel cottages. We turned off the dirt track and parked in a thick grove of cedars. Behind the cedars, next to the shore of the lake, stood a dispiriting old frame cottage, robin's-egg-blue paint peeling off in large flaps, a place where people came to get drunk and try to convince themselves they were having a great summer break.

"Out", the leader said to me, as the two on either side opened their doors and stood facing me.

They led me down to the shore, where a largish boat having a single outboard motor was tied to a decrepit dock. The leader pulled out a gun.

"I'm going to untie you, because you're going to direct us to where we need to be. You know better than to do anything stupid."

He untied my hands and they all stepped slightly away from me.

"To the boat", the leader said.

I looked around at them.

"Now!" he said, with more emphasis but no loud-voiced threat.

We walked down toward the boat; one of the two lackeys climbed in first, moved to the bow of the boat, and drew out his pistol to make it clear that they had all the angles covered. They placed me in the middle of the boat with the third man, and the leader climbed into the driver's seat at the rear. The third man next to me was the only one of them wearing shorts, and I noticed that he was carrying a small satchel in his right hand. So the two pistol bearers were at either end of the boat. The situation looked hopeless.

My despair surged again, but the inner voice came back:

Clear your mind! Don't think of anything! Keep your eyes and ears open!

The leader had some trouble starting the engine, and it was obvious that he was not at home in boats. After a few moments of cursing under his breath, he got the motor running, untied the rear mooring rope, and told the man in the front to do the same. These two knew little or nothing about power craft.

Pushing the boat off from the dock took an inordinately long time, but eventually we were moving slowly out into the lake.

"Where am I going?" the leader said to me.

"You need to turn to star – turn right, and head for the other side, the Indian Point shore, over there", and I pointed. "You need to – "

The leader had held up his hand, cutting off my instructions, and pulled out his phone.

"Yeah."

"Yeah, we have him."

"We're in the boat now, on the way."

"I'll let you know."

He put his cellphone away, then gestured for me to carry on where I had left off.

"Head for the other side", and I pointed again. "You need to be in a position about a hundred metres from that shore", and I gestured toward Indian Point, "but lined up with the church steeple in Largs on the mainland", and here I pointed toward the opposite shore.

We chugged along at a speed that I found surprisingly slow until I realized that the leader was reluctant to open the throttle.

He's afraid of boats, afraid of the water, the voice said to me. But this was hardly any comfort.

It took almost twenty minutes for us to reach the area I had indicated and another five minutes to line up the boat and the church steeple. But in the end, I had to say it.

"This is it", I told the leader.

He looked vaguely over the side.

"Where is it?"

"It's down there", I said. "Somewhere."

"What do you mean, 'somewhere'?"

"I mean somewhere. I don't know exactly where it is. If I did, I would have raised it already."

"Oh, yeah? How do I know you haven't already raised it?"

I looked at the leader steadily.

"If I had already raised it, it would be news. Everybody would know about it. It would no longer be available and we wouldn't be here today."

The leader looked back at me for a second.

"The boss said you could be something of a smartass. Doesn't matter. You don't hold any cards at all."

While this discussion was going on, the man in the middle, the one seated next to me, had begun taking off his shirt. He then pulled a diving mask and a pair of fins out of his satchel.

The leader looked at me, then inclined his head toward the diver.

"Tell him where to look."

"Pretty much right below us is a reef, a rock formation, that extends up to within six or seven feet of the surface. You'll need to look all around that reef. It could be anywhere within about twenty-five feet of the reef. The lake bed itself is about twenty feet down, but it's uneven."

"What's he supposed to look for?"

"Well, I think that it will be gold bars or gold coins. I'm not sure. But it likely won't be just lying around on the bottom. I don't know what they were in when the boat went down. It could have been in one or several leather cases. If so, the leather will have rotted away by now. And whatever they were in, it will all be covered by a layer of silt now.

And it could be buried under part of the physical structure of the boat. So it won't necessarily be easy to spot. The boat went down more than a hundred and fifty years ago."

"What else might it have been in?" This was the diver speaking.

"Maybe a locked wooden box."

"How much will it weigh?"

"Don't know, but it could be a hundred pounds or more."

The diver looked at the leader.

"How do you know that somebody hasn't already found it?" the leader asked.

"I don't."

The diver was now standing, and the leader stood as well. The leader scowled at my last answer, then looked at the diver.

"Better get on with it then", he said to the diver. "Sounds like we might be here for a while."

The diver nodded. But I was no longer looking at him. I was listening.

Within a second I recognized the sound and knew that it was what I had sensed initially. The diver and the leader had heard it now as well. It was a rising tone and it was becoming louder quite quickly.

The diver and the leader both looked around to see whether another boat was approaching. I remained seated, but I could feel my muscles tensing.

It roared out from behind a large and dense stand of trees that grew right out to the water on the shore of Indian Point, about a hundred and fifty metres to the north of us. The two men standing turned when it was almost too late, and the plane closed on us extraordinarily quickly, at a height of not more than twenty feet. Less than a second later, the floats passed over us, little more than ten feet up. I could hear the whoosh of the air flowing past them. I also had a better idea of what was happening because through the plane's windows I could see Kate.

And Mike.

The diver lost his balance and fell overboard. The boat rocked sharply, and the leader struggled to keep his balance while reaching for his cellphone and following the plane with his gaze. The two men in the boat began firing at the plane, but Kate was already more than two hundred metres distant and banking hard for cover behind Indian Point. At that distance, and for a target like an airplane, handguns were essentially useless. The sound of their shots echoed around the lake, giving me some sense of just how desperate they were to complete their boss' orders, apparently desperate to the extent that they had stopped thinking.

The leader now had his cellphone out of his pocket. I stood suddenly and struck his hand causing the cellphone to fly out over the water, and I did what I hoped was a James Bond half-gainer over the back of the boat, such that the man in the front of the boat would have trouble shooting at me without hitting the leader.

In the water, I could see the legs and torso of the diver, who had pulled himself up so that his head was over the gunwale of the boat, likely completely confused and wondering what he should be doing next. I headed underwater for the bow, grabbed the rope to which their anchor weight was tied, swam back and wrapped it tightly a couple of times around the propeller. I then began swimming underwater toward the north, the direction the bow of their boat was pointing. I hoped that they would expect me to swim directly toward the shore, and that they would also be looking south in the direction the plane had flown. I would need to come up for air in less than a minute, I would still be easily within pistol range at that point, and I wanted them to be looking anywhere but the area where I would have to surface. I surfaced as gently as I could, mouth only, took a couple of breaths and then dropped below the surface, swimming once more to the north.

At about six feet below the surface I swam as fast as I could, but my mind was in utter turmoil. I now had a little bit of something that just a couple of minutes ago I had been absolutely without.

Hope.

The urge to breathe was becoming strong again, but I ignored it and ploughed on. My legs were pumping hard and my arms were carving out long powerful strokes, full-length strokes, using up oxygen at maximum rate.

My lungs were now on fire. I let out some air to try to placate the demon that was ordering me: *Breathe! Breathe! Breathe!*

I rose to the surface again, as gently as I could, only my lips breaking through, and breathed in and out, great heaving breaths, seeming to me that I was making enough noise to wake the dead.

"There he is!" the leader cried. He tried to start the engine, it coughed once, gave a strangled sound of grinding metal, and stopped. There were three more ineffectual clicks as he tried again to start it.

I had raised my head as far out of the water as I dared, trying to assess my situation. It was certainly not good.

But then I heard something else. A soft fluttering sound. And I knew what it was.

Kate's plane appeared once more, at treetop level. She had throttled way back, had glided almost silently across Indian Point, and then was upon the boat and its crew once more.

As soon as the plane cleared the trees, less than a hundred metres from the boat, Kate opened the throttle fully. She would cover the distance between them in not much more than two seconds. The little plane roared angrily, was attacking in a shallow, full power dive, and it must have seemed to the men in the boat that it had their number on it. The leader, now phoneless, and probably in the grip of his fear of water, tried nevertheless to focus. I saw his gun hand come up.

Oh, shit! I thought.

But suddenly the plane reared up, the wings practically vertical, the wing on the passenger side of the plane looking as though it was going to sweep both men off the boat. I saw the two of them cringe, now really afraid. In fascination, I watched as the door on the downward side of the plane opened wide.

Something came out of the plane. Or rather, a number of somethings.

Water fountained up on both sides of the boat as whatever it was that came out of the plane entered the lake at speed. There was a very loud clank as something struck the motor, and a series of rapid staccato thuds as the boat itself was hit numerous times.

Rocks!

Mike had dropped fifteen or twenty fist-sized rocks from the plane!

Kate brought the plane back level, gained some height, then made a tight turn to port. Within a minute, she brought the plane down onto the surface of the lake and cruised up close to me. I swam to the plane, climbed up onto the starboard float, gripped one of the struts, and waved to Kate to taxi to the now-disabled boat. The fumes of aviation spirit flowing back at me from the engine's exhaust smelled like nectar. The loud chugging of the engine itself was sweeter than any music I could imagine.

As we approached, we could see that the diver had climbed over the bow back into the boat and was standing in surrender, arms raised. The other two were lying motionless in the bottom of the boat, something Mike confirmed later that he had seen as they had banked away from their bombing run.

The boat's motor had a very large dent, two pieces of metal were hanging from it, and it appeared no longer functional. There was a hole through the boat just behind the middle seat, and the boat itself was half full of water, stern down, but it seemed that the floatation chambers would prevent it from sinking entirely.

Kate brought the plane alongside the boat, and I made the large step across into the boat. Nobody could hear anything above the engine noise, and not knowing what else to do, I stepped up to the diver, smiled, nodded, then struck him in the face as hard as I could.

Now there were three men lying motionless in the boat.

Kate kept the engine at idle while I steadied the boat and plane together and Mike opened his door and stepped down onto the float.

"Nice shootin', Tex", I shouted over the engine noise.

Without giving him a chance to reply, I shouted to Kate, asking if she could take me over to Largs. She nodded, and I climbed into the seat Mike had vacated. Once at Largs, I would collect Wilder's boat, come back, and retrieve our catch: three flounders.

Before closing the door, I leaned out toward Mike.

"If any of our guests awaken from their naps, be nice to them, give them a cup of tea or something, there's a good lad."

Mike gave me a twisted sneer that would have made a Stasi border guard lose all sphincter control. I closed the door, Kate revved up the engine and we were off.

Fifteen minutes later, Mike and I had our three goons in a functioning boat headed back to Largs.

By the time we reached Largs, Kate had the plane tied down and helped us unload our cargo. They were all awake now. The diver had a huge bruise on his left cheek and likely a couple of loose or broken teeth. The leader had been struck in the chest by one of the rocks and by his shallow breathing it looked as though he had cracked or broken ribs. There were no flecks of blood at his lips, so I was prepared to assume that neither of his lungs had been punctured. His chest probably hurt like hell.

Tough!

The remaining man had no visible injuries, but he was having trouble walking, and it looked as though one of the stones had struck him in the leg.

We sat them all in chairs in the garden. Only their hands were bound but none of them was going anywhere.

The pressure to focus on my own immediate survival was off now, but that left a far more oppressive problem. I began slipping into a darker, deeper pit, and anguish filled my being.

Andrea.

Where was Andrea?

How could I possibly get her back now?

I moved toward the back door leading to the kitchen, but before I had reached the steps I found that my hands were shaking almost uncontrollably.

"Mark?" Kate asked, and when I failed to answer she followed me.

"Are you alright?"

I carried on into the kitchen and Kate came in right behind me. By the time I was inside and the door had closed, I was whimpering, then blubbering. Tears flowed down my cheeks.

Kate turned me toward her.

"Oh Kate! I've fucked everything up! Andrea … I let them … Andrea's everything! And I've fucked it all up!"

Kate directed a hard stare at me and shook me violently by the shoulders.

"Stop this Mark! We need to find Andrea! Where is she?"

"I don't … I don't know. Dickson … Dickson has her", and I blubbered some more.

Kate slapped me hard across the face.

"Stop this Mark! Where will Dickson take her?"

To my utter astonishment, my head had cleared.

"I … he won't give up easily", I said. It felt like somebody else was talking. "He'll probably come here. He expects I won't run away. The prize he wants is here."

Mike was now standing in the doorway, looking in at us but glancing back at our catch every second or so. "His connection to the big blond bastard is lost now", Mike said. "Neither of them can contact each other."

"No consolation", I said, wiping my cheeks dry. "If he can't get hold of his guy, he'll know something's wrong. But I think he would make one last attempt to get what he wants. Psychopaths have trouble admitting defeat. As a last resort, he would torture Andrea in front of me."

The three of us walked back outside again, me still wiping my cheeks. Kate walked toward the carport, then past it and disappeared. She told us later that she had gone to the front of the house to check for rubbernecks attracted by the sound of the plane, found two small boys, and told them there was nothing to see and that they should shoo.

Mike was going to the three men separately, and to each one he said "Stand up." As each one stood, Mike emptied his pockets. What he netted was one cellphone that now had a badly cracked face, no wallets or ID, but a huge roll of cash that he extracted from the leader's pocket.

"That's mine", he said to Mike.

"Not anymore, Blondie", and Mike pushed the man roughly back onto his chair.

Mike unwound the roll and looked at me.

"Must be a couple of thousand here. That will go a long way toward covering our expenses for this venture."

Just then, Mike's cellphone buzzed.

Mike hit the speaker option. There were some shuffling noises at the other end.

"Mi-Mike? Mike?"

The voice quavered in fear.

It was Andrea's voice.

Thirty

I grabbed Mike's arm.

"Andrea! Oh my God! Andrea! Where are you? Are you okay?"

"Mark! I was worried sick about you! I was … I was…" and here she broke down.

There was something wrong here.

"Where are you, Andrea? What happened?"

After some sobbing and choking, she brought herself sufficiently under control to say that she was at the Shell station in Rosedale.

"I got away." She said it in a matter-of-fact way as if the "how" wasn't important at that point.

"Andrea! I'm coming to get you! I'll be there in less than five minutes!"

And immediately I turned and began sprinting to my car.

"I'm coming with you!" Kate said behind me.

I raced to Arran Street much faster than was safe, but then I floored it and the tires screamed on the hot tarmac. We rounded the corner at Highway 35 with barely a look to check for traffic. The tires let out another long tortured scream, and this time the speedometer needle was hard against the upper end stop all the way into Rosedale. We screeched around the slight S-bend coming into the village, roared up over the bridge, and the car practically stood on the driver's side front wheel as I braked and turned onto the access road that led back toward the canal. I stopped in a four-wheel skid in front of the Shell station next to the repair bay, threw open the car door, and ran to where Andrea was sitting huddled on a bench next to the little stone building.

In a thankful embrace, I nearly crushed my wife, my life's gem, the world's most beautiful woman, and she dissolved into convulsive sobs. Kate joined us, and the three of us sobbed unashamedly together.

At length, I stood back a bit and looked Andrea over. There were no marks on her face, hands, or arms. She knew what I was looking for.

"I'm okay", she said, still in a very quavery voice. "He didn't hurt me. But he was cold, terrifying."

"Let's go back to Largs", Kate said.

And that's what we did.

During the trip, Kate and I asked Andrea gently how she had got away.

Andrea shivered involuntarily, but Kate had a reassuring arm around Andrea's shoulders, their heads close together.

"He was holed up … in a rough cabin. It was … south of the canal between Balsam Lake and Cameron Lake." But then she broke down and couldn't continue.

The story came out in ragged pieces. At the time, she didn't know where she was. She realized only later where the cabin was. He had tied her into a Muskoka chair, one that had just been made. The edges of the wood slats were rough and unfinished, and when he went outside to answer his phone she managed to use those sharp edges to cut through the rope. There were two doors to the cabin. She slipped out the other one and went into the bush. She headed for high ground, came across a dirt road, flagged down a farmer in his pickup, and he drove her to the Shell station.

"The man there let me use his phone."

She lapsed into silence then, wouldn't say anything more, and Kate caressed her hair.

When we arrived back in our garden, everything was much the same as when we left except that George was now standing by the steps leading to the back door. Andrea and Kate sat next to each other at the picnic table, and Kate comforted Andrea in a long hug. I went into the house and came back carrying a bottle of Metaxa and four glasses. Mike and I chugged our shots; Andrea and Kate both finished theirs in three large sips.

Oddly enough, it was George who broke the silence, directing a question at Mike and me as he walked slowly toward the picnic table.

"Did … did one of … these men kill … kill my brother?"

This surprised me. I had said nothing to George to contradict the story of a boating accident. But George must have guessed from the amount of time and effort I had been spending on the case that something more was involved. I realized now that he wanted desperately to be clear on his brother's fate.

Blondie answered immediately despite the pain that speech was costing him.

"I didn't kill anybody!"

Mike looked at him, walked over, and delivered a very hard backhand across his mouth. Blondie rocked back onto the two rear legs of his chair, almost fell over backwards, and winced again at the sudden balancing effort.

"When we want to hear from you", Mike growled at him, "you'll be invited to speak. Until then, keep your fucking mouth shut! And that goes for you two assholes as well."

They all blinked dumbly.

"Have you got that?" Mike roared.

I turned to George.

"We don't know who killed your brother, George. It might have been one of these guys. It might have been somebody else. But we do know who was responsible."

"Who is he?" George asked. "Where is he?"

"He's somewhere nearby. I think we should be able to find him soon."

George blinked and nodded, but didn't say anything.

I turned to look at Andrea and Kate, caught Kate's eye, and gave her a head gesture indicating the back door. Kate nodded.

"Come on, Andrea", Kate said softly, "let's go inside", and she led Andrea to the back steps, grabbing the Metaxa bottle on the way past. I turned to George and indicated that he should go with them. He hesitated, and my next gesture to him made it clear that it hadn't been a request. He hurried after the two women.

When the three of them were inside and the door was closed, I took Mike aside and we walked back behind the picnic table.

"I need to find out where Dickson is", I said to Mike. "There's no way I'm just waiting around for him to show up. You with me?"

"All the way, brother."

We returned and stood again in front of our three captives. Mike's expression had turned unspeakably nasty.

"Okay, you three bastards", he said. "It's now your turn to talk. Let's start with you, Blondie", and the smile that Mike beamed down at him was utterly evil.

"Would you like to begin?" Mike asked me, as though inviting me to be first to try the potato salad.

"Yes", I said. I walked to the drawer that was fitted under one end of the picnic table, poked around in the drawer for a moment, then came back to stand in front of Blondie.

"Do you know what a ganglion is, Blondie?"

He shook his head, not knowing what was going on, but sensing that whatever it was, it was far from good.

"There are two answers, but the one I'm interested in is simple. A ganglion is a bundle of nerves. We have them at various places in our bodies. Each of us has one just behind his nose, at the bottom end of that structure, near the nostrils. That ganglion is perhaps the easiest one to access. If anything pokes into it, its owner experiences pain like nobody can imagine."

I paused a while to let that sink in. Then I held up a small jeweller's screwdriver in one hand and a crème brûlée torch in the other.

"If I poke this screwdriver up under your upper lip and then jab upwards, it will dig right into that ganglion. Now, I don't want to do that, because I don't like pain, either experiencing it or causing it. I expect that you don't like experiencing pain either, although you're probably a lot less concerned about causing it than I am. But just to give you an inkling of what that ganglion pain would be like, if I heated up this screwdriver to dull red using this torch, then stuck it up your dick, that would be like a feather tickle compared to the ganglion pain I'm proposing."

Short dramatic pause here.

"Now then, you can avoid all that pain, if you tell me everything you know about your boss. We know him by the name Carl Dickson, but that's not his real name. So, start talking anytime, within the next fifteen seconds, that is, and don't stop until you've told me every last fucking piece of information you know about your boss! Do you read me?"

My tone remained calm and quiet throughout this speech, and my hope was that it conveyed to them the careful, systematic, and totally unemotional approach of the professional torturer.

"He found me. Through my contacts. That was five days ago. He called me in Toronto and asked me to meet him. Said he needed me and two others for a job. Needed to find something. Told me his name was David Tiverton. I don't know if that's his real name."

Blondie was stumbling over his words, couldn't get them out fast enough.

"You were staying in a cabin rented from Rick Stinson in Coboconk. Where else did you stay?"

"There was a place in Bobcaygeon, and we met a few times in a vacant office building in Toronto."

"Addresses", I demanded.

He rhymed off the two addresses and Mike wrote them down.

"Very good. Now, where will he be right now?"

"I don't know", Blondie said, just a little too quickly.

"Oh, now, and we were doing so well", Mike said, moving toward Blondie and feigning terrible disappointment.

I brought the screwdriver up to Blondie's face and rested it against the tip of his nose.

"Let's try that again, shall we?"

"No! He'll kill me! You don't know him! He's a vicious bugger!"

Blondie had either seen how casually Dickson could resort to violence (had he seen the execution of the three men behind the hotel near Lindsay?), or he had recognized instinctively what a violent psychopath Dickson was and the extreme danger he posed.

"You have a point there. He'll kill you. But I won't. On the other hand, when he kills you, it likely won't hurt at all, or at least very little. But the pain you'll get from me will be unbelievable, and it will go on and on, for a long, long time. But the choice is yours."

We waited. Blondie was sweating buckets by now and was evidently in agony about what he should do.

"Grab his head, Mike", I said.

Mike went round behind Blondie, and clamped his head in what looked like the jaws of death.

"Last chance", I said. "No? Okay."

I took Blondie's upper lip between my left thumb and forefinger, and began sliding the screwdriver blade slowly up along Blondie's upper gum.

"No! No! Stop, please! Okay! Okay!"

I stepped back, doing all I could to conceal my feeling of massive internal relief.

Blondie began talking and, as I had seen happen during my police days, once he began he sang like a lark.

At the end of twenty minutes, we had just about everything we needed. Mike and I went into a huddle. He agreed to my plan but asked me if I was aware of the risks. I said I was and I asked if he was comfortable with them, but Mike just smiled, patted my cheek, and then he went off to call on, once again, his reliable local man Chuck.

Then we sat down to wait.

It didn't take anything like as long as I thought it would.

Thirty-one

We were counting on Dickson, or Tiverton, or whatever his name was, figuring that he would always be the brightest guy in the room. Both Mike and I had had some experience with his sort. They're not the kind of guys you want to come across often. They are generally very bright, are superb planners, can detect weaknesses in individuals intuitively and with ease, are ruthless, and are not limited by the constraints of empathy, conscience, or remorse. They can be exceedingly dangerous.

Mike and I had a long conference call with Chuck, and we passed on to him all the information we had extracted from Blondie. Chuck was no dummy either; he knew the kind of danger someone like Dickson posed, he had a very healthy respect for the risks psychopaths can present, and he asked many penetrating questions.

"The basic question here, Chuck", I said, "is this: are you comfortable with what we're asking you to do?"

Chuck delayed a moment.

"Yes, I am. If I feel that things are getting out of hand, I'll just back away. But I think you have the right strategy. At the end of the day, it'll be you two guys who'll be running the greatest risks."

"Okay, Chuck. Keep in regular touch. Let us know when you make your first contact."

Chuck signed off, and we waited.

We bound our three landed fish to their chairs, then went inside. I wanted to talk to Andrea.

The four of us, Andrea, Kate, me, and Mike sat together. Mike and I explained what we were doing. Andrea objected right away. It was too dangerous. Let the police handle it. You're putting everything we have at risk.

I began trying to answer her points, but after only a couple of sentences Mike held up his hand and stopped me. He explained the problems and risks in going the police route. He explained how slippery and ruthless Dickson was. He talked in a low, quiet, competent voice. He answered Andrea's questions. She had more questions. He answered them as well. This went on for the best part of half an hour.

In the end, it was Kate who carried the day.

"They're right, Andrea. I saw it today out there on the lake. Dickson had just manoeuvred us all into that situation where he held all the cards. If it hadn't been for Mike's resourcefulness, not to mention yours in getting away from Dickson, I don't know what might have happened. Let them do this. You and I will go to my place in the plane. We'll stay in touch with them right down the line. But we have to let them take out this son of a bitch."

These were strong words, coming from Kate, and Andrea sat pondering.

Kate cleverly moved away from the whole topic.

"Mike, how did you know where Mark would be?" she asked.

"It was a guess, but a reliable guess. The only way to get the treasure is to go out there in the lake and … well, get it. It was clear that Dickson didn't know just where it was, although he had a general idea. Otherwise he would have recovered it already. They had crossed their Rubicon by kidnapping Andrea and then kidnapping Mark, so however it played out it would be only a matter of time before the police became involved. The clock was ticking, so Dickson's best path was to find the treasure and disappear."

"But why just now?" Kate asked. "Why is it that Dickson seems to be suddenly in such a hurry? Surely he's known about this for some time."

"I think", Mike began, "it's because the field seems to have become crowded all of a sudden. First there was Harold. Then the crew who had gone out there in the lake a few days ago. We thought they were Dickson's men, but it looks like they were running their own rogue operation. Dickson dealt with them all ruthlessly. I think he was concerned that some information on the treasure had got out into the world, and he didn't want to take the chance that some other bunch would try their hand and possibly pull it off, whipping the treasure out from under his nose."

"And the rogue group", Kate began, "how did they find out about it?"

This time it was me who answered.

"I'm guessing it was them who tossed Harold's apartment. They probably got the basic information they needed that way. Then Harold was doubly unlucky to run afoul of Dickson's crowd out on the lake."

Kate nodded and thought about that. It sounded plausible. My bit was speculation. I didn't know how much of Mike's explanation had been invented on the spot.

"What would have happened to us, to Mark and to me?" Andrea asked, and it was clear that the nightmare was still bright in her mind.

"I suspect", Mike began, "that they would have taken you to two isolated spots and let you go."

Even though Andrea appeared to buy that line, I didn't. Not even for a second. As soon as Dickson had got his hands on the prize, we would both have been dead meat.

Kate jumped in again, regaining the conversational initiative.

"How did you know what Mark would do?" she asked Mike.

"I didn't", Mike said. "But I knew that he knew I wouldn't be just sitting around waiting for the phone to bring joyous news, and I knew that if they took him out to the reef, he would find some way to disable their boat and give himself a better chance to get away. He's a fantastic swimmer, both on and below the surface."

"When did you have time to collect those rocks, Mike?" I asked.

"He didn't", Kate interjected. "He asked me to bring as many large stones as would fit in a five-gallon pail when he called me asking for air support. Said we might need them."

I nodded at this, notching up my already great respect for Mike.

"There'll be more time for all this later", Kate said as she stood. "Grab whatever you need, Andrea, and let's get back to the plane." They both turned to go to our bedroom to collect some fresh clothes for Andrea.

"One suggestion, Kate", I said, and they turned back to look at me. "When you leave, take off to the south then swing a long way west. He's less likely to see or hear you. Dickson is probably somewhere to the east of us. He won't want to have the large expanse of Balsam Lake between him and us. I don't know what he knows. He might think you're here, either or both of you. But if he doesn't know just where you are, then that could be one more slight advantage we have, another area where he could assume wrongly, make a mistake."

Kate nodded. They went off and returned a couple of minutes later, Andrea carrying a small sports bag.

Andrea put the bag down on a chair and came over to me. Her face was full of the most desperate concern. She put her arms around my neck and whispered in my ear. "Please be very careful, Mark. I can't bear the thought of losing you." She then began weeping quietly.

Kate and Mike both came over to us and we had a group hug.

"Nothing's going to happen to this guy, Andrea. Old Mike will make damned sure of that!"

"I think they're right, you know, Andrea", Kate said. "After today, I don't think there's anything the four of us couldn't handle."

And I think she almost believed that.

I know I did.

We all trooped down to the plane. Andrea and I had another long, desperate embrace, one that left me in emotional turmoil.

"We'll stay in contact", I said. "We'll see each other again in just a few hours. Promise."

Andrea kissed me. And it was a deep and hungry kiss we shared. Then Kate helped her onto the float and into the plane, untied the mooring ropes, climbed in herself, started up the engine, and they moved out almost half a mile into the lake. Kate turned the plane to face south, the wash from the propeller suddenly whipping up the water. The plane squatted and began accelerating and a couple of seconds later the deep roar of the engine reached us. The plane picked up speed, lifted free of the surface, and made a long turn toward the west. It felt almost as though Andrea was leaving for the other side of the world.

Mike and I walked back toward the house. I stopped in front of our three captives.

"Let's untie their feet, Mike."

"Would you like some water?" I asked them. They all nodded.

"And if you want", I added, "you can sit over there on the softer chairs. But take just one wrong step, any of you, and I swear that I'll throw all three of you into the lake, hands still bound. So do exactly, and I mean exactly, what you're told and keep your mouths shut."

I moved the soft outdoor chairs way over to the far corner, behind the picnic table and right up against the house, then waved them over. Once they were seated, Mike held a large plastic bottle of water to each of their mouths until they had all drunk their fill.

"What if I have to take a leak?"

Mike straightened suddenly, walked over quickly, and delivered four massive blows to Blondie's face.

"Did you not hear what the man said, Blondie?" Mike roared. "He said keep your mouth shut! You say one more word, and I really will beat you into the middle of next week! Have you got that?"

Mike's bellowing left no room for any response, not even a squeaky "Yes, sir".

"If any of you has to piss or take a shit, you'll do it in your pants! End of discussion!"

"Since they're too stupid to understand plain English, I think we need to tie them into their chairs again. Do you want the honours, Mike?"

"With pleasure", and he set about his task with a will.

Chuck's first contact with us was at one o'clock. He seemed to be playing his role well. He had no direct contact with Dickson but then he wasn't supposed to have any. He was acting in a way that we hoped would say to Dickson that we didn't know where he was, but that we had his three stooges and they had spilled their guts, and as far as we were concerned, we had won, and the game was up for him. In other words, we wanted Dickson to think that we were cocky and overconfident.

We had a fairly complete description of Dickson from Blondie. After a little coaxing, he had given us a car make and colour and a licence number. We just had to keep laying the aniseed trail and wait.

By two o'clock, Chuck had fallen back to the second of the locations we had agreed on. Time dragged on. A hundred personal concerns and stray thoughts clamoured for attention in my mind, but I swept them aside brutally, needing full focus for whatever was about to happen.

"It's Chuck", Mike said, stabbing at his phone. He listened for a moment, nodded, then said into his phone "Good. Fall back to Hemlock."

"He's on the way?" I asked.

"Looks like he's on the way", Mike said. "Excuse me", and he went into the house, coming out two minutes later carrying a Glock and enough spare ammunition to hold off a battalion.

"You practise with that thing?" I asked.

"Every week."

And so we sat down to wait.

We had tried to anticipate what Dickson would do. He wanted his prize and whether it was today or later probably didn't matter. But he needed to know exactly where it was, and for that he was evidently sure that he needed me.

How he would try to make his way into Largs we didn't know. But we did know he wouldn't come by water. Too exposed. We would see him before he got even close. He wouldn't come in through the village itself. There were too many people there. He might come through the fields to the south or through the trees along the north side of Arran Street. But whichever way he came, he would be trying for surprise. Dickson hadn't had contact with his men for some time now, so his information was stale. I was sure that this would bother him, and he likely would try to compensate somehow. Dickson by now probably had made the conservative assumption that Mike would be here and modified his plans accordingly. That modified plan would likely include elements directed at neutralizing Mike, that is, killing him, as quickly as possible so that he could set about getting from me the information he needed. His plan was by now likely pretty desperate. Under calmer conditions, he could have got the information he needed, vanished for a while, and then come back surreptitiously to get the treasure. But there was great uncertainty here, and he had now left such a trail of bodies behind that, unless he made his move soon, any actions he wanted to take would be seriously constrained by the inevitable police presence. Despite all that, I remained fairly sure that Dickson had utter confidence in his own ability to overcome any obstacles.

"Chuck", Mike said to me, picking up his phone. He listened for a moment then set the phone down again.

"Dickson just turned in at Arran Street. Chuck got a look at him."

"We're on", I said, and we took cover.

Thirty-two

We both heard the sound of a car revving, tires squealing, and then a loud clunk. Suddenly a smallish blue SUV rounded the corner of the house, swung out past the carport, entered the back garden, raced across the grass, smashed chairs and picnic table to pieces, and went head first into the infinity pool, where it stopped.

I almost missed Dickson. He was running in a crouch across the grass toward the boathouse. He must have jumped from the car while it was crossing the grass.

"There he is, Mike! There! Heading for the boathouse!"

"Got him!" Mike said, and then the shooting started.

Suddenly I panicked. The barbecue gas tank!

From where Dickson had taken cover, he didn't have a view of it, but I realized, all at once, that this was probably something he wouldn't have missed in his planning. There is reliably one in every garden in cottage country. Somewhere within me, second thoughts about this whole business started to rise up, but I crushed them back down. There was nothing I could do now about the tank and about the situation we were in.

Dickson and Mike were taking turns firing at each other, and every few shots there was the ricochet whine of a bullet glancing off the stone of the boathouse or our back wall. It's terrifying being anywhere near a firefight, and I was acutely aware that one of us was likely to be hit sooner or later. There was a pause in the firing, the third one by my count, probably for reloading, and it seemed like the shooting had been continuing for a very long time. But most likely it had been not much more than a minute. During this third lull in the shooting, I became aware of the shouts of alarm from Dickson's three men, bound into their chairs and sitting ducks for any stray shots. The firing resumed, and suddenly these shouts of alarm rose to wails of panic. I had no time to be concerned about that. It was just another of the things I could do nothing about.

I had been trying to think of some way we could shift the situation to our favour when a desperate idea occurred to me. I took one quick look at the shooting gallery, just in time to see Dickson duck back behind the boathouse, as another bullet whined out over the lake. There was a smear of red on the stone at the corner of the boathouse, probably blood, and probably the result of one of Mike's shots producing a spray of stone chips that had then grazed Dickson's hand or arm.

I was taking cover just around the side of the house. I had to try to get around behind Dickson. Going completely around the house and into the square would put me in full view, but if I could get through the house – the root cellar! A little further along from where I was sheltering was the outer wall of our root cellar, essentially a cold storage room. That wall has an opening connecting the cellar and the outside air, and I thought I could squeeze through it and into the cellar. That would mean knocking out the heavy metal screening that covered the opening. I ran to the screened opening in the wall. It wasn't large, and the more I looked at that opening the less certain I was that this was a viable plan. *There's no time for this, Whelan*, I said brutally to myself and began kicking at the screen.

The screen was made of heavy gauge wire, and I cursed Jimmy's diligence at fixing it very securely, making sure that no animals would have an easy time getting in. After the seventh or eighth kick, the screen began to yield. Two more kicks, and my foot went through. I stuck my head and one arm through the hole and began squirming. For a moment, I began to panic as I thought I had become hopelessly wedged in the hole, but then both shoulders were through, at the cost of sharp bits of wire shredding the left arm of my shirt. Something was trickling down and off my left elbow, but then two more pushes sent me tumbling headfirst into the cold room, where I landed heavily on a pile of bricks and some sacking.

I made my way through the cold room, limped up the half flight of stairs to the kitchen, went through the house, out the front door, and along the north side of the house. Jimmy had built some storage shelving at a spot beside the path that was shielded from external view by a line of cedars, and on this shelving he had piled irregular offcut lengths of planking. I picked up a four-foot length of two by two, wondering vaguely at the same time what use it would be against the cannon Dickson was wielding.

The firing raged on. I was coming to the corner of the house, the path continuing on ten feet or so to the boathouse between two rows of cedars. Dickson would be somewhere ahead of me. I had no idea just what it was I had in mind to do, and the absurdity of my situation was quite plain. I had no weapon apart from a scruffy piece of wood. I knew the external layout of the boathouse, and as a result I knew that the only thing concealing me was the trees that lined the path. I couldn't just rush Dickson, because I didn't know exactly where he was. Taking a wild guess at his precise location was ridiculous. If he caught me in his peripheral vision, he would have me. And it was clear that it was me he wanted. If that happened, if I was captured, Dickson would hold all the cards again. I inched forward, relieved at least that the noise of the firing would easily cover any sound my advance might make.

Then I saw a movement. Crouching down slowly, my line of sight came to a small break in the foliage. Suddenly, I could see Dickson's arm and shoulder and the gun in his hand. He was half-turned away from me, about four feet distant, firing left-handed. It would have been impossible for me to move on him without him noticing from the corner of his eye.

There was another lull in the firing. Was this a chance? Was Dickson turned away from me sufficiently? Was he preoccupied enough for me to mount a surprise? I had no real way of knowing. And even though I was concealed behind the cedar foliage, I had to be careful about moving, since peripheral vision is very sensitive and Dickson's was probably honed to razor sharpness. And I was close enough to him to smell the smoke from his firing. In the relative quiet of the shooting lull, I had to remain frozen in place.

Shit! I racked my brain, drawing a blank.

Then there was a loud click, and another round of firing broke out.

I heard a cry, and it hadn't come from Dickson.

Mike had been hit! The thought left me cold from dread.

"Give up, Mr. Jefferson", Dickson shouted, the sudden volume of his voice taking me by surprise. "I'm a better shot than you. It's only a question of time."

"Go fuck yourself!" Mike shouted, and I've never been more relieved to hear his voice.

So here we were. Mike wounded, possibly not able to return Dickson's fire effectively, probably not able to hold out much longer.

Shit! Shit! Shit!

It was now down to me, and I could see no good options left.

The firing had ceased for the moment. It was my bet that Dickson was trying to determine how much advantage he had gained by wounding Mike.

Into this silence, between bouts of firing, a loud splash suddenly intruded. I sensed, as much as saw, Dickson turn to the right in a reflex response to the noise. There was a good chance that that action had taken me out of his peripheral vision, but this would be the case for only a second or two. It was now or never.

Stepping out from behind my screen of cedar, I had the sudden fear that I might have dithered too long. But there was no time for second-guessing.

Dickson was beginning to turn back to his previous stance. He had seen me. The man had a sixth sense. But it came just a bit late.

There was a loud crack as my length of two by two struck Dickson's gun forearm, which had just begun to swing toward me. The gun clattered off somewhere, Dickson stumbled a step forward, and then my two by two caught him again, this time across the back of the head.

He went down. I saw Dickson's gun lying on the stone path about six feet from where he was stretched out, and I kicked it well out of reach under the cedar hedge.

It seemed that the gun battle had raged for a long time, but probably it had lasted less than two minutes.

"He's down, Mike!" I shouted, before stepping out where I was visible.

Across the way, Mike appeared and walked toward me, his left shoulder soaked in blood.

"It's okay", he said, registering my alarm and waving his Glock. "I'll get a towel as soon as we've got this bastard hog-tied."

Once Mike and I were convinced that Dickson was securely bound, I went into the house and got a towel and the first aid kit. I soon had a makeshift binding on Mike's wound, which would do until the EMS people arrived.

A subdued chorus of whimpering reached us from our bound prisoners. Or at least from two of them. Those two had tipped over their chairs, trying to stay as low as they could and minimize themselves as targets. Blondie was in the chair closest to the corner of the house and closest to the line between Mike and Dickson. He hadn't been so lucky. His chair remained upright, and he was in it, flopped sideways to the extent his bonds would allow. There was a gaping angry wound where a stray shot from Dickson had opened the left side of his neck. Almost his entire torso was soaked in his own blood.

Jimmy emerged from behind the boathouse. I learned later that he had been working on the marine railway inside the boathouse, had ignored our arrival in that phlegmatic way that had Jimmy written all over it, but took cover when the shooting began. The boathouse doors onto the lake were open, and the half concrete block he had been using as a weight in his repair operation inside the boathouse was what he had thrown through the open doors and into the lake as a diversion. At the present moment, he just stood there, looking on in a matter-of-fact way, as though we had done nothing more momentous than burn out a nest of tent caterpillars. I walked over to Jimmy and embarrassed him horribly by giving him a huge hug.

Though there had almost certainly been a dozen or more calls to the police from people in Largs, Mike now called them from his cellphone. I asked Jimmy to go out in front of the house and direct them to the back when they arrived.

Dickson, Tiverton, or whatever his real name was, didn't sneer, didn't scowl, didn't rant. He just stood there, cool and expressionless. The polypropylene rope that bound his hands tightly behind his back probably hurt like hell, because of his fractured forearm, but he didn't show it. From first sight of him, just a few minutes previously, his presence had chilled me, and even now, immobilized as he was, his expressionless face had me wondering whether he had a Plan B, or indeed even Plans C, D, and E. Did he have something up his sleeve? Were we missing something? At the moment, Dickson gave every impression of simply accepting the situation, not as a final defeat, but as though he was merely digesting the news on some event in which he had zero interest.

Mike and I had only a couple of minutes to grill Dickson. He didn't hesitate in answering. But all his answers, each of them just one word or a few words, were easy, glib, as though he were humouring lesser beings. I quickly came to recognize that what he said was being selected from a palette of possibilities, all of them equally suitable, and none, including the truth, having any special significance or priority over all the others. But none of that mattered. The evidence of the firefight Dickson had initiated was everywhere. Very soon there would be many questions to answer, and before this phase began, I used Mike's cellphone to make a quick call to Cromarty. He would be able to turn this situation into gold for himself, and perhaps indirectly for me, and if I could help him stick it to his cynical superiors, absorbed in their absurd little management numbers games, it would be a red-letter day for everyone who mattered.

A wailing of numerous sirens began to reach us. The police and the EMS crew turned up within a minute of each other.

After providing us minimal information through his essentially monosyllabic responses, Dickson stopped responding. He just looked at us disdainfully, his flat expressionless eyes and his clear, almost cherubic face being enough to cause a chill to run through even anyone who had already seen it. What he had done, and why he had done it, would remain a mystery to us until we found out later, by other routes, just what been driving this whole murderous exercise.

I tried one more time asking Dickson what this whole affair had been all about.

He just looked back at me in that same flat, expressionless, self-assured way. He showed a complete lack of affect. There was not a trace of empathy. Not a sign that he was human in any meaningful way. None of us was ever more than just a tool for him to use or an obstacle to be overcome. Other lives didn't matter. Only his life mattered, but even that must have been a question of "mattering" in the most icy, chilling, and empty psychological surreality. Just as well that Andrea wasn't here. She had seen the "businesslike" side of Dickson, and that had been more than enough. But to witness Dickson's full-blown psychopathic calmness, against all this violence and carnage, would have horrified her to the core, probably triggering both sleeping and waking nightmares.

"How did Harold Barbour fit into all this?" I asked Dickson.

Dickson just shrugged.

Mike moved suddenly to strike Dickson, but I got to him before he could and held him until his urge to beat Dickson to a pulp had passed.

"Easy, Mike. The courts will deal with this bastard."

"Yeah, right!" Mike spat. "Twenty-five years and no chance of parole. Colour television and a library. What the fuck kind of punishment is that?"

"Police! Everybody stay right where you are!"

It was a statement rather than a challenge. Within five minutes, eight armed policemen had secured the scene, determined who everybody was, and led Dickson away.

Thirty-three

At a word from the police, the EMS team replaced my *ad hoc* binding on Mike's wound by something more professional, then checked Blondie and confirmed that he was indeed dead. In accounting to the police for everyone present and why they were here, George's name came up. I explained about George, and once it was clear that he was inside the house, I was told to go and bring him out, one of the police accompanying me. The three of us, Mike and I and George, were questioned for thirty minutes by the ranking detective. George had gone beyond stuttering. He was now mute. At length, it was decided that we would be taken to Lindsay to complete the questioning and to have Mike's wound tended properly.

Mike's Glock and Dickson's cannon were taken away. Mike and I were told, in tones of pronounced disapproval, that there would be many questions to answer because of the gunfight, the death, and what the police considered our failure to bring them into the matter much earlier. PIs are looked down upon by police at the best of times, but when they become O.K. Corral gunslingers, the presumption of innocence falls under serious strain.

Then we were taken to the OPP detachment at Lindsay, where the sergeant in charge said that Mike should go to the hospital right away and have his shoulder tended to. Mike waved that off, saying that we needed to get this over with, so we were questioned further and had our statements taken. After that we went with Mike to the hospital where his wound was X-rayed to confirm the absence of broken bones and shell or bone fragments. After he got stitches, an injection, wound dressing, and a sling, an OPP cruiser brought us back to Largs.

The rest of that day passed but not in the way we expected.

We were besieged by reporters, although the police did a good job keeping them mostly at bay. After a couple of hours, the news hounds realized they had got all they were going to get, and that they would have to fill in any remaining blanks themselves to meet their deadlines. An earlier discussion I had had with Inspector Galbraith of the OPP had been invaluable, and in response to the few questions that reporters did manage to pose to me I just referred them to the police since the investigation was continuing. By midafternoon, we were left in peace.

Of course it was huge news locally. A rampaging psychopath, a Chicago-style gun battle, a man killed, another wounded, and all in the sleepy village of Largs. The residents of Largs were stunned. Elsewhere the locals were also agog. In Coboconk, people stood in knots on street corners, Matthew Dyson's barber shop was full to overflowing, the Tea Room was filled continuously to capacity, and the Pattie House sold more beer in a couple of days than it normally did in a month.

One of the storylines to come out of it all related to the heroine of the piece.

Kate.

A dramatic account of Kate's "bombing run" appeared in all the local papers. Kate was interviewed on television. Somebody had managed to take a picture of the disabled boat as it was towed away by a police launch. Kate made almost no comment except to say that it was all something that should never have happened.

I had called Andrea from our house in Largs, after the shootout and just before the police arrived, to say that everything was okay, and to let her know what was happening next. I had called her again from the hospital in Lindsay while Mike's wound was being treated; we had an emotional half-hour exchange and arranged to meet up later at Largs. Mike, George, and I arrived there first, and Kate and Andrea turned up ten minutes later. When the two women arrived, Andrea and I went into a long, silent, tearful, and thankful clutch. Our house and the garden where the showdown had occurred were cordoned off by police tape, so we asked an OPP officer to retrieve the keys to two of our cottages, and we settled into one of them and sat around in something of a daze. Mike and I explained in detail what had happened. George remained stricken and speechless, and I was able to take Kate aside and ask if she, Mike, and George could share one of the cottages for the night. Kate, who was the least traumatized of us all, but still evidently shaken, nodded her somewhat absent-minded agreement. We sat around looking at each other as the sun outside completed its swing across the sky and we drifted into late afternoon. There was general disbelief in what had just happened. We were all in shock, and it was obvious that for the next while we would have to take things a day at a time.

I made some noises about eating.

Nobody was hungry.

I went back to the house and asked the same officer to retrieve a bottle of brandy from our liquor cabinet. A couple of large shots of Courvoisier relaxed Andrea considerably. Mike declined because of the pain killers he had been given at the hospital. I spent ten quiet minutes with George, and we slowly downed our brandy together. He was on his own in some unhappy space.

We found the sheets, blankets, and pillows we needed in the cottages' linen closets, but nobody slept much that night. I spent almost the entire night lying next to Andrea, ready to help her through any panic attacks that might rear up. By four thirty, when the robins had begun their ever-renewed message of hope, Andrea was in a deep sleep. I knew, however, that I would insist on both of us spending time with a shrink, just as serving police officers do when they have killed or injured someone on the job. Andrea had had shocks beyond anything within her experience. PTSD is real, and it's a horrible and dangerous thing.

I rose quietly just after six thirty and went to our house. The crime scene people had finished sometime in the night and had taken down the police tape. They had also cleaned up some of the mess in the garden, but I got out the hose and spent twenty minutes removing the blood from the chair and cushions where Blondie had been hit and flushing away the last of his blood from the cottage wall and the grass.

In the midst of this zombie activity, I stopped.

What do you think you're doing, Whelan? There's no way you can just walk back in here as though nothing has happened. The route forward was clear.

I selected changes of clothes for Andrea and me, picked up our two toiletry bags, emptied everything I thought might be needed from the fridge into a large cloth shopping bag, and lugged it all back to the cottage where we had spent the night. Andrea was still in a deep, if not necessarily sound, sleep. At the cottage, two doors down, Mike and George were out cold as well, but Kate was up.

I walked outside with her.

"I don't know how to thank you, Kate. You've been a lifesaver for Andrea. For all of us."

"I think there will be a lot more talking needed", Kate said. "Andrea's in rough shape."

"Yes. I know. Will you be able to come to our place from time to time for dinner?"

Kate was nodding and smiling. "Yes, of course."

Kate and I walked on a little.

"That was a good move on your part, getting Andrea to take on house repairs", she said.

"Oh! She mentioned it?"

"After we'd had a couple of drinks and another good weep, I think being able to talk about it helped distract her from all the horrors. She hardly talked about anything else."

"Well, she made it plain to me that things needed shaking up. For a while", I said, "I was becoming really concerned that we were beginning to drift apart."

Kate smiled at me.

"Not a chance", she said. "I know Andrea. She wouldn't let that happen."

There was a short pause here and an attempt by Kate at what seemed unaccustomed subtlety. "She knows there's competition out there."

I looked at Kate in surprise.

"Relax, Mark", she said through a laugh. "There's no way Andrea's ever going to let go of you."

We walked on a bit further.

"Look", Kate said. "I have to go. I've got a big job today, and I don't want to be late starting it."

"Yes. Of course. Thanks, Kate. Thanks", and I kissed her forehead and pulled her into a long embrace of friendship. I then walked back with her to her car and waved to her as she drove off.

By nine o'clock, Mike and Andrea were up, and Andrea and I had changed into fresh clothes. The cottage Andrea and I had spent the night in was a nice one, had a fully equipped modern kitchen and a large outdoor patio table and umbrella. I suggested that we all have some breakfast. They showed no enthusiasm, so I insisted and eventually browbeat them into it. Andrea was reasonably rested but in a flat mood. George was meek, listless, and silent. Mike had seen trauma before and knew what to expect, but he was groggy from the throbbing pain in his shoulder, the result of him weaning himself off the pills he had accepted reluctantly at the hospital and then forgotten about despite his promise to continue taking them for three days more.

I whipped up a monster omelette, cooked a complete package of bacon, and prepared ample toast, then herded Andrea, Mike, and

George out to the garden. It was a brilliant morning. Flocks of birds in the canopy above us told us in no uncertain terms to get rid of the long faces and that if we weren't going to eat all that grub, they would. We picked at the food initially, but then fell on it as our hunger rekindled. George looked at nobody and ate mechanically. To all intents and purposes, he wasn't there.

Andrea laid down her fork on a plate that still had half its original helping of breakfast, and she began to weep silently. Mike and I both moved toward her, sandwiching her in reassurance, and I put my arm around her and drew her gently to me. She responded by laying her head on my shoulder and weeping in choking gasps. There was no point in saying "it's all right" or something similar, because it wasn't all right at all. At length, Andrea's tears tapered off, and I coaxed her into finishing her breakfast. George went inside and stretched out on a couch.

We left the breakfast things where they were and Andrea and I set out on a longish walk around Largs. The gun battle had been impossible to miss, but word had evidently got around to the Largs residents, helping to fill in the rest of the story. People came out of their cottages offering condolences and support. Such gestures had seemed before today to be well-meaning but pointless, useless. However, after almost twenty people had stopped us during our walk, it was clear that we were not alone. Wally Harris placed an arm awkwardly over Andrea's shoulders. James and Gladys Nelson each made a point of giving Andrea hugs and smiles of encouragement. I noticed the strong response of thanks and gratitude that these gestures elicited from Andrea.

We weren't alone.

Thirty-four

In the week that followed, life slowly returned to something close to normal. Kate came by two days after the shootout to collect Andrea, and they went off to spend time together. During that day Jimmy and I disposed of the chair and cushions that had been soaked in Blondie's blood. We also cleared away the debris that once had been Andrea's picnic table. Jimmy trimmed off the shattered pieces and bundled it up to give to James Nelson, who was sure to find a good use for waste mahogany. Jimmy and I went out, bought a replacement table, and assembled it. The police had done the necessary forensic work on Dickson's car while it was in place, half in and half out of the pool, and then they had towed it away.

The following day Mike awoke early, and it was evident that his shoulder was on the mend. He spoke to me about having to get back to Toronto, and I told him to work to his own schedule. But Mike was evidently not ready just yet to assume that we would be all right left to our own devices.

"What are you going to do?" he asked.

Guessing that Mike wanted to know whether I was coming through this mess okay, I explained what I planned to do over the next few days. Mike nodded, sufficiently satisfied, and said that he would be heading back to town the following day. The rest of that day, Jimmy and I started the work needed to repair the damage to the tiles around the pool, replaced the screen in the cold storage room, and filled in the ruts in the grass that Dickson had created as his car had skidded around the carport and slewed toward the pool. Andrea had gone off to have lunch with Kate and returned midafternoon. She and Mike spent a few hours in desultory chat, taking short walks around Largs, and nodding in easy chairs. That evening, I made us spicy ribs, rice lightly flavoured in sesame oil and hoisin sauce, and steamed mixed vegetables.

On Thursday, the next day, Mike loaded up his things, said a long and touchingly awkward farewell to Andrea, gave me a huge bear hug, and then set off for Toronto. About an hour later, Andrea and I drove George back to Toronto, but this time George was in the front seat and Andrea was in the back, keeping up a fairly constant flow of talk with George. Within an hour, George had relaxed noticeably, and we tried as best we could to satisfy ourselves that he was going to be okay on his own and to make him understand that he should call us immediately, even if all he wanted to do was talk. George was quieter than normal, but we didn't read too much into this. He was hardly forthcoming even at the best of times.

When we reached George's apartment building, we convinced him to have lunch with us since we didn't want just to drop him at his door and drive off. Over lunch, George thanked us in his own way, which was almost incomprehensibly halting, but at the same time evidently heartfelt and quite affecting. He said he would take the rest of the day off, and go to work again in the morning. He then said that he would call me at Largs later that evening. This was unexpected, but I took it as a good sign.

Before leaving Largs to take George back to Toronto, we both pondered not returning to Largs that evening, staying instead in our condo in town. But once in Toronto, we decided, practically in unison, that there was unfinished emotional work at Largs and that we couldn't just hide from it. But while we were in town, I did two other things.

First, I took an hour to arrange for a new cellphone. The one Blondie had taken from me was nowhere to be found, and was now likely at the bottom of the lake.

Second, I drove to the hardware chain warehouse where George worked, explained who I was and why I was there, and eventually was introduced to George's manager, an interesting and bubbly middle-aged man named William Owen. At that time of day, George would normally be working at his backroom post, and Owen showed us where this was, where George worked. It was just one of a thousand other nondescript work places. I had explained my connection to George, described recent events to Owen, asked him to keep an eye on George, and gave him my contact information.

During our return drive to Largs, neither of us spoke much. I was hoping for a quiet evening with Andrea to figure out what we were going to do next.

Back at Largs we parked outside the cottage that was our temporary accommodation, and we walked to Wally Harris' shop and picked up the ingredients for a generic but tasty chicken stir-fry. Having offered his good neighbour support earlier, Wally sensibly fell back into his merchant's role, talking about the weather, his son's success in the local baseball team, and several other items able to soothe nerves set ajangle by recent events. Andrea and I returned to our cottage, not yet being ready to face the house. I prepared the evening meal, and Andrea took a long telephone call from Kate. Just as Andrea and I were finishing dinner, Mike phoned, and the force of his ebullient personality was just what I needed. He and I talked about everything and nothing for forty minutes. Ten minutes after Mike had hung up, I was surprised to receive a call from George and even more surprised that he was calmer than I had expected. I promised to call him again soon and arrange a meet up in Toronto, and I floated the notion that he might like to consider another visit to Largs later in the summer.

After that Andrea and I sat out on the patio, in the very mild summer evening air, and killed the half-bottle of sambuca that I had picked up while we were in town.

Friday dawned overcast and cool. Andrea and I had breakfast outside and considered our day. I said I wanted to work more with Jimmy to repair the pool. Andrea surprised me somewhat when she said she wanted to clean up the two cottages we had used over the past several days, do the linen, and move back into our house that afternoon. I wasn't too sure about this, but the sharp electric edges of memory were beginning to wear smooth, and as we had to move back to the house sooner or later, I agreed with Andrea's judgment that it might as well be sooner.

We set about doing the things we had planned, and the day passed surprisingly quickly. Instead of cooking for ourselves that evening, we decided to have dinner at Kelvin Place, and we sat out afterwards on the patio being soothed by the gentle lapping presence of Balsam Lake. That night, Andrea slept deeply.

The next day, Saturday, passed as well.

At the end of that next day, Andrea and I put out the word that we would be spending the evening at Kelvin Place, and that anyone who felt in the mood should drop by. And drop by they did.

Over the course of the evening, almost a hundred people turned up. They came singly, in couples, and in groups, and we sat around over finger food, soft drinks, bottles of beer, and a few carafes of wine. Not many questions were put to us. Instead the residents of Largs simply closed ranks, and in their quiet country way they talked about the everyday things that filled their lives. It was all so practical, so normal, and so full of the importance of day-to-day life that it made the recent violence we had known seem like just an unwelcome irrelevance. This, I realized, was how the wisdom of the country was brought to bear in dealing with life's curve balls. To my shame and embarrassment it was only now, for the first time, that I really appreciated it.

A good-natured argument broke out, a couple of tables away, about the timing and the best methods for pruning apple and pear trees. Once the gardening theme was broached, there was no stopping it. Evidently it was shaping up to be a good year for onions and carrots in the gardens in Largs, and the sandy soil at the eastern end of the village was promising a bumper crop of potatoes. Harvey Wilder's complaint that his pea plants were faring particularly badly for reasons he couldn't understand unleashed a flood of lawyer jokes. There was talk of roof shingling, insulation, water pipe repairs, and other solid practicalities of life that denied any houseroom to the violence of late that the village had known. Andrea and I both smiled at the sheer healthy practicality of the evening.

Andrea's face, in particular, signalled her feeling of inclusion. Although raised a city girl, she had had enough experience living in Largs to understand what was going on without anyone having to explain it. The walk home from Kelvin Place, under the stars and hearing Balsam Lake murmuring sweet somethings just to our right, felt almost normal. As we entered the house, Andrea yawned and said she was off to bed, while I mumbled something about doing some reading. In fact, I spent the time in the den, first of all thinking for half an hour, then jotting down a few things in my good ideas notebook. Although the trauma and violence of the recent past had now faded to an endurable if sinister whisper, there were a couple of loose ends that flapped noisily in my mind. I wanted very much to believe that the entire episode had been put finally to bed, but …

At eleven thirty I turned in, joining Andrea, who clocked a night of sound sleep in our house in Largs, her second night of good sleep since all this had begun. I woke several times during the night, the last time at about four o'clock, nagged by the realization that something important was wrong or missing or unfinished. And I had the strong sense that the feeling wasn't about to go away.

The next day, Jimmy and I finished the repairs around the pool, and Andrea gave the house a thorough cleaning. Just after noon Mike appeared unexpectedly at Largs. Andrea and I were sharing a western sandwich for lunch at our breakfast table.

"*Salve*, fellow warriors!"

Mike had jettisoned the sling, and although he was favouring his left arm slightly, he had full mobility and evidently was able to drive.

"Coffee, Mike?" Andrea asked, rising to get it even before a reply was in play.

"You couldn't charge it up with a dash of elixir, could you?"

"Sure, Mike", she replied, "but the only milk we have is whole milk."

It was one of the few times I have ever seen Mike lost for words.

"Look at him!" I said, in response to Andrea's impish smile. "He's vapour-locked!" I rose and headed to the living room. "I've got some octane here that should do the trick."

A good chug of Talisker caused a smile slowly to replace Mike's expression of a man who had just been bushwhacked.

"Guess I need to watch myself", he said. "She's picking up a lot from you, Mark."

"More like the other way round, Mike."

"I'll leave you two now", Andrea said, collecting our plates and heading for the sink.

"Ah, no!" Mike wailed in mock disappointment, having recovered his repartee balance. "It was just becoming interesting!"

"Later", Andrea sang over her shoulder as she moved off toward the stairs.

Mike and I drank our coffees for a moment. I knew that Mike had not come here just as an excuse for a spin in the country.

"What's up?" I asked.

"Well, a couple of things. Cromarty wants to speak to you."

"Cromarty? He has my number. What's he…?"

"He asked me when you might be back in town. It was pretty clear that he wants to do it face-to-face, whatever "it" is. I really don't know what he has in mind", Mike said.

I pondered this for a moment.

"But you didn't drive up here just to tell me that, Mike."

"No", Mike said, then just looked straight at me for a moment. "Fact is, I just can't shake the feeling that we've missed something."

This comment by Mike was far from welcome. It had reawakened my own similar concern, something I had almost succeeded in suppressing, and it had cut off at the knees the beginnings of a buoyant mood that had begun to replace it. But I maintained a calm exterior.

"Missed something", I said, only half in question. "Such as?"

Mike shook his head in frustration.

"I don't know", he said. "I've gone through everything we know about this. The police have enough evidence, or will get enough, to bang up Dickson for a good stretch. Anyroad, I doubt that Dickson will last long in the slammer. And Cromarty will get enough out of Dickson and his two lackeys, I hope, to be able to trace back at least some distance and uncover more of the details behind how this caper fits into his own cases. We know that Blondie and his crew were just local villains, reasonably successful to be sure, but really just small fry. Ditto for Diver Dan and his mates, but that's where things become murky. I have no idea how Dan and the boys got into this game."

I had risen in the middle of Mike's speech, waving to Mike to continue, while I fetched my good ideas notebook. As I returned to the table and regained my seat, Mike continued.

"The problem here, Mark, and I've come across it more than once, is that the police solve specific crimes. Once they have a suspect and find enough evidence to convict, they're done. But this is all driven just by specific crimes. There's almost always a web of other threads that might well be worth pursuing, but an investigation always has a scope and the smaller that scope the better."

"That's nothing new", I said.

"I agree entirely. But my feeling, and I can't shake it, is that there's still something out there, something that could be important for us, for you."

"You realize", I began, clutching at straws, "that this could be just a free-floating worry, not connected to anything, that there might be nothing at all out there."

"Yes, but you also know, Mark, that in this business it's almost always a serious mistake to ignore strong intuitions."

We sat pondering those two marker posts.

I rose to refill my coffee. Mike sat in silence a while longer.

"Surely you don't think that we've got to the heart of the matter?" Mike said, rather plaintively.

I shook my head, mostly in confusion, just wanting the whole business to be over, but realizing that Mike had put words to my own subconscious unrest.

"What have you got in your Book of Secrets there?" Mike asked at length.

I sat looking at my notes and said nothing for a few minutes.

"When were you planning to go back to Toronto, Mike?"

"Ahh! I see that my welcome has already worn down to the cord", but then Mike held up his hands as I was about to object.

"I need to be back for tomorrow morning", Mike said. "Why?"

There was a long delay before I spoke.

"I did some doodling last night, Mike, but came to no resolution. I was unsure about something. You've just made me realize that the situation is not wrapped up, despite the fact that Dickson has been hauled away in chains."

Another delay.

"There's a big dark horse here, Mike."

An inquiring tilt of Mike's head.

"Harold", I said. "George's brother."

"Harold?" Mike replied, in surprise. "He dayd."

"Yes, but he's a very odd outlier in this whole mess. How did he get involved? If we find out that, I suspect we'll know how Dan and the boys got involved."

There was a short silence at the end of which I pulled out a sheet of paper that I had folded and stuck in my notebook.

"Take a look at this. It's Harold's will", and I passed the paper over to Mike.

Mike unfolded it and scanned it quickly.

"Looks pretty straightforward", he said and began folding it again. Then he stopped and spread it out once more.

"Wait a minute! There's something not right here", and he placed the sheet down on the table where we could both read it.

Last Will and Testament of Harold Manley Barbour

I, Harold Manley Barbour, being sound of mind, here record my last will:

On my death, all my possessions are to go to my dear and faithful brother George.

May George be able to avoid the persecution I have endured.

I looked at Mike.

"That day, in the lawyer's office with George, I looked this will over very quickly. I was in a hurry to get back to our condo and head off to Largs, so I didn't notice the bizarre last sentence."

Mike looked at the document again.

"What do you think it means?" he asked.

"I think we would have a better shot at knowing if we had Harold's computer."

"So you think there's somebody else involved."

"Yes."

"Then why didn't Harold just name him? This will was entirely secure once Harold had passed it over to his lawyer."

"I suspect that Harold didn't name him because Harold didn't know who 'he' was."

Thirty-five

Andrea was somewhat surprised when I checked with her about me going to Toronto with Mike for the afternoon. Once I explained why she just nodded and said to go ahead, that she was going to repair some curtains and spend a few hours on some work she wanted to send off to the office later in the day.

"You're sure? I should be back late this afternoon in time to make us something nice for dinner."

She was sitting at her sewing table, and she rose, came over to me, and we had a little clench.

"Go!" she said and pulled one of my ears.

Mike and I walked out to the carport.

"Where you going?" Mike asked, as I peeled off toward my car.

"What's it look like? If I go with you, I'll have no way back."

"Hmmm. Guess my welcome was worn down a lot further than I expected. Now I'm *persona non effing grata*."

I stood there clueless for a second too long.

"I'm coming back this afternoon. With you, Mark. Back to Largs. Chop, chop, laddie!"

"I thought you had to be in town for something tomorrow morning."

"Rescheduled. Come on. Get in. Winter's coming."

The trip to town seemed to last no time at all, as Mike and I exchanged that relaxed banter that always, for us, carries a large freight of subliminal knowledge.

As we blew down the Don Valley Parkway, Mike piped up again.

"What do you want to do first?"

"First", I said, "we should stop at a decent coffee shop. Then I'd like to go see Cromarty, but I'll need to do that alone. Then I want to pick up what we'll need for dinner tonight, and by that time we should be on our way north again. It'll be into rush hour, but that can't be helped."

Mike pulled in to a Tim Horton's that wasn't too busy, and we bought a couple of coffees and retired to a table in the corner. The leather zip-up documents folder that I had brought along contained my good ideas notebook and a blank pad for taking notes during my meeting with Cromarty. I pulled out my notes and Harold's will.

Mike stared at the will again and wrinkled his brow.

"Persecution", he said in puzzlement.

"What do you think Harold, Diver Dan and his crew, and Dickson's crowd have in common?" I asked.

"Apart from them all being treasure hunters?" Mike offered.

And then, before I could speak, Mike added, "and all being criminals?"

"Apart from those two things, probably nothing. Or, at least, let's lay that out as a hypothesis."

"Okay", Mike said uncertainly.

"And what would those three groups of people need in order to do what they did?"

"Is this going to be a game of twenty questions?" Mike asked impatiently.

"Sorry, Mike. I'm not deliberately trying to be annoying. But a vague theory has suggested itself to me and I want your help in stepping through it carefully. Okay. I'll lay it out for you as statements rather than questions. Harold, Diver Dan, and Dickson don't seem to have much in common. And yet it seems that they were all engaged pretty seriously in trying to find something in Balsam Lake. To spend that effort, and to engage in those risks, it seems to me that they needed two things: information and incentive."

Mike was paying close attention now.

"And the incentive was loot?" Mike asked.

I nodded.

"Hang on, Mark! Are you saying that there's some master puppeteer who's been running this whole show?"

"I'm not saying anything with certainty, Mike. I have a vague idea, and I'm trying to think my way through a fog."

"Okay. Sorry. Yes. It's possible. And I suppose that noticing Harold's complaint of persecution is what started you down that road."

"Precisely."

"And the 'information' you referred to, that would be something that led them all to Balsam Lake."

"Yes", I said. "At least that's what I'm presuming at this point."

"And before we go much further in this speculation, we need some information to corroborate one element of this theory, at the very least."

"I see that we're on the same track, Mike."

"And the source of the information that our villains needed is what we have to find, and if we find that source, we've probably got it all."

"You're my man, Mike! Right on the button!"

We finished our coffee and headed for the door.

"You go talk to Cromarty, Mark. I'll deliver you to his den. In the meantime, I have some research to do."

As we crossed the car park to Mike's Volvo, I raised Cromarty on my cellphone. His invitation for me to come around right away, without a hint of impatience at his day being disrupted, was a good sign.

Bent Cromarty's desk was in a corner of an office that housed six or seven people, and the entire space was surprisingly neat and tidy. I learned later that this was because the woman in charge of this unit was an absolute tartar when it came to dealing with paper: completing forms, filing them, getting them off desks. It took only a couple of brutal public tongue-lashings to convince any wayward novice that they didn't have a better idea after all.

Cromarty downed tools the instant he saw me. He smiled, rose from his chair, offered a warm handshake, and escorted me to the privacy of an interview room. We dispensed with preliminaries quickly and dived straight into business.

"I want to thank you for giving me a prompt inside track on the Dickson business. It could have been days before that information got through the bureaucracy otherwise."

"You're welcome, Bent. Getting a case like Dickson stitched up quickly is in everyone's interest." I'm sure we both recognized also that my balance of personal favours had swung strongly into positive territory. Having debts owing sprinkled about liberally can be an 'open sesame' for a PI, both in terms of finding work and enlisting under-the-table help to solve tough cases. We both made affirmative head motions, reminding me of rear-window nodding dogs.

"I assume you have, or at least the OPP has, enough to put Dickson away", I said into a lengthening silence.

"More than enough." Short pause here. "But I did want to ask how it was that the shootout occurred."

I could see where this was coming from. The OPP had taken the position that Mike and I had been borderline irresponsible in letting things get to the state they did, that we ought to have involved them earlier, and that a shootout in a village was an exceptionally dangerous event to have occurred. Bent wanted to make sure that he could put his own stamp on events and claim some credit but at the same time have solid leeward protection from any political squalls that might arise.

"I presume you have the statement I gave to the OPP? Dickson's three guys abducted both Andrea and me, we were both lucky enough to get free of that, and as a result, whatever those three wanted me to help them find remained undiscovered. So Dickson made a desperate last-minute attempt to retrieve the situation. He had to get past Mike, but Mike was armed, and that's when the shooting began. These events all happened very quickly from end to end. There was no relaxing interlude when some Greek chorus was advising us to call the OPP. But I can give you only our side of the story. You'll have to get the rest from Dickson."

"Alas", Cromarty began, "Dickson is saying very little." Cromarty tapped the table irritably.

"Is there anything you might have done differently in hindsight?" Cromarty asked at length.

"No", I replied without hesitation. "Before the shootout we had no idea just who Dickson was. We knew that whoever was driving the action was ruthless and was becoming desperate. That was clear enough when Andrea and I were abducted. But at the time, there was no big picture. It was all fog. Later, when Dickson's men failed to retrieve whatever they were after, we had no real idea what Dickson might do next. At one extreme, he might have just given up and left us to live happily ever after, or he could do what he actually did do, which was to try to blast his way through. Mike and I prepared for the worst outcome, and that turned out to be the prudent thing to do."

Cromarty digested this, although there was nothing here he didn't already know.

"Once again, in hindsight, was there anything that you think might have been done to avert any of these events? For example, why didn't you alert the OPP when your wife was abducted?"

"You're not married, Bent, so in answer to the second of your questions, I don't expect that the reaction I had would also naturally come to you. Between the time I knew that Andrea had been abducted and the time I was taken hostage was a matter of seconds. If Dickson had got what he wanted out there on the lake, both Andrea and I would have been dead meat. My best chance of keeping Andrea alive, until I could find some way of getting her back, was to stay alive myself and prevent Dickson getting whatever it was in the lake that he wanted. At that point, I had no cellphone, so there was no way I could have contacted the OPP. But I wouldn't have done that anyway, since it probably would have cost me Andrea. That's my answer to your second question. Your first question is a pretty broad one, Bent. I'm not sure just what you're getting at."

Cromarty pondered what I had just told him. Then he resumed.

"Well, Harold Barbour's death appears to have been tied into all this somehow. The tossing of his apartment was hardly coincidental."

"You have me at a disadvantage there, Bent. I still know nothing more than I learned from my fifteen-second glance at the place. If the police found nothing more, I suspect that there was nothing more to be found."

There was another silence here.

"It's a strange case", Bent mused. "We have solid evidence to put Dickson and his stooges away, but at the same time there are massive holes in the overall story."

"Loose ends is nothing new. I sympathize. I know how much this sort of thing bothered me when I was in your chair. But is there nothing you've been able to get from Dickson's stooges?"

Cromarty shook his head.

"No. Nothing important, anyway. It looks as though Dickson operated on a strict need-to-know basis, and his stooges evidently needed to know next to nothing."

"But you have names for them now, I presume?"

"Yes. And I can return a small favour to you", he said and handed me a slip of paper that I pocketed. It wasn't much of a favour, since the names would have come out anyway, and I could easily have waited.

Cromarty and I talked of other things for a few minutes. He was in an expansive mood, and it wasn't lost on me that he was using quite a lot of valuable time here.

"Well, thank you for the information, Bent", I said as I rose. We shook hands. "Let's keep in touch", I added, handing him my card. Cromarty smiled what I thought was a genuine and grateful smile, and it looked as though he and I were onto a better long-term footing.

Once outside, I texted Mike, sending him the names of the two living stooges and the dead stooge. At the same time, I arranged to meet him at a supermarket close to an entrance to the Don Valley Parkway.

Thirty-six

I took a taxi to the supermarket and met Mike as arranged. We went around the aisles together, and it took little time to select some good-looking portions of frozen fish and the ingredients needed to produce a nice pasta accompaniment.

We went through the checkout and carried our supplies to Mike's car.

"Did your research work out the way you expected?" I asked.

"Yeah. Roughly", Mike said. "How was the meet with Cromarty?"

"About what I expected", I said, "but I think he and I now have an understanding."

"Those names were from Cromarty?"

"Yes."

Mike drove out of the supermarket car park, deftly wove through traffic, and within a couple of minutes we were sailing north on the Parkway. It was just shy of three thirty and, although the traffic was heavy and building, it was moving well. In half an hour we were clear of the bulk of suburbia, and after another forty minutes, as we exited at the Highway 35/115 junction, Mike relaxed.

"I managed to get the names of Diver Dan and his crew", he said. "They were like Blondie's crowd, just a bunch of minor villains for hire."

"Any hint of how they came into this business?"

"No", Mike said neutrally. "It looks as though they just appeared out of nowhere. Blondie and his bunch were hired by Dickson, but I haven't been able to find any direct link that brought Dickson into the whole affair. Was Cromarty forthcoming on anything the police have learned?"

"Yes", I said. "He was quite willing to tell me things, but there's not much to tell. Dickson has just clammed up, and the two living stooges know essentially nothing."

"Not surprising", Mike said, looking straight ahead.

"No. Not surprising", I repeated.

Mike drove on and we changed the subject. I asked Mike about his work, and he was happy to expand on some of the more interesting things he was pursuing. I spoke a bit about the usual stable of slightly depressing and salacious problems I had lined up and would soon be working on for clients. Mike suggested, not by any means for the first time, that we should amalgamate our investigative practices, but I deflected that one, feeling that it was better to keep some distance between us, combining forces only by exception.

The discussion drifted off to isolated short exchanges, interspersed by long companionable silences during which I just enjoyed the scenery that was drifting by. We passed the turning into Lindsay, meaning that we would be at Largs in about another half-hour.

"Where do you think all this is coming from? I mean, how have people become so convinced that there's something valuable in Balsam Lake?"

"Specifically, Mike, I don't know. If you do some Google searches, you'll find all sorts of stories about treasure. Some of them are just fantasy, like the one about Cortez burying a pile of gold near Sarnia. Why would Cortez come thousands of miles from Mexico to bury some gold at an unremarkable spot? But there are others that have a least some nominal link to actual history, like the one about French gold being buried somewhere in or around Kingston."

We drove on for a minute.

"I expect", I continued, "that somebody has come up with one of these buried-gold yarns plus several other independent pieces of information to make it more credible in their minds."

"But", I added, "I still find the whole situation hard to swallow. That doesn't matter though. People have died in an attempt to find something. That can't simply be waved off. Dickson and the others are now out of the picture, so they pose no further risk. But if there's somebody else who's been the author of all this grief, well, I can't just walk away from that, not given how it has impacted Andrea and me."

Mike nodded.

"You're concerned that he might just try again at some point."

"Yes, that's what worries me."

The turn into Largs was just a few miles ahead.

"Okay, Mark, my boy. Enough of this for now. We have a meal and an evening ahead of us to enjoy, so let's pick up this thread some other time."

It was just before six and we had begun preparations for dinner and poured glasses of wine when my cellphone buzzed. The conversation was short, and during it I said almost nothing. Looking at Andrea and Mike I said, "We need to go back to Toronto."

"What? Right now?" Andrea asked.

"Yes. George is dead. Cromarty has found something. Sounds like it's important."

I began putting all the food back in the fridge while Mike sent a few text messages.

"I'm coming too!" Andrea said, and to demonstrate that she was not expecting and would not entertain any objections, she immediately set about collecting some things we would need to stay the night at our condo in town.

Having dealt with the food, I went to the hall closet.

"You'll probably need a jacket. The green one?" I asked Andrea as I grabbed mine.

"Yes. Thanks."

We left the house and I locked up while Mike and Andrea strode purposefully toward Mike's car, Andrea carrying a small soft-sided bag. Somehow I had assumed that Mike would come back to Largs after the business in Toronto, whatever it turned out to be, was completed, and Mike's actions confirmed my assumption.

The trip back to Toronto was three parts nervous anticipation, two parts trepidation, and, for me, one part relief. I had the sense that we were in an odd space between one can of worms being closed (the relief) and another being opened (all the rest). The recent violent events at Largs, and the brief period since then, had felt like a climax and a denouement. We had seen the end of something. The exercise of picking up pieces and moving on had begun. Now, however, there was the feeling of fresh tension building, a further climax approaching, the threat of new storm clouds gathering.

During the first ten minutes of the trip, Mike and Andrea both grilled me on my short telephone discussion with Cromarty. I couldn't do more than repeat what I had said already: George was dead and Cromarty had found something. And Cromarty wanted me to be there for the next phase.

"Next phase?" Andrea said in a knitted-brow voice.

"That's all he said. 'Next phase'."

Silence fell among us. I didn't know just what Cromarty had found, but suspected that it would be unveiled in due course. My own thoughts had turned quickly to George, and I found myself wondering, in some distress, just how it was that he had died. And why. I was quite convinced, glancing across at Andrea, that very similar thoughts were occupying her, and I could almost feel the waves of empathy and sadness radiating out from her.

This initial silence lengthened to cover most of the trip, while individually we mulled over our thoughts. When we were twenty minutes out from Toronto, I called Cromarty to let him know that we were arriving imminently. Cromarty directed us to come to his office and to park in the reserved spaces behind the building if we needed to, and he would look after a permit for us. Andrea asked Mike to take her to our condo first, since there were things she had to do there. Mike said he would drop me next and go off to deal with things that had piled up, saying that he would be available instantly by cellphone.

I found Cromarty, but in contrast to my previous visit he now seemed under some considerable stress. Despite this, his lips bore a quirky little smile of incipient victory. He led me to the same interview room, and we took seats across from each other.

"What's happening, Bent? What's the story with George?"

A shadow passed quickly over Cromarty's face as though my question asked him to deal with a minor detail he would have preferred to leave until later.

"He overdosed on sleeping pills. Apparently his manager became concerned when George didn't show up this morning, and at midafternoon he convinced George's super to check on him. The super called EMS and then called us. The paramedics determined that George had probably been dead for at least twelve hours."

"Was there a note? Any indication that this was linked to the events at Balsam Lake?" I asked.

"No, no note", Bent replied. "And we don't see any link."

One might be able to reach that conclusion, I thought brutally, if one ignores the effect on him of the death of his brother, his one family link to the past. But a discussion of that with Bent would be pointless.

"It sounds like you've also had a break in the case, Bent", I began.

"Indeed we have. And we're about to make an arrest." Bent paused here, rather smugly I thought, and it reminded me that people like him were one reason I had decided to leave the police. Instead of prodding him, which was what he seemed to want me to do, I just sat and waited.

"In due course, we'll be arresting Arthur Donaldson, the senior partner at Clarence and Donaldson", Bent said finally, clearly a bit disappointed that I hadn't been bouncing on my chair wanting to know all the details immediately.

"Donaldson?" I said in disbelief.

Cromarty nodded, gratified at my surprise and looking forward to explaining things to a lesser detective.

"Donaldson has been fiddling the books of his own company, siphoning off clients' money. The information we have looks solid. We'll be gathering evidence very soon and I'm convinced that it will point directly at him."

"Well, congratulations on solving an unrelated crime. What about the events at Balsam Lake."

"We're convinced", Cromarty began, "that they were orchestrated by Donaldson."

"Orchestrated? For what purpose?"

"We'll get there. Money has been seen going into one of his accounts, then being withdrawn and vanishing."

"What do you mean, Bent, 'money has been seen'?"

"That's all I can tell you for now."

I thought I saw what was going on here, and I struggled not to let my irritation show. Sure, Cromarty probably had let me know about George because he had been my client. But it seemed that he thought he had pulled off a coup by fingering Donaldson, and he was still trying to pump me for anything that would make his great feat of detection appear even greater. I decided to extract myself from this charade as quickly as possible but with fewest ruffled feathers.

"And what do you conclude from that?" I asked, trying to suppress my skepticism and annoyance.

"As I said. We're working on it." He paused here, fiddled with a pencil, then raised his eyes to meet mine. "Do you have any thoughts?"

"No. They would be just speculation, not worth anything."

"Any speculation, then?" he prompted.

"No, Bent. I'll just wait for you to work the case."

But I had no intention of just waiting.

Thirty-seven

On the street outside Bent's office, I had called Mike, and now we were sitting at a quiet corner table at Il Vagabondo. It's not a cheap place, but that keeps out the army of financial district thirty-somethings whose off-hours seem to be filled by vats of beer and ninety decibel conversations about day trading.

I related to Mike my discussion with Cromarty. He frowned a couple of times but said and asked nothing while I was speaking.

"So what now?" he asked at length.

"Well, first of all, laying this situation at Arthur Donaldson's feet is just not credible. Without even breaking a sweat, I can think of several other possibilities."

"Such as?"

"Well", I began, "there's always the old standbys – blackmail, difficulties due to bad judgment, a frame-up."

We discussed possibilities and approaches. After five minutes, I had laid my pocket notebook on the table and was scribbling in it.

"Have we missed anything?" I asked eventually.

"No. We're good."

Looking at my watch, I said that I thought we had time for another quick glass of wine. At the same time, I had my cellphone out and was doing some searching, finding what I wanted after a few minutes.

Our glasses of wine arrived, and I went over my notes as I sipped.

"Okay", Mike said, setting down his empty glass with an authoritative thud. "Let's go and visit Donaldson."

It was just short of nine in the evening when Mike parked his car and we got out at the address provided by Google. Donaldson lived in a house that was by far not the largest on Vesta Drive, but it was one of the most elegant.

When the front door opened, Donaldson's expression transformed slowly from mild curiosity to complete puzzlement.

"Mr. Whelan!" he said, after a short delay. "What … er … I wasn't expecting to see you this evening."

"Yes, I'm sorry for this late and unannounced arrival, sir. May we come in for just a moment?"

Donaldson's advance into his evening had got as far as removing his jacket and loosening his tie, and he stood in the doorway for a moment holding a small glass of something and looking befuddled.

"Yes, of course. Please come in, although I warn you that I will need to show you out again in just a few moments."

"That's all right, sir", I said. "We'll take very little of your time."

We moved into an exquisitely furnished living room, I introduced Mike, and we were asked to take seats but not offered anything to drink.

Before Donaldson could start questioning us on why we were there, I began putting to him questions of my own. There were eight questions I wanted to ask him. At the fourth question, he stumbled. We didn't get past the sixth question. By then his manner had become very frosty and he simply told us we could leave.

Back in the car, Mike looked pensive. "It was just about what we expected", he said eventually. "It does look like it centres around the nephew."

"It does", I agreed. "But why do you think he's still hanging around?"

"I don't know for sure", Mike said slowly, "but I think we need to be pessimistic. We have to assume that he's going to try again."

Right now we needed information quickly. I could think of only one way to get it in just a few minutes.

"Jocko?" Mike exclaimed in mock horror, but then calmed himself. "But you're right. He's likely our best source."

"Though I can guess what his reaction will be when we contact him this time of night and ask for while-you-wait service."

"If we offer him double or triple his normal rate", Mike offered phlegmatically, "that should tranquilize his pain nicely."

I called Jocko. Even though I used as much diplomacy as I could, I still had to hold the phone away from my ear as Jocko vented his indignation, but the offer of a lavish fee for fifteen minutes of work was oil poured generously onto Jocko's troubled waters. Jocko put me on hold briefly, but we had the information we wanted in less than ten minutes. I jotted a page of items in my pocket notebook.

Mike looked at me as I ended the call.

"Young nephew is up to his armpits in gambling debts", I said to Mike.

Mike nodded, looking pensive, but my bet was that he was thinking at a mile a minute.

"Okay. Here's what I think we need to do", Mike said, and he outlined his plan. I agreed and Mike drove to a small street off Eastern Avenue that had been renovated to a seriously upscale level. Mike parked midway between streetlights.

Consulting my pocket notebook, I made the call.

"Yeah!"

"James Donaldson?" I responded.

"Who's this?"

"My name is Mark Whelan, Mr. Donaldson."

A generous measure of suavity, similar to what I had observed at Clarence and Donaldson earlier that day, immediately flowed from the telephone.

"Ah! Mr. Whelan! It might be late but it's a pleasure to speak to you nonetheless. What could I do for you?"

"I think we both know why I'm calling you, Mr. Donaldson", I said.

"You have me at a disadvantage, Mr. Whelan. Perhaps it's just that I've had a long day."

"Cut the act, Donaldson. I know what you've been up to. Either we discuss a way for you to come clean, or I go straight to the police. Tonight."

"You're speaking in riddles, Mr. Whelan. And your tone surprises me. I don't know what's wrong, but I'm going to hang up now", and the line went dead immediately.

It took less than ten minutes. Donaldson emerged from a house sixty metres up the street, threw a large bag into the back seat, slid behind the wheel, drove to King Street, and turned left.

"Any bets he's headed for the airport?" I asked.

"No point in betting on a sure thing. Time to call Jocko again."

I made the call to Jocko, described what had just happened, and asked him to get in touch with his contact immediately. But I also asked Jocko to check on some travel history for me.

Thirty-eight

We assumed there would be no rush in dealing with what remained to be done, and it turned out that we were right.

Mike drove me back to our condo and then went home himself, but we agreed on an early start in the morning. I spent a couple of hours that night explaining everything to Andrea. She was aghast. There was no question that it made me feel unclean, and Andrea eventually said, with great reluctance, that she also could see no better way for the whole affair to have been wrapped up. But she did end in one strong and heartfelt statement.

"I dearly hope that nothing like this ever, ever happens again." It was part wish, part demand, and part threat.

Given the drained look on Andrea's face, I was a bit surprised when she agreed to join me over an Armagnac. She even smiled weakly at me over the top of her glass as I wished for a brighter tomorrow. Half an hour later we had both fallen into a deep and dreamless sleep.

It was just before eight o'clock the next morning when I joined Mike in his car, not having had breakfast or coffee but after writing a longish note to a still sleeping Andrea.

Mike and I arrived at Bent's office just as he was starting his day, and he was surprised and not really pleased to see us.

"We need to talk, Bent", I said without preamble, Mike and I having agreed that he would be a silent presence.

Cromarty looked pointedly at his watch.

"We need to talk *now*, Bent", I said more forcefully. "Can we use that interrogation room over there?" I began moving toward it before he had responded.

"Hang on, wait a minute", Cromarty said, rising from his seat, evidently irritated.

"Okay. We can talk right here in the middle of your office if that's what you prefer. Arthur Donaldson is the wrong man to go after in the Dickson case."

I knew that Cromarty would not want me to start broadcasting information around the squad room about wrinkles in his case, and he moved quickly to usher us toward the interrogation room.

"I'll give you a minute, then I'm going to have you thrown out. I don't have time for this. The Dickson case isn't the only one I'm working on." Cromarty gave me a meaningful glare before continuing. "So you think Arthur Donaldson is the wrong man. Okay. I'll humour you for a few seconds. Who's your choice?"

"James Donaldson", I said. "The nephew."

"And you know this how?"

"My best judgment. Come on, Bent", I said in response to his dismissive scowl, "old Arthur Donaldson doesn't know the first thing about the underworld. Sure, you have some evidence that seems to point toward him, but the nephew is not only savvy, he's also a slippery fish."

"And where's your evidence?" Cromarty countered.

"I don't have any, and you know very well that I can't be poking around in something the police are actively involved in. I've had ongoing business dealings with Arthur over the past few weeks, and in the course of that I've seen his nephew James up close. He's not the clean-as-a-whistle Ivy League type that he likes to present. I think you'll find that he's the one behind all this."

"Really? And the solid evidence we have that says otherwise?"

"It's just all a fit-up for Arthur."

"Okay. Your time's up", Cromarty said as he rose from his chair. "Just one more thing. Dickson is locked up. Why are you persisting in this?"

"That's simple, Bent. Sure, Dickson tried to kill Mike here. And he and his goons abducted both Andrea and me. And if the buck stopped at Dickson, everything would be fine. But if it doesn't, nothing is fine. So I suggest that you look at it all again, more closely."

At that point, Cromarty herded us out, evidently still not the least convinced.

Back in Mike's car, we discussed the situation. We agreed that we had now done all that we could. We also agreed that the risk was probably past, and if that was the case we would know within the next couple of weeks. But if not, well…

"How about some breakfast at our place, Mike?"

"Sounds first rate to me. Let's go."

When we arrived at our condo, Andrea was up, looking rested and more relaxed than she had been for some time.

"Mike's come by for some breakfast", I said.

"Is it all finished now?" Andrea asked me.

"Yes. Finished." I replied. In response to Mike's quizzical look, I added "Andrea's in the picture, Mike."

"Sit down, both of you", Andrea ordered. "Black coffee?"

"Yes, please", I answered, "but I have to – "

"No! My kitchen! I'm making breakfast! And you're both getting ham and eggs, sausage, home fries, and brown toast. Here's your coffee."

Breakfast included the cooking and eating of it and the cleaning up afterwards. All three of us pitched in on the clean-up, and by then the general mood had swung strongly upward. There were even outbursts of laughter. The pressure had been released, and we could climb out of the pressure cooker.

We looked around at a clean stove, clean table, and dishes draining in the rack, and we were all visited by that feeling one has on finishing a cracking good book that has your adrenalin pumping over its last forty pages, but then it's over. Mike broke the silence.

"You going back up to Largs now?"

"I hadn't thought about it", I said uncertainly.

"Yes. Definitely. In fact, right now", Andrea pronounced.

"Mind if I come along?" Mike asked. "Thing is", he continued, "it's been a long time since I just flopped and did nothing. And business is slow right now. Just a few days?"

"Okay", Andrea said decisively. "Off you go to your place, get some clothes, and be back here in twenty minutes. That's when we leave."

Mike cast a glance at me.

"Don't look at him", Andrea barked. "He's just the cook. Off you go to your place."

"Bugger that!" Mike countered. "We'll stop at Lindsay, I'll buy some T-shirts, shorts, swimming gear, socks. Let's go!"

Including the stop at Lindsay, where I stocked up on wine while Mike fretted over what colour underwear to get, it was three and a half hours later when we pulled into Largs. We got Mike settled in the spare room, Andrea headed straight for the infinity pool, and I did my triangular swim and had a long-delayed commune with Balsam Lake, the great water spirit of my youth.

I had just towelled off and was sitting at the picnic table soaking up sun when my cellphone buzzed.

There was a great deal of background noise, but the message came through clearly enough. I agreed most willingly to Kate's self-invitation to dinner later in the day. Kate said "I'll see you there" at about the same time as her plane roared past us out over the lake. Andrea's eyes sprang open, but I told her to relax, that Kate wasn't about to land, and relayed the arrangements made for that evening. I didn't mention that Kate had asked if we could have prime rib for dinner.

Things settled down then to one step up from somnolent. Andrea continued to unwind in the pool. Mike had dragged a large chaise longue down close to the lake and was lying immobile behind his sunglasses. By two thirty, Andrea had gone inside to lie down and get rid of the prune wrinkles from her long soak, and Mike had dragged his lounger into the shade. I dressed and took myself off to Wally's place to see if he could provision us for the evening's feast. To my delight, he had an excellent prime rib, a little too big for four of us, but I took it anyway. After picking up the vegetables we would need, I walked back home, put everything in the fridge, then worked out the timing for getting dinner ready.

Kate arrived at about six o'clock, when the meat and vegetables had only about another half an hour left of their slow roast in the barbecue. The evening was the usual random romp through that delightful mental landscape that emerged when we four got together. The time flew. Kate, having arrived by car, agreed readily to spend the night with us, and even though Andrea, Mike, and I had spent a day of almost zero stress and less effort, by eleven o'clock we were ready to turn in.

Of our originally planned two weeks at Largs, Andrea and I had less than a week left. Her business partners, well aware of what had been happening, didn't hesitate at all when Andrea said she wanted more time.

And we made good use of it.

We relaxed. We went for walks. We did a fair bit of impromptu and desultory socializing with people in Largs. But we did more than that.

We talked. Often well into the small hours. Sometimes there were three of us. While Mike was there, he proved to be an acute and sympathetic listener. Kate dropped in fairly regularly. And then there was John Woodhouse.

Naturally we discussed what had happened and why. It was in one of these three-way discussions that Mike prodded us, obviously interested to be sure that we really had come to terms with what had happened and that loose ends had been dealt with. Mike did this in his usual way: head on and after few preliminaries.

"I guess that we have Cromarty to thank, when it comes right down to it", Mike said.

"How do you work that out?" I asked.

"Well, we were focused almost entirely on Dickson, why he was so obsessed with the treasure, and what made him so certain that it was there. It was only when Cromarty broke his news that the police considered Arthur Donaldson to be the real kingpin that we were nudged into a different line of thinking."

"Well, no, Mike. It wasn't that simple. You and I began wondering whether Dickson as kingpin really was the full story not long after Dickson was hauled off in chains."

"You're rewriting history again, Mark. What we really were concerned about was how ragged the story was and whether we'd missed anything. The whole 'Third Man' thing was just one possible missing piece."

"That's not the way I remember it, Mike. But just suppose that you're right. Where does this discussion lead?"

"Well, it forced you to assess Arthur Donaldson as an archcriminal, and for him that role was just a ridiculously bad fit. So then you focused on what else might be going on. The key here is the evidence Cromarty said he had, something that pointed straight at Donaldson. We know nothing about this evidence, although we can surmise that it was probably unearthed by some accounting sleuth. The real point here is that Cromarty wouldn't take such a strong stand unless he had something solid, and so we couldn't deny that there was something there. You believe that Donaldson is incapable of that sort of chicanery, and that led you to the conclusion that the most likely person was the nephew, James. That's when and why our whole focus changed. Jocko's information was enough to shore up that view."

"I don't understand, Mike", Andrea said. "Where are you going with this?"

"It's mostly for the benefit of the redoubtable Mark Whelan. He had a career in the police, and he came away from it with some excellent knowledge and street smarts, but those skills are getting a bit long in the tooth now. He has a lot of really good nuts-and-bolts experience with everyday human failings – lipstick on shirt collars, torn stockings retrieved from unlikely locations, condoms found in the jacket pockets of men whose wives are on the pill – but that doesn't translate too well to serious firefights and dealing with unpleasant heavies. I want Mark to understand that what we did, and the way we did it, was dangerous. I want a debriefing."

"Why are you attacking me like this, Mike", I spluttered. "Why do you think that – "

"Mike is right, Mark! Can't you see that?" Andrea was distressed, almost pleading.

Andrea shook her head. "Maybe you never could see it! But you've always been too confident, too wrapped up in yourself, too…"

I was in turmoil, but before I could say anything further, Mike rose, wine bottle in hand, and came over to sit between us, pushing us apart by his sheer physical presence.

"Time for a pause and a drink", Mike said quietly, filling our glasses.

"You are two of my favourite people. You've just been through something that nobody should have to endure. But it happened. Now we need to understand it. Did it happen because of anything we did or didn't do? Could we have avoided it? Did we just narrowly avoid it being something much worse?"

There was a pause here while Mike looked at us in turn. Andrea was now looking concerned, stricken, and withdrawn. I was still seething from Mike's unexpected broadside.

Andrea was the first to get her voice back.

"Tell me first, please, either of you, that this really was an outlier, something we might expect will never happen again."

"That's reasonably easy", Mike said, jumping right in. "It was indeed an outlier. Many policemen go through entire careers without ever having to draw their weapons, let alone shoot at somebody. But I think all policemen are very much aware that the potential for that sort of thing is always there and can't be avoided if you want the job. It's far less likely that PIs will be caught up in something like that. So, to answer my own questions, I don't think this was caused by anything we did or didn't do, and I don't see how we could have avoided it short of just ignoring George and probably throwing him under the bus, but yes, something much worse might have happened."

This had the effect of cooling things down somewhat.

It also made me aware that there was a chasm open at my feet, a chasm that might have been there for some time. I had pretty much failed utterly to consider seriously the effect that extremes in my working life could have on Andrea because I had made the assumption that my work could never lead us into this sort of danger. This realization was so sudden, so cold, and so blunt that it left me speechless. I looked up and realized that both Mike and Andrea were regarding me expectantly. I looked back at them. I shook my head. My mouth worked. One hand made ineffectual motions in the air. I had a great deal of personal work to do.

Over the next two hours, Mike showed great skill and sensitivity in carrying out his debriefing. Andrea and I went to bed, but I felt completely disoriented. At about four am, I fell into a deep sleep, and when I awoke just before nine, I found Andrea looking at me calmly and sympathetically.

We had not come off the rails.

Thirty-nine

Breakfast outside, sunshine, birdsong, and the quiet lapping of Balsam Lake brought the three of us together.

Cromarty called later that day with news that had taken him, Cromarty, a while to digest. A body had been found. It had been shot once, execution style. The details had entered the police system, had worked their way through channels, and then a sharp-eyed detective in Cromarty's office had noticed the name "Donaldson".

James Donaldson's body had been found in a drainage ditch behind a small shopping plaza on the outskirts of Milton. Not only had there been no effort made to conceal the body, but it appeared to have been placed where it would be found soon.

At the risk of being accused of interfering, I placed a call to Arthur Donaldson. Yes, he had heard about his nephew James. Yes, he admitted, after a lot of coaxing and cajoling on my part, James had been embezzling money from the firm, but James had disguised it well. Arthur was appalled that clients might learn about the fraud, so he made up the financial diversions from his own private funds. Drawing on the information I had got from Jocko, I asked about James' gambling. Arthur had been unaware of this. I didn't relate to Arthur my sense of what really had happened to the money James had pilfered, and I said that I would be happy to stand by him as the police carried out their eventual forensic audit.

The rest of that day the three of us spent in discussion. Mike and I worked our way through what we understood or could surmise about

James Donaldson and his role in the whole affair, and as we stepped through what had happened, we laid out the details for Andrea.

"Yes", I said in response to Andrea's question. "James Donaldson was indeed Arthur Donaldson's nephew. The elder Donaldson told me that himself when I went to meet him. And as we passed a few minutes, James Donaldson was quite happy to reveal that he had been working with his uncle for about six months and was keen to learn more about the business."

"But why did he come to work at Clarence and Donaldson just when he did?" Andrea asked.

"Well, I don't know for sure", I said, "but I'll bet that he got wind of a 'McCleod gold' story and wormed his way into the office to see if he could find out whether it was true. Evidently he learned enough to convince himself that there was a fortune out there and it could be his for the taking."

"But how did Dickson get involved then?"

"I'm doing quite a bit of guessing here, Andrea. Jocko's information indicates that James was not only a gambler but a player on many fronts. A very slippery fish. My bet is that he got to know quite a few underworld types, but he also dug out their backgrounds. I doubt very much that James would ever get his own hands dirty, and it would also be my bet that he would dig out the backgrounds, all the warts, on anybody he hired to do something. He seems to have been accomplished both in dangling the carrot and in wielding the stick."

"So", Andrea said, after a long pause while she reflected and looked out over the lake, "how did James convince Dickson to play along, and how did he know he could trust Dickson?"

"I'm pretty sure now that James never did trust Dickson. And I expect he got him to go along by giving him almost the complete picture on the gold and making himself look, in Dickson's eyes, like a sucker who could be duped."

"But how could he … how could James be sure about…?"

"I believe that the basic reality here, Andrea, is that Dickson and James Donaldson were both psychopaths, but in the psychopath stakes Dickson came in second. Dickson probably thought all along that he was outsmarting James, a sissy who wrinkled his nose at any wet work, but really it was James in the driver's seat all the time. I doubt that James would have let Dickson get out of it alive no matter what happened."

"But now James Donaldson is dead. Was all this just pointless violence? At the end of it, Dickson didn't find the gold, so James Donaldson didn't know where it was or even if it existed. Seems like he wasn't that bright after all."

"That's where it gets interesting. We assume that James didn't know where the gold is. But that assumption likely is wrong."

Andrea blinked, in stunned silence, trying to make sense of what I had said.

"Just listen to this guy!" Mike said through a huge grin. "I just love this stuff! He can spin these tales without any effort. But the kicker is that most of the time he's right."

Andrea shook her head, not really listening to Mike, trying to fit all the pieces together.

"It appears that James Donaldson was a gambling addict", I continued. "But he was also, I suspect, a very accomplished white-collar criminal. I doubt that he ever lacked for money. And like a lot of high rollers, I expect he enjoyed the thrill. But McCleod's gold would have been the real deal for him. All he needed to do was wait until the fuss over Dickson died down, then he could quietly go and collect his gold."

"But couldn't Dickson have just come clean and told the police about James?"

I shook my head.

"Dickson almost certainly didn't know him as James Donaldson, probably never even saw his face. Dickson might well have worked out that he had been screwed, but he had no credible story that the police would buy."

"You told me earlier", Andrea began, "that you thought James was headed for the airport. Where do you think he was going?"

"I'm not entirely sure, but he might have been off to hide in the Caribbean until things settled down."

"What makes you think it was the Caribbean?"

"Jocko did some digging for me. He found that James had made six identical trips over the past four years. He had flown to London then taken a flight from there to Aruba."

"Why not fly directly to Aruba from here?"

"I think he wanted to stay out of the direct view of US authorities."

"Why Aruba?"

"I doubt that he was interested in Aruba", I said. "I think that from there he probably hired a plane to fly him to a financial haven, likely Grand Cayman. I suspect he had quite a wad stashed away there, and once he had converted the gold to currency it would have ended up there as well."

Andrea just shook her head.

"It's incredible! How did you work out all this?"

Mike was about to say something, but I held up my hand to stop him.

"It's patterns. I see patterns. And there are key points in patterns. If you can confirm that the information at those points is correct, the probability that the pattern reflects something real goes way up."

Andrea didn't ask how it came about that James was eliminated by the crowd that held his gambling debts. I had already told her how, with Jocko's help, I had planted the suspicion that he was about to vanish, and the chances were very good that once that happened he would have been impossible to find.

So, indeed, I had condemned him.

Forty

Our remaining time at Largs was well-spent. One of those days stood out. Andrea spent it with Kate. I spent it with John Woodhouse. And that evening, all five of us, Andrea, me, Kate, Mike, and John, got together for a memorable meal at The Repose.

And I did a lot of thinking about the future.

Mike remained with us the whole time, and we had one more session thrashing through the remaining details of the case.

It was a representative warm late summer afternoon. Andrea, Mike, and I were out at the picnic table, nibbling on raw vegetables and dip, sipping wine, being soothed by lake sounds, and drifting toward an evening meal of grilled fish.

"At one point", Andrea began, "it seemed to me that you felt this whole business revolved around the *Daniella* and where she had settled out there on the lake bottom."

"It did look like that", I said. "At one point, we considered ourselves lucky that Dickson had access only to general public information. We felt that he might have twigged that the Toronto Archives would have something worthwhile, but it seems that he never did make that connection. I think it was the newspaper article that made the case for him. The one where McCleod lamented the loss of his favourite lake boat, the *Daniella*, and then went on to say that there was only one occasion when he suffered disaster. He didn't actually say that he had lost something of great value when the *Daniella* went down, but he made it very easy for anybody to think that was the case. The assumption that old McCleod's comments invited was not only plausible, it was convincing. But it was aimed at people in the middle of the nineteenth century."

I paused here.

"But at that point, we knew nothing about James Donaldson and the role he might have played. By then it might also be the case that Dickson's mental state was crumbling. Maybe he had begun to suspect that he'd been hopelessly outflanked by James, or whoever he knew him as. Maybe he was losing his grip on the world, or maybe his ability to process information was degrading. I don't know. He might just have been descending into the most horrific psychopathic darkness. Or maybe he was just overwhelmed by his own greed."

"What was it that McCleod actually had done?" Mike asked.

"Well", I began, "he was so secretive and devious that we might never know that. But I think that he was concerned about getting the value from his land in Hastings County into a bankable form and getting that money into his bank in Toronto."

"But what's so special about Hastings County?" Andrea asked. "Why would land there be particularly valuable?"

"In the normal course of events, land would have low value there", I said, "but there was a gold rush there in 1860, and old McCleod took advantage of it."

"Gold? So he was after gold?"

"No", I said. "He knew that going after gold was a mug's game. He bought a lot of land before gold fever really got going, when it was still fairly cheap. Then he sold it when land prices skyrocketed and everyone wanted someplace, any place, to stake a claim."

"He really was a crafty old devil!" Andrea said, almost admiringly.

"He certainly was", I said. "But he was surrounded by a strange social landscape that he had to navigate. Everybody knew of McCleod then. They knew he was successful, and they knew he was rich. Given that nobody ever seemed to know just what he was up to. I doubt that anyone considered him an easy target, but I think he worried about being exactly that – an easy target. So, he wanted his rivals and his enemies to be unsure about what he had done with the money he had extracted from his land holdings, which they would assume had been converted to gold. That gold might have been lost somewhere in Balsam Lake or might be somewhere else. McCleod was almost paranoid and a master at disinformation. He might have overestimated the risks from his rivals and those who envied him. He almost certainly did. He could have had no way of knowing that his disinformation would set in motion a series of events a hundred and fifty years later."

Mike was nodding.

"But then", Mike said, "we know a fair bit about what happened when and where concerning the *Daniella*, or at least we think we do. Why has it proved so difficult, then, to locate this sunken boat and to find the place where its treasure might be, if that treasure actually exists?"

I pondered Mike's question as I got up to refill glasses.

"We need a baseline here. And that baseline is that almost nobody today is interested in the history of steamboats on Balsam Lake. Hell, very few people even know that they existed. So, far from there having been an army of treasure hunters out there over the years, the reality is almost complete ignorance. The Balsam Lake of yesteryear, and what happened on it, has pretty much sunk without trace today."

I paused here, as much to formulate what I would say next as to let what I just said sink in.

"It's against that background that we need to distinguish between what Dickson knew and what James Donaldson knew. Dickson apparently wanted jam today, and he would do anything to get it. James Donaldson likely was in no rush. If he knew only the approximate location of the *Daniella*, that would have been good enough for him. He could wait until the excitement over Dickson died down and then come back and search at his leisure."

"But the question still remains", Mike said, "why Dickson apparently couldn't find the *Daniella.*"

"I've thought a lot about that, Mike. And I'm afraid that I just don't know."

I refilled all our glasses, then looked at my glass contemplatively.

"It might be just that – ", but then I stopped abruptly.

Andrea told me later that it had taken me a while to answer her prompts and that finally Mike had poked me with an elbow.

"Hey, kid! Wake up! You can't just fall asleep like that in the middle of a discussion."

But it was Andrea who tuned in first.

"I don't think he was daydreaming. You weren't, were you, Mark?"

"No. I wasn't. And I think I might just know the explanation, at least to *that* question. It's your glass of wine, Mike."

Their expressions were nonplussed.

"Refilling the glasses just now made me recall something. And I think it might be the key. When they completed the Trent-Severn Waterway, they made some changes. One of those changes was needed for the Kirkfield Lift Lock to work. They had to raise the water level in Balsam Lake by eight feet."

"And?" Mike asked when I failed to continue the explanation.

"Prior to that change in lake level, the reef out there", and I pointed toward the lake, "would have been visible. It would possibly have stuck several feet out of the water. That's not something that anybody could have driven a boat onto unknowingly."

We all looked at one another.

"But those numbers that were on the sheet Harold passed to George. They pretty much pinpoint that very reef!"

"Yes", I said. "They do, Mike. But even that number of decimal places doesn't pinpoint a location exactly. At best it indicates a range, and that range varies depending on latitude. Plus, we don't know where he got those numbers from."

"So where do you think the remains of the *Daniella* are?"

"No real idea, Mike. But I'd wager that the high point of the reef extends quite some distance either way from the point we've been focusing on. The *Daniella* could be anywhere along there."

Mike nodded, convinced. He didn't need anything more detailed than that as an explanation.

In due course, Mike got ready to go back to Toronto. Andrea gave him a long thank-you hug and extracted a promise from him to spend time with us later at our condo in Toronto. We had one more beer together, and then Mike asked his one remaining question.

"How did McCleod get so much gold to Largs?"

I had spent a lot of time thinking about that.

"Well, there's no certainty that there was ever any gold here at all. When McCleod sold his Hastings County stakes, he did have to get his profits back to Toronto. The most direct way was south to Peterborough and then by one or more routes to Lake Ontario and on to Toronto. But there were other possibilities. The Gull River was always a good north–south travel route. And McCleod had a lot of dealings in furs, so he had trappers and agents through what is now northern Victoria County and parts of Haliburton, Hastings, and Peterborough Counties. It wouldn't have been difficult for some of his agents to pass through or near Madoc. A steady trickle of McCleod's profits from land sales, probably in the form of gold, could have, and I stress *could* have, made its way from Hastings County to Largs. You can imagine what kinds of problems would be associated with that approach, but it's conceivable. It's not hard to imagine that there were quite a few unscrupulous buggers who had suspicions about what McCleod was up to, knew that he had to get his profits out, and would have been more than prepared to help themselves, and that McCleod was aware of all this. But old McCleod seems to have kept everyone guessing."

"So", Mike said, after a short pause, "there might never have been any gold at all, shipwrecked or otherwise." He shook his head a couple of times. "Just a siren song. With consequences to match."

"That might be the case. Or maybe there was gold, at least here in Largs, and McCleod managed to get it all out in the *Jackson* on one trip or in several trips. Or maybe he really did lose it somewhere out there in the lake. He made a big public deal about the *Daniella* going down, and everyone knew that it had gone down. They just didn't know what was on it. Even the story about a steam leak could have been a ruse. Old McCleod really did keep them all guessing."

"Are you going to keep looking for it?" Mike asked.

"Well, I can hardly *keep* looking for it because I haven't *been* looking for it. No, I think I'll keep going through McCleod's records. There's a good chance that I'll be able to show that all his profits did make it to Toronto and that there wasn't any gold lost here in the lake."

"That likely won't stop people speculating and thinking that there really is a store of lost gold out there on the bottom of the lake."

"You're almost certainly right", I said. "Look at the story of the Ghost Island treasure, still alive and well after two hundred and fifty years." And it was precisely because of the attraction of that kind of story that James Donaldson would have continued to be a serious potential danger to Andrea and me.

After Mike had left, Andrea and I continued our own personal discussions. Some of these discussions were long. Some of them were full of anguish. Over the previous two weeks, I had come to the searing realization that too much of my thinking and too many of my actions – far too many – were self-centred to a degree that had put Andrea, the best thing in my life, at serious risk, and that Mark Whelan had a lot of reflecting to do.

Consequently, many of these discussions were about my work, about me, about us.

But these soon expanded to cover the world we lived in and continue to live in, about the people who inhabit it – good people, blameless people caught wrong-footed by events, innocent and defenceless people, irresponsible people who are neither particularly good nor particularly bad, amoral and grasping people, twisted and damaged people, and then the people who could really be called nothing other than evil. The whole glorious and ghastly spectrum offered by the human race.

We talked about George. About what had happened to us as a result of my taking on his case. About what might have happened had I decided not to take him on. About the many possible ways that evil can rise up from the muck and engulf us. About the limited extent to which we can prevent this happening. About how far we should go to help other good or innocent people and how much we should put ourselves at risk.

There were no good answers. There were few answers that were even marginally acceptable. There was mostly just a big grey area where nobody really knew what the hell was going on.

I had spent a lot of time, on my own, going through what had happened, trying to determine whether there were things I could or should have done to change the outcome. Many things are possible in hindsight. Putting myself back into those times in the past days, would a less self-centred outlook have made me less willing to assume that everything would work out all right? Possibly. But I honestly couldn't see what alternative actions I might have taken that would have made a great difference to the eventual outcome.

It was clear that Andrea had spent a lot of time reflecting as well. She faulted me for not letting her in on the whole picture earlier, but eventually, reluctantly, she came to the conclusion that this, by itself, likely would have made no real difference to the ultimate result. She knew why I did what I had done, but she still was unhappy, unsettled. She knew that we were not the ones who had suffered most, far from it. We talked a long time about this, particularly about our responsibilities to each other, given how our lives could be invaded in the ways we had just seen. We spent time considering our responsibilities to others. I spoke at length about my responsibility to Andrea. And I ended by saying that it would be best for me to wrap up my PI business and do something else.

As she does frequently, Andrea surprised me.

"Mark, I don't want you to give up on what you do. You're really good at it and it gives you a lot of satisfaction. But you do need to take a very different perspective."

I lapsed into silence at that point.

After a few minutes, Andrea brought up the subject of George again, our representative Other.

George.

In many very real ways, our brother.

Poor, defenceless George, sucked into a maelstrom by forces he could not resist, for reasons he didn't understand, dragged down into a fearful darkness and a desperate final personal gesture of defeat, perhaps in response to the unfairness of it all, perhaps in despair that his brother had been deprived of any natural justice.

Compared to what George had had to face, the impact on us was minor. But even so, it would take some time for us to recover from that impact, and in one sense we never would, never should. As opposed to being just intellectually aware of what is out there, this case had been a graphic visceral reminder that the world has its horrific side. We had seen it and couldn't pretend that it didn't exist. We couldn't fix the world, protect people from all the possible downsides, and indeed could not even be sure of preventing horrors being visited upon us personally.

But the world also has its exquisite, brilliant, elegant, subtle, and hopeful side. That was it. Hope. It really did spring eternal. It had to. Without some source of hope, we had, well, nothing. And while we had to hang onto that thought, we also had to know that the Good and the Evil are inextricably intertwined in events, in things, in technologies. And in people.

We had attended a funeral of sorts for George. There were just four people there: Andrea and me, Mike, and Bent Cromarty. It was really nothing more than a burial, an uncomfortable goodbye to someone we basically had not known, someone whose life seemed to us to have been an unimaginable confusion, but someone who, for all that, had touched both Andrea and me deeply. But, even then, we didn't know him.

We had both made a new friend, John. And John had intrigued me by saying, obliquely, that he needed my professional help. I asked him for details, but all he would say was "in due course". The events had brought Andrea and me much closer to Kate. We, Andrea and I, were also much closer now to each other. I had also caught glimpses of an unflattering picture of myself.

My own shortcomings, serious fault lines that I had failed to recognize, or refused to admit, were now squarely in front of me. Once I mustered the humility needed to accept that, what I felt was relief. And release.

In our last days at Largs, we met John and Kate three times at The Repose for dinner, and on each occasion we talked far into the night. John and I also had three long one-on-one sessions during the day. John became fascinated at my fascination over Balsam Lake and the area around it. John talked much more about his past, the past that had been unknown to him until just a few months earlier. He was discovering things. And the more John and I talked, the more I came to the hazy realization that in some strange and interesting way we, the two of us, were a microcosm of what was happening all around us. A larger historical reality was unfolding, and we were becoming aware about where we live and its pre-colonial past and about the betrayals and inhumanity that had been committed against the indigenous people over almost two centuries. To anyone who chose to see, it was blindingly evident that all this needed plenty of attention, some process was needed, and there was no clear or simple answer on where this process might lead or how long it would take. The only certainty was that the discussion had to occur, the whole business was messy, and it all had to be driven forward to some common understanding and outcome.

Over a surprisingly short period of time, John and I had grown quite close, and I found that I had much more in common with him now that we were grown men. And one of the things we had in common was the path we were following through our personal lives.

John kept being drawn back, irresistibly, to pondering the course of his life thus far as John Woodhouse. From his teen years, John had accomplished what he had expected to, and that accomplishment unfolded normally, naturally. While the path John followed was in public view and praiseworthy, it had been expected given John's mental endowments. He had done well academically. He was considered successful by almost any measure.

"But what if I had remained John Longfeather?" he asked. "What path would I have followed? Where would I be now?"

There were others that John could have emulated. James Bartleman, for example. But would he have done that? Would he have been able to do that? Just based on the statistics, it was highly unlikely.

And how was that fair? John Longfeather and John Woodhouse, apart from being on different tracks, would have been, in essence, the same person.

There was a lot that needed fixing here.

In the weeks after these events, Andrea and I spent more time at Largs than we had in previous years. It was partly Andrea's newfound appetite for house repair. It was partly our shared deeply felt connections to the place. But for me it was also the recognition that this place, this area, its history and its essence, forms a central part of my own extended personal being. And this background was something I wanted to get to know better.

It was now late August. The sunsets were just as spectacular, but they arrived earlier in the day. Over the summer, John had spent many evenings with us, both in Toronto and in Largs, and Andrea and I had also reached out to people in Rosedale and Coboconk, and in Largs, in ways that we hadn't done before. The people we contacted in this way didn't all become bosom buddies; not everyone is destined to become one's fast friend. But we got to know their country rhythms, the things that made their lives tick, and the things from our world, Andrea's and mine, that were too distant, too rarefied, too much lacking in meaning, to be of real interest to them. We got to know them reasonably well, and some of them became people we welcomed and spent time with. We also found people we had underestimated, interesting people, thoughtful people, and these people became regular visitors at Largs.

And then there was Balsam Lake. It was simply there, pondering, reflecting, reaching out to us, almost a living thing, changing continuously, but seeming to be eternal, timeless. It was as complex, rough, and subtle as its surroundings, the Land Between. It laughed in the sunlight, brooded to match overcast skies that loomed above it, whispered lines of wonderful, luminous sunset poetry, lay bathed erotically in moonlight, and always reminded us that the great life force moves through everything.

Gitchi Manitou.

Andrea and I sat at our picnic table in the back garden. A late evening breeze ruffled the surface of the lake, the hesitant and clipped conversations of night birds rose and fell in the woods around us, and a loon voiced a long exotic air that no oboe, shawm, or any other musical instrument could ever duplicate, a cry that echoed hypnotically over the water, off the land and trees, and through the warm air.

Andrea stirred beside me.

"When I first met you, you talked a little about this place, and it sounded so wildly lyrical to me that I thought you must be nuts."

We sat silently for a few moments, looking out over the water, now metallic and brooding, over the fractal shadow that was Indian Point, toward the glow in the western sky, preparing for its grand finale.

"But you were right. This is a magical place."

Another short silence.

"What's that German word again?" Andrea asked.

"*Dämmerung.* Twilight."

"It had something to do with the gods, didn't it?"

"Yes. But that doesn't apply here."

I looked out over the water.

"In a way we're lucky. We have an advantage over places like Europe. Being here, in this place, we're not fenced in by a dead weight of minutely recorded history, not yoked to knowledge of land soaked in blood, not burdened by myths that are magnificent but sometimes oppressive. You know how irritated I get when anyone says we don't have any history here. Everywhere has history. We have history here. It's just not European history. Sure, we're tied to European history. But there's our own history too. It's here. It burrows into our collective psyche. And it's fluid, deep, subtle, numinous. I think that's one of the things that makes this place timeless."

"And there's no treasure in the lake?" Andrea said, half in question.

"Oh! There's plenty of treasure in the lake. It's full of treasure."

Make no mistake about that, I thought. Make no mistake.

"Where we're most likely to go wrong, and disastrously wrong, it seems to me, is when we become too literal about things. Things like treasure."

I stopped and looked for a long time over the surface of the lake, now an incredible shifting artist's palette of indigos, reds, pinks, golds.

"Our first reflex is to turn to the European tradition. That's natural, I suppose. But it's not the only wellspring we have."

Another long pause.

"Many people are obsessed by the spiritual drumbeat of things like the Lorelei and the Rhinegold."

The colours continued to shift and blend before us.

"But they're nothing compared to this."

Acknowledgements

My thanks to my wife, Maggie, a sure-footed reviewer.